Praise for *Simone in Pieces*

"In the tradition of Lily Tuck and Jayne Anne Phillips, Burroway's *Simone in Pieces* interrogates trauma, memory, and identity mapped across a life's movement toward wholeness. Gripping and painful fragments allow the reader to fill in the blanks that Simone cannot—the result is both compelling and rapturous, a novel that gives voice to a life spent fulfilling but never quite becoming. Austere and haunting, this addictively compulsive novel is a must-read portrait of our age."

—Adam Johnson, Pulitzer Prize–winning author of *The Orphan Master's Son*

"A capacious novel. For more than sixty years, Simone navigates her career and relationships, working through traumas and fragmented memory, and strives for self-realization during a precarious time for a woman academic. Moving, courageous, and thought-provoking, Simone's quest is both a love story and a triumph over her childhood tragedies."

—Yang Huang, author of *My Good Son*

"If there were such a thing as a cubist novel, *Simone in Pieces* would define the genre. Every chapter captures the woman at its center from a different angle, each a dazzling surprise. Burroway has found a brilliant way to portray a woman in search of herself and her dire history, lost and found many times over."

—Rosellen Brown, author of *The Lake on Fire*

"This book is stupendous. I loved it so, so much. An assemblage, fragments that bring vividly to life a woman, an era, a world—or rather, many worlds—this book is a marvel and a delight."

—Ayelet Waldman, author of *Love and Treasure*

Simone in Pieces

Janet Burroway

THE UNIVERSITY OF WISCONSIN PRESS

The University of Wisconsin Press
728 State Street, Suite 443
Madison, Wisconsin 53706
uwpress.wisc.edu

Printed in the United States of America
This book may be available in a digital edition.

Library of Congress Cataloging-in-Publication Data

Names: Burroway, Janet, author.
Title: Simone in pieces / Janet Burroway.
Description: Madison, Wisconsin : The University of Wisconsin Press, 2025.
Identifiers: LCCN 2025006650 | ISBN 9780299353841 (paperback)
Subjects: BISAC: FICTION / Literary | LCGFT: Fiction. | Novels.
Classification: LCC PS3552.U76 S56 2025 | DDC 813/.54—dc23/eng/20250331
LC record available at https://lccn.loc.gov/2025006650

For Peter

for the rest of time

Memories are killing. So you must not think of certain things, of those that are dear to you, or rather you must think of them, for if you don't there is the danger of finding them, in your mind, little by little.

—Samuel Beckett

I'm so interested in different points of view . . . how, in a small town, we think we know someone, but we only know them this way, and someone else knows them that way. . . .

—Elizabeth Strout

Do you think it is possible to write a life of anyone? I doubt it, because people are all over the place.

—Virginia Woolf

Contents

Simone in Pieces

Transit: Ostend–Dover

1940/1964

Four times that summer we brought back boatloads of the refugees. The Vicar organized us. They didn't mind I was a woman because I was able-bodied. We traveled down from Teddington once a month to make the crossing, and we had the use of Duck Henley's trawler and half a dozen meeting points along the Flemish coast. Underground runners all through Belgium setting up the rendezvous.

It's a wonder what you remember. Great blanks, and then some daft thing bobs up like flotsam. Such as, I'd never worn a pair of trousers, and what I couldn't get used to was the twill going swish between my thighs. Is that camera running? Don't show me saying *thighs*, will you? Anyway, that and the smells. Tar, old fish in the wet boards. Seasick, of course. And a bit of metal smell, with a sourness like fireworks. When they say "sweating bullets" I expect that's what they mean.

More than once I've been told it didn't happen. *You must have got it muddled*, people say. *Not with the channel full of mines, nobody would've risked it.* They reckon without our Vicar, and the grit of those Resistance—and our ignorance, I suppose.

That must be twenty years ago—oh, well, that's what you're up to, isn't it? Twenty-five years! and high time you do the women, if you don't mind me saying. But you know—*Women of World War II*—it's not how I fancy myself from one day to the next. *Borough postal clerk*, now, *grandmother, Church of England; dab hand with a Yorkshire pudding*—for someone reared in Clapham Common. *Widow.* Twenty-five years!

The ones we ferried came in every sort—rich man, poor man, tinker, tailor—always drained-looking like they hadn't been out of doors, although most had been living rough. I said it at the time: every one of them gray, and eyes like drain holes that the color washed right down.

It's the children stick in your mind—a wee tiddler with its eyes wide open and its mouth tight shut. I remember one boy landed crooked off the dock and broke his shin, so the bone stub rolled under the skin like a tongue in a cheek. Somebody gave him a mouthful of coat sleeve to keep him quiet.

It was that same trip we were expecting a father and daughter that didn't show up, and we about pushed off without them. We'd heard dogs, and you never knew the meaning of dogs—it could be the patrols, or just somebody's mutt in a furore. One thing I've never understood: you pick a night with no moon and a piece of shore without a light, and you can't see a whit. And then there's a click, like, in the back of your eyes, and you can. Sandiford was pressing off the piling, and the Vicar said, *no, steady on*—and then Duck felt it too and had them put up the oars. The waves were thick, and the black shore, and now there's this girl, maybe nine or ten, gawky little tyke, slogging into the water up to her coat hem. Sandiford signaled her to go round the dock and fetched her down with her shoes full of water. Skinny as a rail she was, and her coat too small, though it was posh—velvet collar and that. I wrapped her up, and she says, po-faced, "My father arrives not. I arrive alone." She says, "My fah-zer." I knew better than to ask.

From there across—you understand, nobody said *U-boats.* Nobody said *mines.* All the same that's what was in everybody's mind. Well, of course I was frightened! Spitless, we used to say. But you lot want me to show you frightened now. And I'm not, you see. You can't be afraid of the past, can you?

What I remember is, we had a little paraffin stove, and usually when you got out far enough to rope the motors into life, they were all glad to settle down over a cuppa. But this skinny one didn't leave the stern maybe eight hours of rough crossing, looking back where we'd come from in the dark. She held one hand tight, and I thought she had some money in there, maybe, or a bit of jewelry, something she'd been told to keep from harm. Well, eight hours is a long time to be standing; your mind must be doing something. I remember I tucked the blanket tighter around her and held it there, which she let me, and we just stood till it was lightening a little down by the horizon. She sagged against me and bit by bit her hand relaxed. There was nothing in it. Not a thing. I cupped it in my own and chafed it back to life a little.

There must've been a thousand like her, cut off and set out some other direction altogether, but she's a one I do think about from time to time. I wondered, all that way across, how *she* would think of it, looking back—the wet and the dark water and, maybe, this woman that held her bundled against the wind. I suppose I hoped she'd remember me now and then. And I thought how we must have looked to God, that greasy little trawler in the black wake, like a clot being washed from a wound.

ONE

Anglo Erotica

CHAPTER I

The Love Song of Johnny A. Purdy

1944

Lt. Johnny A. Purdy has let himself get adopted by a Limey family, and this December Saturday he splits off from the boys at the George and Dragon and heads up Warrington Hill. There's a cold drizzle, though Army Weather said it would be clear. Johnny is singing under his breath, not knowing it:

Praise the Lord and pass the ammunition,
All aboard, we're not a-goin' fishin'.
Praise the Lord and pass the ammunition,
And we'll all . . . stay . . . free.

Almost at once he passes Reefer Ruth and gives her a salute smart enough to cut her off. Reefer Ruth is wearing a tatty black fur wrapped across her bony chest, a black bowl of a hat bent so far to one side it skims her scrawny neck.

"There's a poppet," she calls after him and sways seductively on her high heels.

Johnny is in Supply, U.S. Army Air Corps, stationed just outside Hove with the Eighth Bomber Command, proud of being a cog in a crack machine. Mostly he desk-jockeys, but every couple of weeks they get pressed for personnel, and he'll be sent aloft to load up plasma or insecticides or parts. He is six-foot-two and thick-chested, known to be shy but tough. He will crack a joke when they swing up into the belly of a stripped Boeing Stratoliner, heading for Prestwick, New Brunswick, Goose Bay. He is nineteen, from Abbeville, Missouri; also married and the father of a six-month-old baby girl he hasn't seen—didn't even see Joyce Milner Purdy from Jepson (the next town over) lose the flatness of her belly, and—she says—get it back again.

It is not strange to be sitting in the bare fuselage, heels wedged against the webbing, steadying the crate of a Flying Fortress engine—or at least it isn't stranger to be there, doing that, than to think: *married, father, belly, six months, girl.*

He got tall late and it's only the war that has muscled his shoulders. "Rabbits under a rug"—who said that? Some sports announcer on the radio, of DiMaggio maybe. And this hardening has happened out of sight of Joyce from Jepson, so that now he's more man than she saw in him. The girls on the seafront turn their eyes.

He climbs the hill between high white buildings with their windows blanketed. The locals call them *terraced houses,* which means stuck-together-in-a-row but always makes him imagine that, behind, they open up onto verandas with railings and rocking chairs. The Toffats also live in a "terraced" house, but tiny, stuffed with wallpaper and cheap figurines, a long hike up from the expensive seafront.

Johnny is not the Toffats' only stray. They have also got a war orphan named Simone Lerrante, which is Belgian and pronounced *Lay-rawnt.* Auntie Toffat got the orphan at the Processing Centre where she used to volunteer. Supposedly all the refugee kids were evacuated inland, away from the Blitz, but this Simone threw a tantrum and wouldn't leave the coast. That's pretty much all Johnny knows about her—that, and that she's not a Jew like most of them. She's fourteen, tall and twig-skinny and nothing like the Toffats. Sometimes she's smart-alecky, but sometimes you'll say something you don't have any idea what, *looks like rain* or *pass the potatoes,* and she'll disappear inside herself like a sunk stone. Johnny's heart pounds when he thinks about her because she is who they're here for, the ones that have lost everything. This one lived in Liege till '40 but claims to know nothing about how she got to England. Twice she sleepwalked and woke up in the coal yard in her nightgown, which the boys thought a hoot and which required Auntie to box their ears. Auntie Toffat says she's "got holes in her memory."

The climb gets steeper and the railway bridge comes in sight. He passes a restaurant where the door opens and laughter and a yellow glow spill out. Farther on, a man in his shirtsleeves is smoking, outlined by the bare bulb. Off to the west Johnny hears the drone of the night-raiders taking off, and he damps down a pang of envy and then a pang of dread. If they send a supply-drop to that downed DC-3 in the flats of Greenland, he has to decide whether he'll volunteer. Should he or shouldn't he? That is the overwhelming question. All the guys say only a fool or a suicide would sign on in that kind of weather. But they don't know the men that went down in that plane. Johnny does.

He tucks his collar against the wet. He has a letter from Joyce in his pocket that says she's making a corduroy vest for the Lutheran Synod intramural pep squad, and this nags at him. He wouldn't begrudge her the games. Joyce has a lot of fun in her and that's her best personality. It's just weird to think of football going on, teams full of kids and dads, missing all the best players because they're over here in this toy town, toy country. Except that it's Abbeville that's starting to seem not a serious place to be from.

This bothers him. The other boys hang around in the mess hall waiting for the mail. They carry pictures of their girls and wives even if they have Betty Grable on their locker. Johnny dreads another set of snapshots. Joyce takes pictures of the baby every Sunday and sends them in numbered batches. He lays them out one after the other, trying to get some idea who this baby *is*. But he can't put the photos together so as to come up with a single idea of his one kid.

The Toffats' is over the railway bridge and back of the furniture factory making field gear now. You go around and in by the kitchen yard.

"There now, Johnny Purdy!" Mrs. (but always called Auntie) Toffat confirms from her wing chair in the dining room. "It's about time you gave us a look-in." For somebody sitting she puts out waves of fat energy. "Ada, here's John Purdy! decided to grace us with his presence. We've had the welcome banners taken down, thinking you was never coming to call again. Sarah Dana, set the kettle on." Her voice is cheerful with plaint. It is her note.

The littlest boy screams "Chocolate!" There are two others not much older, and a girl about ten. The war orphan is not in sight, but Maggie, eighteen, is here with her baby, all of them crowded between the kitchen stove and the dining room coal burner, the boys waiting with cowlicks at the alert.

"What d'you hear from your grease monkey?" he greets Maggie, whose husband is a tank mechanic on the Continent somewhere and hasn't seen his baby either.

"Bleedin' all," says Maggie. All of these Toffats—all but Mr., not home from the factory yet, and his sister Ada, sitting next to Auntie—have thick arms and ham thighs, pendulous parts. Ada, in retreat from a bad marriage, is ropy like her brother and given to whining.

The boys stand one foot on the other, patiently. Their grubby sweaters are knit in stripes from wool-ends of other knittings. The girl has her lower lip caught in her teeth, and even Ada has a light in her eyes with the hope of chocolate. The boys at the George and Dragon like to laugh at England's oddities, the awful coffee, the warm beer. But for Johnny the primroses on this wallpaper, the oily reek of cabbage in the air—they're pure down-home, and this is the moment he loves best. It makes him aware of being U.S. Army Air Force, Christian, open-handed, clean and strong. He tousles a head and breaks the Hershey bars in halves, handing them round. The war orphan comes in from the cold parlor.

Simone. Today she is schoolgirl shy but mindful of herself in her navy pinafore, the way she leans against the doorframe one foot rubbing the back of the other calf. She has long straight legs chapped at the knees that disappear into cable-knit blue socks. She has a habit of lifting one foot and twisting the delicate ankle.

"Hello, Johnny Purdy," she says, shy and daring, "Here you are arrived for playing Father Christmas."

Her speech is the strangest thing he's ever heard. She makes grammatical mistakes; her *r*'s are in her throat and her vowels are off.

And yet she speaks a more formal English than either the Toffats or the Purdies in Missouri; more words, more phrases, more flourish. "Are you bereft of your baby?" she asked him once, and he knew only in the vaguest terms what she was asking, but it also seemed exactly to describe that tingly dread. His baby. He was bereft. He offers her the largest chunk of Hershey bar.

"Johnny, Johnny!" the boys compete, and Ada strains forward in her chair. At the PX there's always Spearmint and Juicy Fruit, always Hershey with and without almonds. There's always Ivory and sometimes Camay. Sometimes there are Realsilk stockings, which are not real silk but are the most desirable of all to the women—Auntie, Ada, Maggie—who undo the paper packets and bury their fists in the slithery tubes of them, pulling back out against the grain of their rough fingers. The orphan does not expect to be included in the stockings. Johnny is aware that his best present to her is tucked in the inside pocket of his pink-and-tans. For now he opens his palms and tips into hers a bar of Camay, which she lifts to her face to drink in the scent. Her skin is not like the skin of the Toffats, who live on sausage fat. It's girl-skin, an ivory teacup you can almost see through. Her hair is dark blond and curly, fastened with a barrette.

Then Mr. Toffat is in the back door, smelling of machine oil: "We thought you'd fallen down the hole!" and the girls are squeezing one more place at table, ladling a sour bowlful for each of them. Simone says, "Ada has made egregious turnip soup."

There is always an awkward moment at grace because the orphan won't bow her head. Simone says she is a *humanist*, but Johnny does not think this is her fault. In America there are more conveniences, the water is cleaner and there are better electricity and cars, so you would not hear an American girl saying she didn't believe in God.

"God bless this food to its intended use, Amen." Maggie's baby bangs the saucer with a coffee spoon, which it would not be allowed to do if it was Johnny's kid. Mr. Toffat takes his whole week's cheese ration and sticks it in his mouth at once.

After dinner they sit hunkered over the wireless, over cups of steaming tea and news of the stalled advance. In the room the women come and go, talking of how hard it is to boil diapers on the fuel allotment.

Simone should be helping with the clearing up but keeps a foot wrapped around the chair rung.

"It's not that they haven't got supplies," Johnny says. "It's just a huge operation, and we have to sit it out." He could brag how huge—six hundred tons of rations and medicals a day, eight million ammo rounds a month—but he has learned to button his lip. The supplies have been dropped all over Belgium and northern France, but there aren't trucks enough to run them to the forward positions; everywhere the roads and bridges have been blown, little pockets of crazy Germans ambush the routes.

"The Jerries are dug in," Mr. Toffat explains.

"They don't know when they're beat," Johnny agrees. "We've had Antwerp since September, but we can't supply it because the Krauts still hold Scheldt Estuary." The war orphan bucks her head, and he bites his tongue, remembering that she came from Belgium.

That's not all. There is something else he wouldn't know how to tell them, even if he was allowed. Last week he was pressed into service with a hospital transport of American wounded en route to St. Johns in Canada. The job was basically the same as with a cargo of parts and shells: load and unload, make sure the inventory doesn't shift. But when the cargo is damaged men you fill with pride like helium in your lungs, because these are not flyboys who think of themselves as Errol Flynn; they're the citizen enlisted infantry, salt of the earth, and their salt blood is in the earth to prove it. They are burned or shrapnel-stuck, the wounds are black where there was no way to clean them, and still they joke. If they have only one eye to smile with they smile with that.

There were fourteen evacuees, their cots lining the sides of the fuselage. It was an old Douglas DC-3, commandeered from TWA and stripped; cold and loud, clumsy to walk through between the exposed struts. The weather was bad over the Midlands and a couple of the wounded were sick. One of them was a narrow-faced kid with blood coming through the bandage on his foot. An NCO, hit in the groin but chatty, told Johnny that the kid was in a bivouac caught by a machine gun round, the others on top of him so he was left for dead.

The kid didn't remember a thing about it. And didn't know yet that he was going to lose the leg. He made a moaning sound over and over, and when they hit a hard bump starting the descent into Prestwick he shat himself.

What Johnny loves is this: that although these men teased each other rough—one private told the NCO he was bald and finished in the sack besides, and the NCO gave back that the private couldn't get it up *before* the war so he wouldn't know finished from fuck—although that kind of thing went on for the whole three hours, nobody ever said a word to the kid for either the moaning or the shitting. The private perched on a strut holding the elbow of his sling and talked to the kid about how sweet it's going to be back home, the *tomatas* starved for men and all the best jobs going begging.

"Hell," said the NCO, "I had an uncle came back from the Great War, owns his own factory."

Johnny said, "I've got two uncles that were at the Battle of the Marne." This is true, though one is a clerk in a hardware store and the other barely scratches a living out of too few acres of corn. "Battle of the Marne," one of the wounded farther aft repeated for no apparent reason. That was when the DC-3 hit the air pocket and the kid let loose, the putrid stench they call field-ration-fart. "Hell, yes," said the NCO, casual, taking a pull of his cigarette. "We got it made in the shade."

By the time they got to Prestwick Johnny would have followed these guys to the pole. But the damn dispatcher switched crews and sent the wounded men on to St. Johns while Johnny got to load tin cans, boots, and Wrigleys on a C-46 for the trip back south.

It was the next day—though Johnny didn't hear about it until Wednesday—that the Douglas went down over Comanche ice flats in Greenland. Last pilot contact reported engine sputter. Looking back, Johnny thinks he should have known that plane was due to conk out. Reconnaissance is lucky to have spotted it in that waste of rock and white, but the sno-gos are hundreds of miles away and ATC can't send a sled-team before April. So they have no choice but to try the drop. He has a choice whether he's going to volunteer.

"This war is over," he says now, bravado. "We just have to convince the Krauts."

"You should bomb some chocolates bars on the Germans," Simone says, "for sweetening them." Her tone is cool but her eyes flick away from him and back. She cocks an elbow over her head to scratch under her collar, and her torso makes an arc.

"People back home don't know it," Johnny says, "but the Air Age is already started. I know a guy, a dispatcher from Louisiana, has a scheme for spraying the cane fields with insecticide—out of airplanes."

Simone giggles. She picks Johnny's hat up and cocks it slantwise on her head. He lunges for it and she shies, squealing.

Maggie says, "'Ere, mind the creamer!" Auntie Toffat is unraveling an old knit waistcoat, and she insists on Johnny trotting out his latest pictures. It's embarrassing. In one of them, Joyce is holding the baby between his mother and her mother. He has known Joyce's mother all his life. It never occurred to him that Joyce could come to resemble her.

"You always say *the baby*," Simone observes, still acting smart. "Does she have no name?"

Johnny mumbles, "Olivia."

"Lydia! That is elegant."

He doesn't correct her. The name *Olivia* is nothing of his choosing. He'd told Joyce that whatever she wanted would suit him fine, and she claims it was the name of somebody in *Gone with the Wind*, but to him the name has an oily, Italian sound. It reminds him of Olive Oyl, not any notion you'd wish on a kid.

Now it's Maggie's baby that's yowling upstairs, and Ada is in the kitchen doing the dishes. The boys pummel Johnny into another chorus of "This Is the Army, Mister Jones." It's gone nine and time to leave, but Johnny wants to give Simone her present. He stands, swiping the flattened rectangle of his cap against his thigh. As he hoped, she bounces up, one foot dragging in that uncertain way she has. Ada in the kitchen is still singing, "*No more private rooms or telephones.*"

"Well . . ." says Johnny.

Simone says, "You should see my new words before you go."

Maggie scoffs, "*See words.*"

"Sure, I'll be glad to, and then I've really got to mosey."

She disappears into the parlor, but Auntie Toffat detains him with a plump hand. "There now, Johnny, there's a duck. See if you can't talk Simone into coming to the candle-lighting service."

Toffat says, "Yes," with surprising sarcasm. "You're the hero. You bring her to religion."

Auntie Toffat pats her husband's arm. "She's just trying to do like her daddy taught her."

"I don't give a toss. I'm all the daddy she's got for the duration."

It comes stray into Johnny's head what it would be like to be as lean as Toffat and to mount that hippo of a woman. Or be mounted by her.

"Well, any road, Johnny," Auntie Toffat says, "see if you can't convince her."

Johnny says he'll try, though he's wary of mixing into anybody's family ruckus. He follows Simone into the front parlor that has been sacrificed to her. It has a whatnot full of china boats and quadrupeds, a treadle sewing machine, and lace curtains over black-out paper. The couch is made up with a shabby comforter.

In front of the fireplace is a table spread with a thick English dictionary and what Simone calls her "vocaboolary." There are cardboard rectangles in stacks, neatly inked with a word on one side and its definition on the other. Simone stands with her back to him. The down on her neck is darker than her hair and forms two whorls below her curly bob.

"Do you know this one, Johnny Purdy: *opsimath*?" she asks. "It is from the Latin, for a person who begins learning late in life." Johnny laughs, and she bends her long nape. "Here is *gobsmacked*! Have you heard such a thing?"

"You're nuts," he says. "You already know more words than the rest of us put together."

She turns to him, flip. "It this *rebarbative*?"

"I don't know about that, but I do know it's my language."

"It is your *mother tongue*," she amends. She leans a fist on the dictionary, bites tongue to lip, and he drops his eyes from this.

"You know," he says, "I think Toffat is trying to be a good father to you."

She eyes him coldly. "He is not father to me."

"It would be a, a—gesture of goodwill, for you to go to the Christmas service."

"My father is dead, or he would have come for me."

"Maybe not. It's not that easy just to push off for England, you know."

"And however, apparently I did so."

This seems so clearly the last word that Johnny doesn't press it further. He reaches into the pocket of his pink-and-tans and extracts the manila cards. Unlike the stockings, the Camay, these cards are pilfered from the U.S. Army Air Corps.

She takes the packet in both hands, lifts it to her face as she did the soap, as if to smell it. "Thank you, John Purdy. Pasteboard is so hard to obtain." The air seems thin between them, a pressure-drop. Simone turns away. She gives off a scent of damp wool and unwashed girl, and he's rushed with a memory of Abbeville High, a moment in particular just after sophomore gym, when he stood behind a girl (not Joyce; he can't now remember who) and with a sense of imminent danger poked a Butterfinger over her shoulder into her locker. He's aware of Simone's bony body inches from him, the body of a tenth-grade girl whose gawky beauty used to make him sit in the back of the class and ache.

She says, her back to him, "I don't have a picture. Not a snapshot." For a minute he thinks she is asking to see his photos again. Then he realizes she is talking about her parents. "I don't have a letter. Nothing."

Her neck is rigid. He reaches back into his pocket and slips out one of the baby snapshots at random, opens her dictionary and folds it in with a comic flourish. "There!" he says. "Now you do." He doesn't know which picture he's just discarded. But she has barely glanced at it. He straightens and makes his face serious. "The war will be over," he assures her, "and you'll go home again."

At some point she has put on a brown cardigan, and she stands now with her fists deep in the pockets of it, pushing it down her thighs. "I will never go back there."

"You will," he soothes. "You don't think so now . . ."

"Belgium is *gone*," she says. *"Elle est disparu!"*

This is the first time she has ever used French on him. She whips her averted head, and Johnny reaches out to touch her shoulder. "Naw, it's not gone," he says. "You've just got holes in your memory. I know a lot of guys who get in bad situations, they can't remember how they got out." He is thinking of the kid on the plane who didn't remember what happened to him in the bivouac. "It works out okay," he says. "After the war is over, they'll rebuild from the ground up . . ."

But in fact he suddenly believes her. Why would she go back? She has nobody waiting for her. She could go anywhere—Australia, Panama, the North Pole. She can be anybody she chooses. She can have any life she makes up for herself.

She begins shuffling at the cards again, and he has a thought as large as any that has ever come to him, muscular as a fish. *There are two kinds of people in the world: those who will go home after this war, and those who won't.*

He says, headlong, "You can be anybody you want."

But her hands dither among the cards. "If you can be anybody then you must be nobody."

He wants to tell her about the men who were pulled bleeding out of the Belgian dirt only to crash onto the glass-hard top of the world. But he doesn't know how to say it so it will mean what he wants to mean. He can't tell a girl what she would never understand, the large love among men who sit at the edge of death.

"Edification," she reads, spreading cards. "Oblivion."

For a second he thinks she has said "Olivia." *Those who will go home and those who won't.* Suddenly he is revealed to himself as having no choice but to return to his old life. He sees himself back in Jepson County, Joyce slowly fattening, other babies born in rooms where he is not wanted, growing up into strangers. He sees the fields of dry grass crossed by macadam, Wednesday Rotary, Sunday at his folks' house lining up for the camera. There will be the intramurals in the fall, and in the summer picnics at Lake Ozark, where his belly will sag year by year over his swimming trunks, and the girls will get younger and younger, giggling and calling. He doesn't think that they will call to him.

And as suddenly he is resolved that he will volunteer for that supply-drop over Comanche Flats, no matter what the weather. He'll take that one risk, for the men, for his youth, before he settles in sales or tobacco like his uncles who spend their whole lives looking back.

Simone flicks the cards. "Peregrination," she reads. "Hankering."

Transit: London–Hertfordshire

1946

The girl in the window seat is a familiar sort by now—broadcloth coat gone shiny at the seams, flip-brim hat, her ankles crossed in shoes blacked over the scuffs. British working class, probably headed to see her granny, or maybe she's a home help on her way to a new job. She stares out into the bustle of King's Cross, wearing the stillness of anxiety contained.

It's the sort of train with a corridor along one side giving onto compartments with six seats each. She's presently joined by a fat man in waistcoat and fob, who takes the far seat on the corridor side, and then a weedy college boy carrying a *Times* crossword. Just before they pull out, a woman gets on in a rush, slides into the other window seat and presses her laughter against the glass. Outside on the platform, some good-willed young neighbor or relative lifts a baby up to the glass and takes its hand to pat against the window. The baby screams.

The mother turns, laughter rippling out of a plump mouth, and appeals to the three of them. "Such a kerfuffle!" she says. "I'll only be gone two days!"

The undergrad gives a glance upward, the fat man chuckles. The girl in the cloth coat squints, and the baby screams.

The baby screams. Clawing at the glass, smearing its snot-soaked fingers on the pane, its face a red rubber ball of grief and rage.

"I'm sorry!" the woman appeals to the compartment. She has her dark hair rolled into a neat chignon under a tilted hat. She tucks one coat lapel beneath the other and makes a kissing face to the baby's rage. "What can one do?" she says. "It's not as if I'm *abandoning* the poor sausage."

"They have to learn," the man avers. The woman's infectious tinkle offers itself. "Poor poppet!" the man says, and the mother, "Yes, but he's a boy!" The three of them laugh fondly.

The baby's sobs have become an engine now, implacable and rasping, louder through the glass than the woman can compete with. She shrugs, making a show of giving up. The baby screams.

The woman leans to take the girl into her confidence. "They carry on like the end of the world, but they get over it in a minute. By tomorrow he'll have forgotten me entirely!"

The girl, Simone Lerrante, sixteen, on her way to Little Chatswade, Herts., keeps her eyes on the baby, whose red face has begun to blue although she has seen infants enough to know that it will not strangle itself entirely. That much is true. Mouth stretched to the tonsils, thrust after thrust of noise and blame honk out.

"Lord, lord!" the mother says. She appeals to Simone, even patting the girl's cloth-coat knee. "He'll be laughing by the time we're out of the station." The girl's expressionless expression seems to challenge her. "By the time we pass the first back garden!" she insists.

And they are pulling out. The baby, no sign of subsiding, claws toward the window and slowly disappears backward down the platform. Simone imagines the face appearing once in each windowpane, clenching and bellowing down the length of all the carriages, as if the train were a strip of film.

The mother arranges herself. "Such his-tri*on*ics!" she declares, and glitters at her audience.

They settle back. The sooty station walls suck them north and, as the woman predicted, the gardens start. Little workman's cottages, coal bins, the scabby rows of bean sticks, and here and there more enterprise, more hope, in the form of peonies or a dahlia bed. Soon there will be factories, and then fields and oaks, neat hedgerows to separate the placid sheep. The baby's drool dries on the windowpane.

CHAPTER 2

Home Help

1948/1978

I was eleven before we got a home help. Daddy was made Headmaster at the Saint Alban Grammar School and no longer had time to oversee my sums. And Mummy was—well, now we would say *depressed,* or possibly *fibromyalgic.* Daddy said she was *fragile,* though, in the event, it was Daddy who died young and she who carries on a martyr in the pensioners' home and no longer recognizes me.

But at the time I'm talking about, just after the war, Daddy was active while Mummy lay on the sofa in a blouse with languid sleeves. It's not that she drank—or at least that is not this story. She bathed and dressed, she powdered her jaw and tackled this or that patch of bookish clutter. But she was in some elemental sense increasingly not *there.* Daddy would bring her tea. Seven days a week he wore a narrow three-piece tweed with his Cambridge fob across the vest. And when he was promoted, he signed on for a home help up from Sussex with good references.

I was apprehensive. Daddy said the young lady came from an academic family herself, back in Wallonia. Wallonia to me suggested a moated castle where a Gothic nanny would stand over me with a ruler while I spent hours improving my handwriting.

So it was a pleasant letdown when Simone arrived, an ordinary-enough-looking girl not much older than myself, dirty-blond and slim, apparently thrilled with the attic room that had been set up for her. Daddy and I took her round the house, and she exclaimed over the lion's-head umbrella stand and the Chinese sideboard that had belonged to Grandma Moxham. She passed her hand along the book spines in the library.

"Would I be allowed to borrow a book now and again for my spare time?"

"Certainly, certainly!" Daddy was chuffed at that, of course. I may have been jealous that she pleased him so handily. I had expected her speech to be Francophone. In fact she spoke fluent English in a flat southern accent—"doon" for *down* and "aroon" for *around*—which, however, climbed the social scale during the years she spent with us.

There was in that period after V-E Day a scum that attached to the skin. Coal and gas were still rationed, the soap full of grit, the light bulbs placed stingily. Simone cleaned with a quick wipe and let the dishes drain, but Mum didn't correct her and mainly got out of her way, hiding out in her room with a book or one of her endless jigsaw puzzles. Simone started out to make tea the same as she talked—mushy peas, bangers, Sunday rolled roast—while Daddy introduced a smelly Devon Blue cheese now and again, or a wild hare, and after a while she was doing omelets *fines herbes* instead of over-easy on fried bread.

It was Simone who invented the Do Drama Company and turned a lark into a passion. Oh, I had always liked dressing up, and had since I was a toddler begged Mum's castoffs, which I kept in an old trunk. Daddy even added flourishes from time to time—a bombazine cloak that had been used for some school pageant, or a feather boa from a long-ago Cambridge ball. So I would parade as a grand lady or a wicked witch. It had never occurred to me to justify the swagger with a *plot*.

Simone was charged with meeting me at the bus stop after school and would fill the longish walk with whatever she had read the night before: Scott, Dickens, Hardy, du Maurier. Then, three or four evenings a week we would play back the nub of the plot to the audience of two. Daddy clapped with his hands raised high; Mummy nodded and said an occasional *Bravo*. At the time it both seemed my due and made me strain with eagerness. I *did* so long for my mother's grudging praise.

"Let's do drama," I would beg, and after a few weeks of this, Simone christened us the Do Drama Company Limited.

"*Limited* means we only have two actors," Simone said, which I think I did not recognize as a joke.

Simone Lerrante herself—you would have thought I had no reason to envy or emulate her. It was I who had two parents, a safe and comfortable life with the promise of a university education; and I was very well aware that it was I who had the bronze glints in my hair. I was happy-natured and pig-ignorant, and even then I had a rather larger than average head, which has served me well in the West End and the Royal Shakespeare. Whereas she was pretty enough in a bland way, skinny to the point of underfed.

But in fact Simone had extraordinary powers of transformation. It was in the Do Drama sessions that I first conceived how one could truly *make believe*. She could hold forth as frog or monarch. She had a way of moving that made the lift of an arm seem full of meaning. She could express loss with a quiver of her lip. What she taught me was the gift of concentration, that loss of self that makes this mundane world disappear.

It must have been the first spring Simone was there that Daddy received an invitation to a May Ball at Cambridge. He was Kings College and was sometimes asked back to chaperone. But on this occasion he said no, it would require a new gown for Mummy, which they could not afford. The discussion took place at tea. I remember being ashamed that he would say this in Simone's presence. I wailed in protest. I would find Mummy a dress in the costumes! I would empty out my savings bank! But no. A warning look. I was stricken.

But it was his game. Over the next three weeks Simone and I were invited to watch him assemble in secret a décolletage gown in stripes of grey on ivory, shoes with diamanté buckles, a fall of curls that was miraculously the exact color of her hair—an outfit lovely and also a fantasy of her.

Most of the clothing he brought into his study, where he assembled it on the back of the door. But the hairpiece we were taken to inspect one afternoon in the Étienne Rousselle Ladies' Salon, where it was being kept until the day. This was the first time I met Étienne himself, a man of dark beauty (though not in fact French, as I learned when Simone later tried to speak to him in that tongue).

On the evening of the ball we three went into Daddy's study and draped the dress over the wing chair with the shoes poking underneath and a writing table pushed up to hold the wig form that Étienne had lent us. Then Daddy went to fetch Mummy, and Simone and I waited in a thrill of anticipation.

We should not have expected much. Mummy said, "But I will have to bathe." And then, "Poor Ted, you must have your charade." As if to accept a gift was one more sacrifice. The air went out of the girl joy.

They changed the film twice a week in the local vaudeville house, and the three of us had gone occasionally to one of those Hollywood dramas that flooded Europe after the war. But after Simone came, she and I made a regular Saturday afternoon trek of it, and then also Wednesdays, when my school let out at two.

Simone was adept at remembering plotlines. We switched off the male/female parts, ad-libbing the dialogue, rehearsing in the garden in summer, later in greater secret in her attic room. She could sew, and haunted jumble sales to come home with old curtains or big-brimmed hats or, once, a marabou capelet that I commandeered.

We did equally smart-mouth, historical, and *noir*. We learned how to be courted, how to be in love. We also learned to covet the scrubbed and moneyed look of American living rooms. I developed a Barbara Stanwyck stare and a Katherine Hepburn slouch, also a Cary Grant double-take. Returning shell-shocked soldiers gave rise to a bunch of amnesia movies that Simone favored, especially *Love Letters*, where Jennifer Jones's memory is restored by the love of Joseph Cotton. But my own greatest success was *The Major and the Minor*, where, at twelve, I got to be Ginger Rogers at thirty, pretending to be Susu Applegate at twelve. I did it mainly by doing a bad job of being twelve, with saucer eyes and a pout, my voice in the top of my mouth. Then I would suddenly make my tone throaty: "He's going to war so the same thing that happened to France doesn't happen to us." Daddy gave us a standing ovation for that one, and Mum said, "Darla; very *good*."

I called her *Simmy* and she called me *Darling*. She read gulpingly, the classics on Daddy's shelves, the romances Mummy brought home from the library, the movie magazines at the news agent. She bought a box camera and took pictures of me as Cary Grant and Ginger Rogers. She said, "I'm going to Hollywood when I have enough money saved." She said, "If I can't make it as an actress, I can take the pictures. I can sew the gowns." These plans seemed daring beyond the exploits of the adventurers in our movies (though when I actually came to making film, I found it a tedium of waiting and repetition. Give me a good three-hour run at *Hedda* or *The White Devil* any day!).

What Simone would not do was talk about Wallonia, which I now understood to be a part of Belgium. I asked gingerly, "Do you have any brothers or sisters?" to which she replied, so that it sounded like something she had learned, "No. I was the only child of only children."

"Well," I asked, "what was it like back there? You know, school, and friends."

"I don't remember."

"But I mean, just the ordinary."

"I don't remember!"

Thinking of Jennifer Jones, I suggested, "Maybe you have amnesia."

"Don't be silly! That only happens in the cinema."

I asked Daddy about her one Sunday, by the fire in his library as he was making out his lesson plan. It was dark by four these winter days. He said we should be delicate in speaking to Simone of her early life. He said that sometimes it's hard to remember the things that cause us pain.

This was a curious notion; I could not forget the things that caused me pain: Mummy's distance, boys' taunts, the hard pebbled surface of the playground. Daddy picked a pipe from the rack and started grinding out the bowl with his penknife.

"But what happened to her parents?"

"I gather her mother was lost to illness. About her father I don't know, though she apparently believes he is dead."

"She isn't sure?"

"That's not for us to ask, Darla. Sometimes remembering the past is like trying to remember a film. You know—which part came first, or what happened then."

"She's going to Hollywood!" I burst out, but he just sighed and put down his pipe.

"Darla, your playlets are enjoyable recreation. Simone is very bright, and should go to school. But how many girls do you think, all over England, fantasize about going into moving pictures?"

Jealously I imagined these other girls who might dress up and replay scenes from films. "If Simone isn't *discovered*," I said, "she can run the camera. She already *has expertise* with her Kodak."

Daddy sighed again. "Sweet girl, you must realize that people are set on a certain path, and don't deviate far from it. In Simone's case, there is the misfortune of being born into war."

"Some people change their path!" I protested. "Your Shakespeare, your . . ." Shakespeare was the only genius who came to mind.

For a time he studied the fire, and I felt excluded from his mood. "Ordinary people make ordinary mistakes." He picked up the pipe and began scouring its black interior again. "Most of us make peace with our situations, and that is a good thing."

And I suppose he was right. I've tried finding any mention of Simone in such movie magazines as I can still find, but she doesn't seem to have made any name for herself in Hollywood, though it sometimes annoys me that Daddy died before he saw how thoroughly *I* have deviated!

Some weeks after the surprise for Mummy, Daddy took us to have our hair done at Étienne's. It was in those days a miracle to have a hairdresser on a village high street. I remember that the water was heated on a little gas ring, and Étienne poured it over us to rinse out the soap. Still, it was glamorous enough. A mirror stretched from window to wall, two ponderous chairs swiveled in front of it, a Medusan contraption trailed perm wires. There were two dryers like diving bells and an array of evil-smelling chemicals.

And Étienne Rousselle: his handsome features over my head in the mirror, his concentration absolute. "What would please you, mam'selle? A marcel? A chignon?" He was, I realized, the only man I had ever seen who was as beautiful as a film star: his perfect symmetry, his treacle eyes. I can still hear him, slightly breathy, in an accent vaguely European: "This hair is the color of ancient amber! I think we shall trim gent-ly to the shoulder. Just a lit-tle."

Dazzled, I said, "You know best."

"Oh, yes! Because beauty is the only option." He reached to pinch my cheeks. "Just the faintest touch of rouge, perhaps."

Daddy laughed. "Take care. You'll have me in serious trouble."

Étienne cupped my chin. "Nothing is more natural for a woman than to use makeup. No, you laugh, Teddy, but just look at a woman in love. Her eyes are deep, her skin glows. What could be more natural than to emulate that state?" I had never heard anyone talk like this.

Étienne engaged my eyes in the mirror. The two of us were caught in a silvering of reality, framed large, as if on a movie screen. I became rigid with self-consciousness—and then he guided me to the basin, tipped me back and began to wash my hair.

"En-joy it. Let the follicles re-lax." His fingertips traced the circumference of my ears. Lather burgeoned. I re-laxed the weight of my head into his palms and felt my brain bounce sensuously.

Eventually he wrapped a towel where his tender fingertips had been and helped me to the swivel chair, where I waited in a stupor while Simmy was treated to the same seduction, and Daddy and Étienne chatted easily over our heads.

All this lasted a long while, since I must sit through her cut and set, and she through mine. We sat under the helmets in the blare of warm air. Then, for Simmy first, because my hair took longer to dry, he unwound the metal tubes, smacked lotion between his hands and palmed it on her neck.

She said swooningly, "*Ça sent bon.*"

To which Étienne replied, "Bo-coo, bo-coo."

I understood at once that he was not French, and the shame I felt for him was shot through by a fierce protectiveness. Then he unveiled me to myself, older by ten years in my Joan Crawford waves. My posture had matured as well; I found myself brisk and competent walking out onto the High Street and toward home.

"As if the cinema doesn't put ideas enough in their heads." Mummy clattered the kettle. "What would that have cost, I wonder?"

I had been in a fog all afternoon, but when this tone overtook the evening tea my brain was thick as socks. Mummy made sniping jokes. "And you, Simone, are you going to do us a Busby Berkeley chorus?"

"She's more Jean Harlow, I'd have thought," Daddy defended her 'do.

By now I was thirteen. I saw myself in the mirror in the one bath we all shared, and I was proud of flexuous limbs and little scoops of breasts. Simmy too saw me naked as a matter of bedtime routine, though what she praised in me was "natural style."

We had been to see *Pimpernel Smith*—Leslie Howard again, my pattern for a Hollywood version of Daddy, coolly performing tricks for the Resistance. The deliciously dark Ludmilla Koslowski comes to him for help. Simone played Horatio ("The Pimpernel") Smith—Horatio, which is the name of the perfect friend.

Many war plots could be recycled into the relationship of the brave Polish lady and the ice-cool spy who could disappear in the smoke of his own cigarette. Ludmilla and Horatio huddled over the wireless under the stairs, hiding from the proto-Gestapo, whom Horatio confronted among the bare rose bushes: "You are doomed, captain of murderers!" We made rendezvous at the end of the hedge, passing surreptitious touches.

We kissed first in the garden under the clothesline, me trailing a curtain as Ludmilla. I mouthed, "Beauty is the only option," and brushed my lips across her cheek. Simone leaned back against the clothespole and reached her arms around my neck. There was threatening sky beyond the fence. I put my arms around her and the clothespole both. The metal hurt my wrist. I kissed her on the lips and leaned my head into her neck.

"Ludmilla," she said. My heart pounded against her pounding heart. "My darling. Take care."

She called me *Darling* every day; she had often called me *darling* in our playlets. But she had never called me *darling* when I could feel the breath of it. "I must be away for France," she warned, "but I'll be back," and then reverted to our favorite line: "For England's the one land I know / Where men with splendid hearts may go." We both sobbed, and kissed again.

I put on a furry shrug and said goodbye on the back step. "Don't forget me," she teased as I turned inside. But once in the hall to the back stairs I went up not only the first flight but the second, into the narrow passage to Simone's room. I divested myself of jacket and then capelet and blouse, and got into the bed in my singlet, one strap of which I let fall.

I heard her on the stairs. She appeared, tentative, at the door. "My most dear," she thrummed in her fake accent, "we cannot leave each other thus."

When I thought about Leslie Howard or Étienne Rousselle I felt queasy in my stomach, but when I saw Simone taking off her camisole, the skin between my legs contracted.

"Quickly, before we must part," I said.

She knelt on the bed and spoke in movie-talk to disguise our panic. "God will forgive us, my darling Ludmilla, for God only knows how long we have to live."

I don't know how many times this happened. I know that it was a period of energy and aliveness, with an undertone of constant anxiety. In spite of the banality of our sources, I saw Simone's beauty in the act of its becoming. I watched her bones become more defined, her carriage more confident. Yet in our embraces I never lost the sense that this was *playing* love. That I should kiss her was required by *story*.

I remember the smell of the attic—paraffin and starch, her breath on the frigid air. The seizure of little muscles over my lower back when I cupped her scant breast in my hand, put my mouth on it, pretended the passion that in fact I confusingly felt as she arched her back pretending passion. "My most dear Ludmilla!" I remember that I became aware of another tread on the stairs just one moment too late in the dense fog of that concentration. Or much too late, because what could ever have stopped us except discovery?

Mummy. The sound she made was of the wind being knocked out of her: "Haughhh!" She stood in the narrow doorway leaning against the frame with both her hands. A string of spittle attached me to Horatio's breast. Mummy gasped for breath and I thought after all that she was *fragile* and would die.

"Mummy, we're doing drama!" I stupidly said, and pulled my singlet on. Simone scrambled among the bedcovers for her camisole.

"Go to your room, Darla Moxham."

I had to pass her to obey her, and couldn't make myself do so. I hung there chattering, "It's Pimpernel Smith, Mummy. The Germans are after him. He may never see Ludmilla again!"

"I cannot," Mummy said, her usually sallow face florid, "I cannot speak to you at present." And to my relief she turned and fled.

This is the way disaster was handled in a British household: Simone cut the crusts from watercress sandwiches. I set out the sugar caster, the scones, the gooseberry preserve. At table I chattered brightly between mouthfuls. Mummy fingered her temple, her shorthand for incipient migraine. Daddy played Abstraction. Simone played the Hired Help. She washed up and put the tea things away and disappeared. Daddy went to his study, Mum up to her room, and after a while I closed myself carefully in my own. I was unwilling to go back down to the WC so I peed in my basin and lay stiffly down to sleep.

And did sleep, for a time. When I woke I could smell my urine in the close air. I heard voices downstairs. The weight of my shame, for sheer heaviness, might have broken the bedframe. I found the smell of my waste intolerable, and I had to find an excuse to get closer to those voices. So I took the basin and descended, sliding against the wall.

I stood outside the door to Daddy's library, which was ajar, holding a bowl of my own piss in both hands like an offering while he sat in front of the cold fireplace and my mother stood at the window where a branch of linden bounced.

And they were not talking about Simone and me at all!—but about him, his failures. Or at least, the first thing I heard was her voice, tight with contempt, saying "The whole atmosphere is poisoned," so that for a moment I thought they were talking about my pungent burden.

But she continued, "I won't be your beard."

She said, "You've taken my life and wiped your feet on it."

She said, "It's a scandal you being headmaster to all those boys."

At which I heard his chair creak. There was a hush. Then he said fiercely "I am. Not. Interested. In. *Children*!"

The floor fell away. I went to the WC and tipped out the bowl.

How could he not be interested in children? He spent hours with me bent over my little projects, teaching me insects and the Kings and the subjunctive. My *mother* was perhaps not interested in children, but his pupils sought him out, praised him for fairness. He gave his life to children! In short, the idea was so impossible to fit into my feelings about him that in the end I did not fit it. For that sleepless night the sentence echoed through my head, and then it receded, and then I thought of it no more.

Meanwhile the Do Drama Company was foreclosed. Mum took me to Leicester to visit Grandma Moxham for a week. She took me down to London to see proper theatre done by proper actors. I knew I was being kept from Simmy, but the daily tenor of our friendship did not change. We were teasing, funny, and offhand. Only there was no playacting and without playacting no attraction, as if my passion was not for her but for the making-up.

Within a week or two Daddy informed us of a generous arrangement he had made for Simone. He was friends with the Chief Education Officer of Cambridgeshire, a man much interested in the intellectual opportunities of young women. This personage had arranged that Simmy should be enrolled in a grammar school in Bidborough, leading to a Higher School Certificate—which could mean, if she was diligent in her studies, a possible place and bursary at Cambridge.

Daddy had also arranged that she should be housed with a math master and his wife who lived in nearby Suttling, Mr. Charles and Lydie Heywood. I had heard Daddy speak of them. I knew they had lost their only child, at something called the Battle of Arnhem. Now Daddy indicated that Simmy would be a comfort to them.

Of course I knew that she was being exiled. I also knew it was a chance for her to go a different path. *A gift from Daddy*, who was not interested in children.

I am remembering a day before all this—but after Étienne had massaged my head and transformed me for the silver screen. We were walking, Daddy and Simmy and I, one Saturday home from the market, Simmy with a bag of necessaries and Daddy with another which he held against his shoulder so that the tops of a dirty-fen celery brushed his cheek. I was larking about, spinning some project for the afternoon, when we chanced upon Étienne. We stopped to chat. It was one of those crisp spring days under a hurtingly bright-blue sky. I danced about, Simmy stood listening as the two men bantered, the celery shoving against Daddy's cheek so that it left a black smudge along his jaw. He reached to wipe it, but Étienne was quicker. Étienne's fingers were long, the nails blunt and buffed. He brushed the dirt away, and then surprisingly brushed the backs of his fingers lightly from Daddy's jaw up his cheek. He gave Daddy a sad, ironic look—such a complicated look as Horatio would give Ludmilla at their parting or when they were in danger—and my father's eyes filled with tears.

Then Étienne smiled, and Daddy laughed. Simmy said something bright, and Étienne bent to fluff my hair. For that moment I experienced perfect happiness, there in the company of the three most gorgeous people I knew in the world, the three I loved.

Being at thirteen self-centered in the way of thirteen-year-old girls, I had never noticed that anybody loved but I.

CHAPTER 3

Straight Home

1950

Simone free-wheels down Suttling Hill, legs out in front although she has tucked her wide skirt under her, in which position she shows a bit of thigh. The bicycle belongs to Mr. Heywood, and Mrs. Heywood did not think it proper for a girl. But if Simone was to go up the shops as a matter of course there was no alternative, and in this instance Mr. Heywood prevailed.

Everybody in Suttling says "go up the shops" though the village is in the valley and almost everybody must descend to them. This kind of thing makes Simone laugh, and when she points it out to the greengrocer and the bakery lady, they laugh with her. She is well liked in town—an enthusiastic presence. She has once or twice deliberately forgotten something so that Mrs. Heywood, after a "Tsk!" of exasperation, will send her freewheeling down Suttling Hill to go up the shops again.

At village center is a curving hedge leading to a row of half-timbered commissaries, a pub called The Green Knight, and an arched stone bridge over a stream locally referred to as the River Wen. There is a whitewashed church with a steeple and a four-hundred-year history. The rectory garden is full now, in early autumn, of faded beauty. Simone leans and scoops a handful of rose petals into her basket, then hurries to the baker for soda bread, to the greengrocer for a pound of sprouts, and on to the butcher shop, where massive Spencer Duff stands in an apron as wide as her bedsheet.

"A half a pound of chicken livers," she says to Duff, and wrinkles up her nose at the shiny knobs of offal he presents to her. This makes him laugh, but he thinks she is a lucky girl. A decade ago there were all kinds of volunteers to take in the little refugees. Now it is a generous oddity for the Heywoods to be housing a young woman who spends the bulk of her time in *school*. The labor force needs women, and she could make a useful shopgirl or a nurse. But he beams at her. She's bright, and the bright can be lucky in this postwar economy.

Simone stows her bag and pushes off, detouring to the little bridge, where she stops and squints upriver in the hope of a swan. Sometimes there are swans.

"Mind you come straight home," Mrs. Heywood always says.

What now serves for home is a brick bungalow called The Gote, which is not a misspelling of the animal but an ancient term for a water channel, in this case basically a ditch along the garden.

Mrs. Heywood is a person of wide-ranging skills. She can sew, embroider, needlepoint, knit, tat, cook, garden, organize a charity jumble or a wedding shower and arrange the flowers on the day. Now, having acquiesced to Teddy Moxham's (and her husband's) notion of taking in a student, she has determined to teach Simone the skills of which the girl is so obviously in need.

In the town, Mrs. H.'s tea roses and compotes are much admired. Simone admires them. She admires Mrs. H's perfect posture and the perfect organization of her larder. The problem is that her talented hostess is owed a debt of gratitude—and Mrs. H. conveys an awareness of this debt in every gesture. It permeates the air of the kitchen like a smell.

"An orderly home is a happy home," Mrs. H says. "You'll thank me when you have a home of your own."

Today there are no swans. The hill that is so free and wind-rushed on the way down must be pedaled up one effortful footfall after another.

The room could be nice. There's a narrow metal-springs bed, which leaves space for a wing chair and a table under a window that looks out onto the back garden. But when Simone asked if she might remove the plaid spread and replace it with the blue quilt in the airing cupboard, Mrs. Heywood looked as offended as if she had proposed knocking down a wall. Nor may she put the cricket trophies away, nor remove the shin guards from the back of the door, nor the portrait of Nelson at Trafalgar. She understands keenly that she is living in the dead boy's shrine.

She rises at six to make breakfast for herself and Mr. Heywood. He will drive her the two miles to Bidborough in his Morris. After her classes she must walk straight home to help in the house till teatime at six, and after tea go to this room to study. Saturday morning is for the weekly cleaning; Saturday afternoons she has free. Sunday mornings while the Heywoods worship, she bathes, washes her knickers and hangs them in the airing cupboard.

She is least lonely in those few hours she is alone. At school, when she sees the other girls heading off, the girls who would be her friends if she could linger, she cannot bear to return where under Mrs. H.'s eye she has become awkward with implements she could handle easily in the past; or to this room that she may not make her own because the walls themselves speak of the fallen boy. Because she "must" be grateful and is not, she is resentful, and then ashamed of her resentment, and resentful of that shame in a carousel of exhausting loneliness. The distance between what she knows and what she feels leaves her sometimes balancing in thin air.

To get to Cordwainers Grammar she crosses through a nineteenth-century graveyard with moss on the stones. Cordwainers Hall itself is shabby-grand, so named because it used to house the shoemakers' guild when that was the primary employment of the parish. Now it is divided into the Girls' High School on one side and Cordwainers Grammar on the other. The more dignified name means that the boys are headed for Cambridge, whereas the girls are preparing for marriage, though in fact the classes are shared, and more girls qualify for the universities every year.

Just before the columned portico there's a horse-chestnut tree the boys climb to pick the huge hard seeds. Even at nineteen years old they still have conker wars, slamming the seeds into each other on long threads. Serious prestige is at stake. Inside the hall there are cubbyholes for books and for the plimsolls required for gym, and which the girls call tenny-pumps. There is a formal assembly hall for matins and the occasional play—not that there is any great tradition of drama; it's just *ad hoc*, when a teacher has the notion to put together a production.

Unlike Simone's primary school back in Hove, which was chaotic and peremptory, the Cordwainer staff are knowledgeable, the demands diverse. She is the oldest of the girls, having missed out on part of her schooling, but the teachers are used to older boys interrupted by the war, and do not mind her. Simone struggles with maths and is put back a year to catch up on algebra. History reorganizes time in her head.

It is in stories she feels at home, just as she did at the Moxhams. Reading, she becomes Dorothea Brooke, Tess Durbeyfield, Lady Teazle, The White Devil. She writes her essays over and over. At the end of her second year she is awarded the English Prize, which is a hardbound notebook with leather at the spine and creamy unruled pages such as an artist might use. Mr. Thaddeus, in bestowing the prize, says that Simone should "beware the sentence fragment" but that she "can put an idea on paper."

But when she finds herself facing the page there is not an idea in her head. And when she finally begins it is with the few facts she knows of herself, copied from the birth certificate that was saved and ironed flat by Auntie Toffat in Sussex:

> I was born 21 September 1930 in the Maternité Publique of Liege, Belgium, weight 3.18 kilograms, to mère Françoise Broissard Lerrante, housewife; and père Gaston Lerrante, Professor of Philologie.

She thinks, rolls her pencil on her tongue, and writes:

> There are other things I know without knowing how I know them: That my mother died of liver failure during the war, and that my father

also died some time later. That my father's real subject matter was English literature, and "Philologie" some way of making it academically respectable. These come to me as facts. Whereas when I try to remember my mother her features weave in and out, ghostly. I *seem* to remember a perfume bottle. A dish shaped like a cabbage? A pottery animal? I try to put these images together to make sense, but there are too many pieces missing.

After which she must go for provisions for the Christmas pudding: figs, prunes, raisins dark and light, eggs, carrots, flour, molasses, and three cups of suet, which Mr. Duff tells her is the fat off of cow kidney. Later, turning the handle of the metal grinder where the fruit and offal mix, she learns that this Christmas pudding is not for Christmas. No, this year's pudding was made last Christmas, and this one will be set alight next year. It's hard for Simone to consider year-old kidney fat as a holiday treat, but Mrs. H. says the pudding "lasts forever" owing to its ample rum content. She says that every woman should know how to make a Christmas pudding. Mr. H. says he will provide the rum.

The Heywoods are both short. The buttons of his waistcoat strain; she is girdled tight. But there the resemblance ends. Mrs. H.—Mr. H. calls her *Mother*—stands up straight and offers the correct way to accomplish anything. Mr. H., called *Big Chaz*, is slouched and often muddled. It's hard for Simone to remember that he teaches *mathematics*.

Nevertheless he also teaches her useful things. In the spring he shows her how to stake beans and tomatoes. In winter one afternoon as he makes the fire, he offers her a cider and asks if she knows how to make Welsh logs.

"No? You open a newspaper and roll it from the corner, tight, until you have a long, tight tube." He demonstrates, afterward coiling the tube around his plump hand. "And tuck the end into the middle so it stays. Eh? It's near enough good as kindling. Ha." She tries it, and her coil holds at first try.

Mr. Heywood shows approval in the form of bilabials: "Mm, nn, mm," and she imagines him in the classroom, articulate as to numbers but unable to manage ordinary speech.

In the Lent term there is a new fifth form teacher, Mr. Fintan Quinn. Simon mouths the sound of *Fintan Quinn*, which seems to her musical-Irish. Mr. Quinn is tall and craggy-faced, with sea-blue eyes and a tousle of dark hair going gray along the sides. His cheeks are pock-marked as from a serious case of acne back when he was the age most of his pupils are now. His voice is deep and mellow, and also natural in some way that teachers are not usually natural. He talks as if he is making conversation.

"Simone Lerrante." When he calls the roll, he pronounces her name with gutturals on the r's. Does he speak French? Or is that a brogue? Claudia, who seems to know things, says Mr. Quinn has been to America on a "fellowship," to study, but she doesn't know what. She says he has an American wife and a baby boy. Simone imagines the wife with the swaddled boy on her lap, Fintan Quinn with one hip on the edge of the chair, his arm holding them in a tweed crescent of adoration.

The first day, when Mr. Quinn has finished with the roll, he leans on the lectern the same as Mr. Trevor did. But he has no notes in front of him, and instead of beginning to lecture, with the dates and events and biographical facts they must write down, he begins straightaway:

> My heart leaps up when I behold
> A rainbow in the sky.

Mr. Quinn *talks* the lines, as if it were he, and not Wordsworth, whose heart was doing the leaping. He sounds like someone confiding in you.

> The Child is father of the Man;
> And I could wish my days to be
> Bound each to each by natural piety.

All of them are pen in hand, waiting for the lecture to begin. Instead, he indicates Joel and asks, "What do you think Wordsworth means by, 'The Child is father of the Man'?"

They are all embarrassed. What is a teacher for but to tell you what Wordsworth meant? However, Joel, and then Pamela and then all of them struggle to come up with the meaning of the lines as Mr. Quinn seems to want them to, arriving after some forty-five minutes at a merely tentative conclusion. But most of them will remember it, and some will locate it in their lives.

Simone is one of these. She leaves the class unsettled, thrilled. She copies the poem into her special notebook. She memorizes it. She thinks, fearfully, how she might be now setting a life pattern for herself, learning how to dust baseboards and make Christmas pudding. *The Child is mother of the Woman.* Then she thinks how the poem opened like a daffodil as the discussion hour passed. And then, failing of any further insight on the poem, she thinks of Mr. Fintan Quinn. She writes:

> My heart leaps up.

Now five days a week she waits ardently for one o'clock, not somehow slighting her other classes, which have become the satellites of Romantic Poetry.

Coleridge, Byron, Shelley—Mr. Quinn never offers them a lecture. He knows all of the poems by heart and never stumbles voicing them. Instead, they grope their way forward, heated in defense of this idea or that. From time to time he asks a student to read aloud, but passes no judgments on either the reading or the interpretation. If some of them—if Simone—suspect that he is subtly leading them one direction or other with a lift of eyebrows here, an affirmative "Ah!" there—well, that is his way of teaching. If some of them, girls and boys alike, are in love with him, well, teaching has always included that form of education. When Stephen L. gets up the bravado to ask why Mr. Quinn never gives them any *facts*, Fintan Quinn says, "Oh, those are in the book if you want them. It doesn't alter that *a poem says what it says.*" Claudia, whose mother works in the front office and knows all the gossip, says Mr. Quinn brought the New Criticism back from America.

Simone copies each poem into her journal and memorizes all of them, because Mr. Quinn says memorization strengthens the muscle of memory. She suspects her memory-muscle is in need of strengthening. Fretfully, she tries to exercise this organ, to call up a credible and stable childhood memory, but all she can come up with is an unspecified scent of perfume and a—is it? a pottery rabbit.

At one o'clock five days a week she takes her seat in the classroom. There is a hollow in her midsection that sets the rhythm of her heart awry. She's afraid the other girls can see it. She goes straight home, where she's afraid she'll drop a plate, and after tea sits absorbed—*sponged up*—into the lines she memorizes, whispering because the Heywoods would think her daft to be mumbling away in Young Chaz's room.

> My heart aches, and a drowsy numbness pains
> My sense, as though of hemlock I had drunk,
> Or emptied some dull opiate . . .

She cannot completely separate the sound of the poems from the sight of Fintan Quinn, blue eyes and wounded cheeks. She wants nothing from him but that he should know her to be a kindred spirit. She understands that all the girls must have a crush on Mr. Quinn. But no one, she thinks, is so crushed as she.

One night she dreams that she is standing at an upper story window; beyond it lies flowing water. She is waiting, for what, is not clear, but the intensity of the waiting pervades everything. When she wakes she goes to the window and leans forward over the potted geraniums. The threat is gone but leaves behind a melancholy sense of *wrong*. She solaces herself with the thought of Fintan Quinn, his little family, the wife strong and beautiful for him.

And then disaster. She writes in her journal:

> I have humiliated myself with Fintan Quinn and all the class. We were doing "Ode on a Grecian Urn." Mr. Quinn asked, "Why does he say,

> 'O, Attic shape!?'" I said, "Where else would you find a Grecian urn but in the attic?" Mr. Q. laughed, the whole class laughed. I knew I had said something stupid.
>
> Now I am the dunce. O God.

She can't leave it alone. She can't. When they have done with Keats she waits after class until the others have left, then goes to his desk, heart in mouth. Fintan Quinn looks up.

"Yes, Simone?"

And she tells him the thing she wouldn't say in class, "What *I* thought Keats meant—

> Beauty is truth, truth beauty—that is all
> Ye know on earth and all ye need to know.

—what *I* thought he meant was, 'That's all *you* know.' As if there's another truth, but humans couldn't handle it."

He leans his chin on his curled fingers. "That's an interesting idea, Simone. Why didn't you bring it up in class?"

She hesitates. She can see the corona of blue points around his pupil. She says, "I was too embarrassed after that stupid thing I said about the attic."

"Oh, that. We all thought you'd made a joke. You should have gone along with it."

Such kindness, Fintan Quinn.

"By the way, Simone. I'm going to direct The Arts Club production of *The Agamemnon*. I hope to see you at the tryouts." He smiles, mischievous. "It would be good to have a *tall* Clytemnestra."

A little laugh catches in her throat. He sees her. He has asked her to "do drama." But of course she can't. And she can't for the moment tell him how she couldn't come to rehearsals. How she's the one who doesn't pay school fees, because she pays with her obligation day after day to stand in for a dead son.

"That's wonderful," she says.

She goes at once (*Come straight home!*) to the library, but the three copies of *The Oresteia* and two of *The Complete Greek Drama* have been checked out.

There's also, she knows, a set of the Greeks in Mr. Heywood's study. She goes back to The Gote but doesn't want to incur extra debt by asking to borrow the book. However, Mr. Heywood has a streak of bumbling kindness in him. So she tells him, "It's for school," and he pulls *The Oresteia* off the shelf. An old translation, dated before even World War One.

Allay her anger, still her frenzied tongue
E'er she exact a recompense beyond
Capacity of Argos to repay.

She reads when she ought to be doing parallelograms, perplexed at the choice of play. She does not like the action or the message.

You heard me say the words I spake of yore,
But now the meaning of such speech is fled.
Or ne'er could I have spilled this sovereign blood,
My husband and my mortal enemy.

She doesn't see why, in this day and age, the Cordwainers Arts Club should pick a heroine who is hideous in her power and cruelty, or why Mr. Quinn should want to direct it, or should see her in the character of Clytemnestra, tall or not.

Her vexation gives her courage, and the next day she holds back after class again and tells Mr. Quinn why she will not be taking part.

"I couldn't go to rehearsals. I have to go straight home."

Fintan Quinn doesn't turn a hair. "Well, in that case, why not have a go at designing the set? That's something you could do in the evenings, isn't it, in your spare time?"

"But I don't know anything about design."

"Neither does anyone else in the class. You've seen plays."

She hesitates. "I've been to the cinema." And he says more gently, "Never mind. I've got a book on the amphitheatre at Athens. To see what the original looked like."

Afterward she wracks her brain trying to imagine a stage set where this particular murder might take place that would not be just a copy of the one in Mr. Quinn's book. She would so like to please him! Opening night he would introduce her to his wife. He would praise her: *This is the pupil I told you about . . .*

The room where she sits scribbling is alien. She's tired and cold. It's theoretically been spring now for ten days, and tomorrow April starts. And she is still in double socks.

But on the third of April she sees it right in front of her. On the windowsill she has propped a snapshot of Cordwainers Hall that she took with her Brownie when she first arrived, its Grecian columns and the horse chestnut tree. Speculative, she takes the snapshot and draws quick black lines over it, leaving white pillars with prominent capital and base. In front of this palace she converts the conker tree into a few curves, like a cloud on a prong.

When she takes this idea to Mr. Q. he guffaws. "Good girl!" he says. "I thought you'd figure it out."

He says they can use a grid for scaling up the sketch. He suggests using Greek letters to say "Cordwainers Hall" on the pediment. The Watchman can have a conker on a string.

Simone is late to British History and takes a demerit, happily.

There are four Saturdays between now and the production, four afternoons when she may take part in the building of her design. Mr. Quinn stays in Cordwainers Hall from morning to night. Rehearsals are relegated to mornings; in the afternoon he teaches the crew how to scale up her cartoon. The crew consists of four boys, two of whom she knows from class. First they build a flat-frame, then stretch over it an enormous canvas. She considers it a matter of pride to handle the boards and the heavy cloth. Her skirt is sometimes awkward, but these boys don't pay much attention to her, which means that they accept her on the team. Mr. Quinn takes her sketch and puts it on the enlarger in the Art Department. Then the crew apply a half-inch grid to it and draw a twelve-inch grid on the canvas. Everyone is assigned a number of squares to draw on the canvas exactly as they appear in the enlargement. When the drawing is done and pronounced good by Mr. Quinn, then they paint, in tandem, checking the canvas against the cartoon as they go. Simone sweats though the hall is cold.

The second Saturday she comes "straight home" more than an hour late, fingers full of paint and glue, her blue jumper ruined.

"You're in a good mood these days," Mrs. H. observes, as if a good mood is an affront. She sits by the fire purling a green and purple jumper into being. It occurs to Simone that Mrs. H. has talents but no taste. The dining room wall has two wallpapers, all roses below the picture rail and sailboats above. What is skill if you have no sense of life? She eats a cold chicken thigh over the sink and does the dishes. She hears Mrs. H. say something and hears Mr. H.'s sharp reply.

By the time she comes out, Mrs. H. has gone off to bed, but Simone thinks this quarrel is between the two of them and it is not her business to address it. The fire has burned low, and Mr. H. says she can try restarting it if she likes, so Simone sits making Welsh logs, then squats to shove each one with the poker under the grate. The coils smoke, smolder, and go out.

Then suddenly the flames leap and lick beyond the aperture. Simone jumps up, arms flailing for balance. She takes a step back and runs up against Mr. Heywood, who reaches around under her arms and grasps her by both breasts. Simone shrieks, but immediately stifles the sound. He is already apologizing, "I didn't mean . . . I'm so sorry."

And she is covered in confusion, does not know whether it was an accident, whether he only meant to steady her, or whether she somehow invited what could not have been more absent to her mind. He seems as confused as she, keeps apologizing while she continues to say *no, no, my clumsiness,* but also mumbles that she must work. She leaves for Little Chaz's room with the fire now merrily roaring on the grate.

The Cordwainers curriculum is not meant to include any Americans, but Mr. Quinn has added several poems each by Walt Whitman and Emily Dickinson, which he passes out mimeographed. One day in class, when they are discussing Whitman as the poet walks from this soldier to that in the hospital, Jared says in a stage whisper "He's a bloody Communist."

Mr. Quinn trains a calm look on him. "Do you mean Communist, or do you mean Soviet?" Jared shoots back, "Same thing!" Several of the boys—and girls, too—grin and nod. So Mr. Quinn stops and tells them how the real Communism is based on the creed, "From each according to his ability, to each according to his need." And how the Soviets, especially Stalin, have subverted that. He talks about fundamental rights of the weak. He says, "And in that sense, Jesus Christ was the first Communist."

Nobody says anything but the feeling is electric. Then Mr. Q says, "And tomorrow, one of your parents will call the Headmaster to tell him I said so."

Simone has already copied the Americans into her journal. Now she tucks the journal between the mattress and the springs.

Simone has no interest at all in the progress of the *Agamemnon* rehearsals, no envy of Pamela, who is also tall, in the role as Clytemnestra, and whom, on the third Saturday, she hears shrieking. This compartmentalized indifference is shared by the rest of the crew, who wait impatiently for the histrionics to subside, then stand the set up on its braces, and walk back and forth admiring their handiwork. Mr. Fintan Quinn looks haggard but excited.

The boys are chuffed. "Hip-hip, hooray!" they shout—ironically, to mask their self-satisfaction.

It is on this third Saturday that Mrs. Quinn stops by—with the baby, who is in fact a toddler. The boy hides behind his mother's skirt, just beyond the wings, where Mr. Quinn goes to talk to her. She is nearly as tall as Mr. Quinn, bony but somehow substantial, with very black hair swept up into a bun. She is fretful like the child, and Mr. Quinn a little querulous. He walks them deeper into the wings.

Simone sees that she has mis-imagined the woman and the marriage. Her head full of Clytemnestra's bloody raving, it comes to her that marriage is stupid. Who would call the Heywoods' house, for instance, a *happy home*? Or the Moxhams'? Or for that matter Auntie Cox's back in Sussex? Better never to marry! But at this point she stumbles up against the images of the two women teachers in Cordwainers Hall, Miss Harley and Miss Olmstead, one pinched and the other embarrassingly buxom, married to botany and anthropology, respectively.

Mrs. Quinn disappears, and when the boys disperse Simone hangs back. Fintan Quinn seems in no hurry to shut up shop. They sit on the edge of the apron and he produces a leather flask half full of Scotch, which he calls "malt." He offers her a cigarette, which she declines; lights one himself, which is against every rule she knows. And then, feeling like a prude, she accepts the bottle and drinks after him. Malt has a dark taste, as sweet as sharp.

"It's a marvelous set you've designed, Miss Lerrante," he says.

She says, "Thank you," and then has nothing more to say. Unable to let the silence stretch, she blurts, "Your class has changed my life."

He says, mischievous again, "Is that so? And what poem or poet?"

"Emily Dickinson," she says at once. "'The Soul selects her own Society . . .'"

"Very good," Fintan Quinn returns. "'Then shuts the door.'"

"'Unmoved, an emperor be kneeling / On her low mat.'"

"'I've known her from an ample nation. / Choose one.'"

Simone finishes, "'Then shut the valves of her attention. / Like stone.'"

Her chest wall slams.

"Well!" he says. "And does attention have valves, then?"

What? "No. The heart does."

"Are you saying that the heart is in the poem even though it is not in the poem?"

She thinks it's a test, even a trick. "Yes, I am," she says.

"There," he grins. "And that insight, Miss Lerrante, you may call by the name of Literary Criticism."

The playful note confuses her. It takes her a minute to follow his meaning and be torn between disappointment and joy. This was, after all, what she wanted of him, wasn't it? Acknowledgment? Affirmation?

Then he says sharply: "Don't be *too* adorable, Simone. I'm only human."

The skin of her face stings. But it's also a compliment, isn't it? Her face settles into a smirk against her will. "I'm human too," she mumbles.

And soon, but not soon enough to let him know how she smarts, she rises and says that it's late and she must go straight home.

That night she copies more Whitman in her journal:

> Reexamine all that you have been told.
> Dismiss that which insults your soul.

On the night of the play she finishes the dishes slowly, wipes down the counter and puts the leftover roast in the fridge. She makes sure to take long enough that the curtain is well and truly up, that there is no possibility to change her mind. She goes to the room—she can't call it *her* room—and sits idly at the desk. The garden is deeply dark. The alley light must be out again. She can't sleep yet—the image of the figures falling into water comes to her—but neither can she study. The last warmth she has felt in this house is gone. Her relationship with Mr. H. has become wary and unnatural, as will from now on her scholarly dealings with Mr. Fintan Quinn. Still, she made something that was worth building. The snapshot was nothing in itself, but she saw something else to make of it. That matters. And she has money of her own, from back at the Moxhams' when she got real wages. She need not take the two-and-sixpence "allowance" doled out from Mrs. Heywood's fingers. She will tell Mrs. Heywood that she no longer requires it.

Maybe she will buy a book. She wishes she had a different one tonight than these in the bookcase, all boy's books. *Kings of Fortune. Treasure Island.* Only the well-thumbed dictionary is hers. She wishes she had a long novel, or a book of American poetry. This school book on the desk stops at. . . . she opens it at the back and sees that it ends with Rupert Brooke, 1887–1915. Well, at least that is this century.

If I should die, think only this of me:
That there's some corner of a foreign field
That is forever England . . .

Stupidly, she is crying. Stupidly, longing for this England the poet experienced but she cannot, its "richer dust," its flowers and "English air,"

Wash'd by the rivers, blest by suns of home.

Home. Home. Angered by her emotion—because she understands she is not weeping for the soldier but for herself—she lies down on the bed and then, realizing that this spread was lain on by the dead son, she gets up and goes restlessly back to the bookcase where there are only boy's books.

And the cricket trophies. She has turned on only the desk light, and the bulbs in this room are in any case of middling strength. She has paid scant attention to the boys at Bidborough on the pitch. Nor in this light can she really read the words stamped in the cheap tin, but she has learned them "by heart" without knowing it.

Charles Heywood,
"LITTLE CHAZ"
Cordwainers First Eleven
Championship 1939

There are similar trophies for 1940 and 1941. That was the year she came to England, and sometime then or thereafter he crossed the other direction, to Holland, and some time in the next year or two, at Arnhem, fell.

The portrait of Nelson hangs above, his white trousers immaculate in a scene of smoke and gore, collapsing back against a uniformed aide. Nelson is surprisingly small. And she sees the boy Little Chaz, short like his parents but ambitious to be a champion, itching to leave this constricted home, this little village, to become something larger than himself.

She slips off her shoes and her skirt and slides under the worn coverlet: brown and green plaid, a boy's choice—no, a mother's choice for her boy—and sleeps.

CHAPTER 4

Lady Lazarus

1956

There was nobody on the High Street until he turned into the lodge and that weedy wanker of a porter said, "Terrible, isn't it, sir? But that's fen weather for you." And handed him two square envelopes—Christmas cards from the aunts, no doubt—and a notice about the Atheists Club.

There hadn't been a gas fire lit in the whole college since break began. There were crystals edging all his windowpanes and a cobweb outside lined in hoarfrost. He'd saved up eight shilling coins and stuck five of them in the meter, then turned on both the waffle grate under the mantel and the gas ring in the gyp room. There was nothing but a tin of spaghetti sauce, a half bag of fettuccini and several damp McVities. He sat by the fire in his overcoat, not wanting to go out again but wanting a meal at least. Lyons would be closed, but maybe the Chinese place on Magdalene.

Down the steps again, thinking again of the very thing he wanted out of his mind, the bastard whom he was biologically obliged to call his Father: *And where was the sauce for the veg?* Then Mouse Mum: *This was Brussels sprouts, meant to be eaten plain.* And the bastard: *Well, it* tastes *bloody plain.* Mum's defense, the bastard's rant, his own rebuttal rant, the tears, the bloody frigging *inconsequence* of it all. Thinking of that. So it brought him up short when he saw her on Clare Bridge.

She was leaning on the balustrade, long body propped against the stone ball that had suffered a major gouging at some point in its seven-hundred-year history. Flat shoes too thin for the weather: a Scholarship Girl. Wearing her gown over her coat although the proctors wouldn't be out until term started: a Good Girl, then. Simone something. Closer, he saw she was aiming a little Box Brownie at—what?—nothing to take a picture of, the murky water lapping at the pier. He remembered that when she took pictures for the Amateur Dramatic Club she didn't pose people in their costumes but snapped them backstage in their skivvies, poses no use for the programme. He couldn't remember her last name.

So he said, "Simone the Beauvoir," and she turned.

"Hullo, Jamie."

"What are you doing here? Didn't you go away for hols?"

"I went to Helene's for Christmas. Which was nice of them, but . . ."

"Posh."

She gave a shrug, "Work to do. You went home?"

"Mmm."

"That was posh as well."

"Oh, no. We're nouveau, barely ascended to the local council." He saw his father stretching his wattles.

"Why are *you* back early?"

"You know: work to do."

The politic thing was to ask her along to the Chinese place. But if he suggested it, he might be required to pay for her. He could foresee all the problems he'd face this term for having rejected the bastard's pocket money—though it had felt good, seeing the allowance in that outstretched hand, to turn on his heel and leave the house.

"Look, I've got some spaghetti and a jar of sauce upstairs. And some plonk, I think."

He'd chatted her up at Andy's once, to no particular purpose. He'd seen her at the Atheists Club last term too. She had eyes and a smile, but no breasts. And she was wary now. Wary Mary the Scholarship Girl.

"No strings," he said.

Still, she seemed willing. Between them they scraped the pan and he opened a second bottle. She plunked down beside him on the tatty carpet and laughed when he called his mother Franny Fogwhistle.

She volunteered that things had been awkward at Helene's too, the little rituals of gratitude. So he offered his theory of language à la Hobbes; you never know if what you mean by a word is what I mean by it, so every conversation is a ragbag of approximations.

"Hobbes, eh?" she said.

"I'm very taken with Hobbes at the moment."

"'Nasty, brutish and short,'" she offered.

"Nasty British shit, the lads say."

"You're Philosophy."

"And Politics and Economics."

"Was PPE a good choice for you?"

Oddly personal thing to ask, that. She was an odd girl. "Why do you ask?"

"Well, you seem very keen at the ADC."

"Amateur dramatics is my sport. PPE is supposed to prepare me for real life."

"And does it?"

He was a tad unnerved by the solemnity, though it might be a good sign. He laid a forearm behind her back and cupped a hand at her shoulder. "I'm fine with the philosophy and politics, but I'm buggered if I get the math. I'll get a second-class degree and be stuck in my father's shop for the next millennium, hawking Gentlemen's Bespoke." He said this lightly, and despaired.

She turned toward him, suddenly arch. Flirting? "There's a certain nobility in cloth, though. Think of the centuries of artists painting robes and their flowing folds!"

He said, "Thank you, Aldous Huxley," and she laughed. So far so good. He nibbled at her neck just as his brother Trevor had told him about, back in Ealing when he was too young to hear it. But it had stuck in his mind, and it had stood him in good stead before this. Now she stretched her jaw aloft. Inviting his mouth?

"I'm swotting up for a scholarship to America," she said. "If *I* get a second, I'll end up teaching in some polytech."

Her mood was slippery, serious to flip. They broke the Hobnobs in shards and downed each with a swallow of the cheap red. She stretched in a limber, unself-conscious way. Provocative? She said

Arden House had emptied out for the holiday, and that only the British would think of stuffing all the foreigners together in one digs, and that she liked Amrita the Pakistani but not Nadila the Turk; and that the most un-English student in Arden House was Dodie the American, who went off for holiday to Paris and Vence—"Vence, not Venice"—in a red checkerboard skirt and a bandeau with a Samsonite overnighter.

He pictured Dodie, lanky and full of herself, fashion model, author of lush and in his view overwritten poetry. Envious girls were always ready to discuss her vulgarity.

But Simone's tone was admiring. "Dodie's not trying out this term for the ADC. She says she has to devote herself to her writing."

He asked if she herself hadn't wanted to go home for Christmas, but she shrugged and ducked her head, not answering. She said instead, "I have this phantom in my mind, somebody who is me and not-me, going about Liege, wearing a cloth coat bald at the pockets, and a flat hat. But if I were there now, this is not the way I would look. It's the way twenty-five-year-olds looked when I *was* there, before."

He felt pity for her. He remembered that she'd been a refugee. He asked if her parents had died in the war. She said, "Oh, what does that mean? We say: *in the war, in the morning, in the seventeenth century*. What does that explain?" She was an odd girl. He kissed her—she let him—and slipped his hand down to her ribcage. She smelled of bread.

His shillings were gone now, and she'd contributed just one; the chill was spreading. He reached up over the sofa, dragged the blanket off the back and tucked it around her. She huddled under.

Her head wagged and her speech began to slow. "'R you..trying out for . . . *Troilus and Cressida*?"

"No, I'll stage-manage; stick to what I'm good at."

"I thought you'd audition for Thersites." And then—showing off her Thersites voice—". . . *how if he had boils, full, all over, generally? . . . And those boils did run?*" Immediately she reddened. "I di'n't mean . . ." Well, he had acne pits. So what? She had a spider nevus on her cheekbone. She rushed on, "I'll have a go at Cas-sandra, but of course Victoria will get it, and I'll be fobbed off with taking the pho-tos."

That was probably true. "There's a certain nobility in camera work, though," he said. "The play must close; the pictures are forever."

She said, "Thank you, Cecil Beaton," and they both giggled.

"But. Apart from Cassandra and America, what do you want?" He waited for her to say what girls always said, even the smart ones, even the Scholarship Girls: *a home and family, a good husband.*

"Stil-letto heels and a set of Samshonite."

He guffawed and emptied the bottle into her glass. St. Mary's chime had sounded ten and the porter would close the gates early, it being vac. There was nobody to disturb them, but all the same he felt exposed if he didn't shut the outer door. He got up, unsteady, opened the baize door a crack, reached out and closed the oak, closed the baize again.

Now her head was lolling. "Ceiling going 'round. T' mush plonk." He inserted himself under the blanket and shifted her head back onto a pillow on the floor. She hiccupped a little. He hadn't managed this all that many times: his zip, her garter belt, the blanket tangle, her moaning, "Sloo-ow . . ." But when she started pushing his chest away, his anger excited him. He found the elastic of her knickers and stuck two fingers up into her, at which she bucked and the cushion slid, her head bouncing on the floor. She said, "No!" and he said, "Your mouth says no but your eyes say yes," which Trevor had told him always worked. She said, "Can't. Can't" or "Cant. Cant," or was it (his mind flailing), "Kant, Kant." She shoved him sideways and again his anger aroused him so he pulled at her knickers and had them down with one hand, the other pinning her forearm on the floor while with her free hand she scratched his collarbone above his vest, drew blood.

A memory came unbidden out of his childhood: a pond somewhere; he sat in the prow of a boat while his father stood midships pulling at Mum's shoulders trying to get her to step in, which made the boat wash away from the dock, and pulled her into the widening water.

This image was no use to him. He thrust it out of mind and got his free hand under her jumper, clutched at her boob—surprisingly soft after all—and latched his mind onto the first film scene that came:

a Yank soldier comes out of the palm trees toward a girl wearing a wrapped skirt and a bikini top, boobs fruity, and she comes at him, sloe-eyed, wanting it.

"Stop. Stop now!" Simone rocked her hips side to side so he couldn't manage to get in. His anger intensified and intense was good, good and then urgent. Between pinning her arm and fending off her flailing other hand he couldn't get inside her. So he pressed his member against her belly, pushed once and came. Needed. Huge.

He collapsed on her, and she too went limp except for her thrashing head. But he felt okay about it. She wouldn't get pregnant, or be able to say she did.

He went for a towel in the gyp room and wiped her and then the rug. She was still now, hand over her eyes, but when he went to pull her knickers up she said, "Don't touch me!"

Oh, for Christ's sweet sake.

"Stay away from me!"

Nevertheless, he was a gentleman. "Look. Come on to bed," he said. "The gates are closed, and there's no way you can climb the wall. You can get some sleep and make it back before they miss you in the morning."

She rolled away from him. "Come on," he said. But she stayed wrapped up there, so he got in his bed in the recess and pulled the curtain.

But once in bed his anger—a sense of being wronged compounded with a sense of having somehow failed—had him by the teeth, morphed into his bastard father and back to Hobbes, *nasty British shit*. How dare she? Get him hot and then act as if he'd violated her unlikely bloody virginity. It was not as if he'd be bragging about her in the showers. The starch-stiff sheet rasped and twisted against his legs. He would be ragged tomorrow for lack of sleep.

When he woke she was already gone.

He put it out of mind. Why should he care? Bitch. She knew the rules. She'd been with him right up to the last minute, with her stretching and kissing and all that "slo-o-ow" stuff they all think they have to do.

He didn't run into her, there's a blessing, not at the Mill nor on the High Street, not even at the Atheists Club meeting, where he'd planned to cut her dead.

But January fourteenth, a Saturday, he went along to the ADC tryouts as scheduled. This morning was for the girls. The men would scramble another day, but, Shakespeare plays being replete with male parts, they would all be cast. The girls sat in the front row, pulling on their skirts and making bright faces, fourteen of them to read for four parts. She was there, all right, head down, book on her lap, twisting at her hair.

He was in charge of passing out the audition info and calling the hopefuls up by turn. She accepted the page without lifting her head. Simone *Lerrante,* it said on the roster. Good. Halfway through the alphabet, so by the time they got to her she'd understand she could expect no special treatment. Geoffrey St. John handed round the scripts, which caused Miss Simone Lear-rant to lift her own dog-eared Penguin paperback, showing off. Oh, and then, of course, she gave Geoffrey that doe-eyed look, that panting-dogface of the Sin-jin Fan Club—whereas it was no secret Geoff was lusting after Dodie the Yank Wonder Woman.

They went through the first four Cassandras leisurely, Geoffrey letting each of them "try it again with a touch more urgency."

> "Look how thou diest! Look how thy eye turns pale!
> Look how thy wounds do bleed at many vents!"

"*Die-est,*" Geoffrey said. "Dra-a-aw out the syllables so we feel the weight of the dying." His forelock *would* flop in his face. It was his gambit just to shove it back.

The pace picked up a bit, which was usual. After the first few lines, the first fifteen pentameter feet, you know at once who's in contention. Also you get bored. You couldn't spend half an hour with every one of the fourteen.

It was after lunch break before Simone came up. She got up on stage not by going round to the wobbly steps but by sitting on the proscenium edge, swinging her legs over and pushing up on hands and knees.

She moved well, he had to give her that. She had presence as soon as she took the stage. And her voice was clear, and carried. All the same. He could have told her exactly what was wrong with her audition. What was wrong was being an immigrant, if you didn't mind his saying so. She read Cassandra as if she was Barbara Stanwyck in shoulder pads and a canted hip. Whereas the English girls had got the Bard in their bones, so you got natural speech and natural poetry at once. The whole time Simone was reciting—for she had it all by heart—she never turned in his direction. She focused here, there, every chance toward Geoffrey. But she never came within of a yard of catching his eye.

Victoria was last, a fortunate accident of the alphabet, since it was clear from the start she was the one. A short, stolid girl, fierce-faced in spite of a nubby nose. Yes, Victoria won it fair and square. Geoffrey thanked them all and lied about the difficulty he'd have in choosing, and said that if you were cast he would be in touch by Wednesday noon.

He stationed himself at the door to take the audition info back, but she hung at the stage chatting to Geoffrey, so he had to decide whether to wait or not. He stayed where he was, uncertain, until she finally came toward the exit. He put his hand out for the page. But halfway down the aisle she draped the sheet on the arm of a chair and veered off toward the side door, her head held high to make obvious the snub.

It wasn't clear when or how he got the idea. One minute he thought anyway she'd get her comeuppance in the casting, and the next there it was, fully thought out in his mind. It was during the meeting, where Muriel was picked for Cressida and Victoria for Cassandra. Or was it in Hall when Rupert turned over a forkful of lumpy mash and said, "The purpose of mashed potatoes is to keep the noodles on your fork."? Or was it at Ian and Thom's on Green Street up over the ironmonger's: booze, sausage rolls, six kinds of cheese, an urn full of Sharp's Creamy Toffee? Ian served the best wine and food because he came from old money, but he shared the house with

Thom, a scholarship boy with a cockney accent, because both were Communists. *Workers unite* and all that. Nobody pointed out the contradiction between the politics and the French cheese.

The room got crowded and full of the sour smell of breathed-out wine, and then somebody brought up the question of identity, post Sartre.

Ian said, "All your cells are changed out every seven years, so on the level of matter you are an entirely different person."

Thom said, "And on the level of politics, everything you believed seven years ago is bollocks."

Firth said ardently, "People can't change. They can only be *redeemed*."

No wonder, with a drip of drivel like that, he retreated into the wine, a Beaujolais his father would have made a great fuss over, and then a raffia-wrapped Chianti some tosser had brought. Drank so much of it that he drifted into Ian's room, lay on Ian's couch, the ceiling meandering over his head, tossed back into a rage that seared his eyes.

It could not have been simpler. On Tuesday afternoon when he knew the Lit-Crit classes met, he called Arden House and asked for Simone Lerrante. Mrs. Guinea said she would take a message, so he asked her to write it down. Mr. Geoffrey St. John was pleased to invite Miss Simone Lerrante to accept the part of Cassandra in the upcoming ADC production of *Troilus and Cressida*. Her presence was requested at first reading Sunday the twenty-second at ten o'clock.

He hurried through the lobby toward the stage, harsh under work lights that momentarily blinded him. They had drawn study tables together, but they were not seated yet. Geoffrey stood at the head with his director's notebook splayed, and Muriel and Keith pored over their lines; others were sitting on the apron bumping their heels against the rise, or lounging in the seats whose velvet upholstery was pocked like divots on a golf green. Some were still missing; Geoffrey would be giving his oration about the sacred rules of promptness.

Then she was there, out of breath, blinking from the dark lobby, full of agitated joy. Oh, yes: she had made herself a new Dodie kind of skirt, flared tweed instead of the mole-colored kind of thing she usually wore. She teetered there on her thin ballet flats. A few lifted a hand to her. But it felt wrong. Everyone looked at her, quizzical. Geoffrey was first to break. "Simone?"

"Hi," she said, still breathless. "Sorry I'm late. What a day to have a flat! I had to borrow someone's bike."

There was a hiatus. Geoffrey took half a step. "Hullo, Simone. Can I do something for you?"

She shook her curls with a little laugh. "Is that the rehearsal schedule you have there?"

Victoria drew her face back. Muriel's smart-chopped hair sat along her jaw like a scimitar. Geoffrey, when he was unsure of himself, moved as if he were clumsy once and had incorporated clumsiness as a part of style.

He said, "I'm afraid we have exactly as many as we need for the cast."

Sometimes you can see the process of realization as it unfolds. They were all looking at her now. She picked up her shoulders in a shrug, pulled back the corners of her mouth.

Geoffrey went to her. Oh, he was kind! "Simone—I'm sorry if there's been some kind of misunderstanding."

She wavered, barely. "No, no. I just thought," she said, "I thought I should just come along and let you know. That I won't be able to take thc photos this production. I won't have time, you see. I have to, I have to, devote myself. To my studies."

And turned and ran.

The production was a success, the reviews good and the houses full. He felt secure in his place among them, this community of creatures in fear of being singled out and frantic to be seen, in terror of the thing they most desired. His was the mundane part, the keeper of times and places, seeing to ropes and tea. It suited him.

Troilus closed, and just when he ought to have started cramming for the Tripos, he contracted the bugger of all colds. He huddled in his room in a pathological avoidance of his books. Days he lay on the sofa, evenings he got himself upright and dragged down to The

Mill, where he drank till last call. One night he dreamed his head was forcibly tipped back and his nostrils plugged with a rubber-tipped bottle like those they used at school. Mucilage ran into his sinuses, his ear canal, between his skull and brain. In the dream he must lie very still or it would harden and glue his eyes in place. When he woke he told the words over in the dark: acedia, anhedonia, abulia, anomie: *spiritual torpor, a lack of the capacity to experience pleasure, the inability to make a decision, deep malaise.* He had the thought that definition was befriending, though why this should be so he couldn't say. And it did not get him to the books that would have given him the definitions his exams required.

April was a little better. His sinuses cleared. The crocuses came out on Clare College Backs. He began to hear the odd rumor here and there that Simone Lerrante and Geoffrey St. John were an item. And then that she'd been accepted for supervision in The English Philosophers (*from Plato to Sartre,* the wags said) by Professor Daiches at Jesus College—a rarity for a Newnham girl. Someone said that American Dodie had disappeared at a magazine launch with Leonard Hawk, and when they reappeared he had bite marks on his cheek. He himself had a couple of successes, one with a Girton girl who was known to put out, and one with another Newnhamite who invited him to her row-house, where they had to suppress any noise on account of the thinness of the walls.

One more odd thing. One night at The Mill, John Wing told him he had seen Simone straddling her bike on Mill Bridge and throwing her little Box Brownie into the Cam.

One cold day he had to deliver the ADC accounts to the sponsoring don; and he spotted Dodie brushing snow from the shoulders of the bronze boy with the dolphin on Sedgewick fountain. Dodie's nose was rubbery and her hair stringy under a babushka scarf.

"We've both been ill, apparently," he said.

"D'you think? This rotten climate."

"You live at Arden House," he blurted out, "like Simone Lerrante." He had no idea he was going to say that.

"Oh, Simone," said Dodie. "She's just got a Fulbright to America, you know."

"No, I didn't know. Well, good for her. Brilliant, is she?"

"Bright enough for America anyway!" Dodie laughed.

He said, "She's tight with Geoffrey St. John, I understand."

"Oh, nah, I think that's over. He wasn't going to go to America, and she wasn't going to stay here."

"Ah, right, she's strong-headed."

But Dodie said, "I don't know about strong-headed. She's just mad that her daddy died."

Over the next few days he began to think that he had made wrong assumptions. Other people seemed to find her admirable: Geoff. Daiches. Fulbright. Dodie. And quite suddenly he leaped ahead to something like remorse—for he didn't know, really, what she thought of him or what, from her point of view, had really gone wrong that night. Maybe he even hurt her by not calling on her afterward. He was sorry he'd made her spend the night on the couch. Why had she thrown her camera in the Cam (*Cam-camera*) in such a public way?

As to how had she and Geoffrey St. John got together, he could imagine Geoffrey stopping Simone after lecture to say something consoling. He could see them going to Lyons for a coffee, Simone confiding about the trick, the two of them even figuring out who might have played it. But this did not make him feel "caught" or worried for his reputation. Geoffrey had apparently found out for himself what S. L. meant by "no." If he felt remorse, it was shot through with slivers of pride that he had been led on and then dumped, like Geoff, by an apparently famous girl.

Just that week he had a letter from his Mum enclosing thirty pounds; a princely sum, which she had probably scraped together out of the grocery money. Her note said that he needn't mention it to his father. No fear. He bought another case of plonk and, on impulse, a dozen red roses not from the stalls in the market but from a proper flower shop, half a crown a stem, to be delivered in a box to Miss Simone Lerrante at Arden House on Barton Road. He took a long time over the card, in which he did not want to say anything directly apologetic or, God knows, to suggest he wanted to take her out again. But something friendly, one scholar to another. In the end he wrote, "Congratulations on your Fulbright. Well done!" He signed it "James" and let it go at that.

It was when he got back from The Mill just before curfew that that wanker porter stopped him at the lodge. "'Ere, sir, there's a package for you, dropped off personal by a young lady on her bicycle. She'd've had a dicey time to balance it."

The long box was still tied with its satin ribbon. He carried it up the stone steps wondering if the shop had got it wrong, if they had delivered it to his address instead of hers. But he did not really think that. He thought she had sent it back. Or brought it back. And it was no real surprise, when he'd fed the gas meter and laid the box on the counter in the gyp room, to find inside in their brittle green paper the dozen roses, each of their heads chopped neatly just below the hip. Not chopped either, but deliberately sliced; each limp head severed with the precision of an X-acto knife.

TWO

Zoological

Transit: Southampton, England–New York, NY

1957

Now adrift.

There's a flute's worth of champagne and half a snifter of Remy Martin—warm in the belly of her lean and solid, long, *presentable* body—that is submerged in a foot of bubbles in a porcelain bath in Cabin Class. She's a new person. She has shed her old self like a skin. She's her American self; optimistic, even sassy.

The steamship is a city unto itself, complete with streets, shops, restaurants, and ghettos; and though she may have been assigned to the wrong side of the waterline, she has bootstrapped herself up into the cordial comfort of the professional class. Exactly as she intends to do.

Here she is roomily ensconced and en-bubbled by the grace of the Arthur Collinses of Hatsfield, South Dakota—because, when the Fulbright bunch on D deck dared her, she sneaked up the stairs past the rope and took the first *chaise longue* she came to. Which turned out to belong to Mrs. Collins, who, when Simone confessed, had invited her to lunch (purser's table: a couple from Rhode Island with a teenage boy, two New York sisters palpably moneyed, and a retired Marine Major with a guffaw)—and then offered her a decent bath.

So here she is. Champagne inside her body, her body wafting in the water sloshing in the tub on the ship that wallows in the ocean that is cradled by the underwater mountains of the planet Earth, which is a bubble adrift in the solar system.

Adrift. Far from the angst of essays, far from the tribulations of the Suez canal and the uprisings of Hungary—between decks, between continents, between lives; no strings attaching her to anything but disyllabic Mrs. and Mrs. Arthur Collins of South Dakota (farm machinery franchise) who *lu-uv* her accent and are sure she'll do *jus' fie-uhn* in America.

Now is not the time to think about what she will do. Now is the time for feeling she is already fine. The time is now. *Now is the time for all good men. Here on this bank and shoal of now. If it be not to come, it will be now. Now is the winter of our discontent made glorious.*

She dangles her foot against the stopper-chain, splashes her legs like calipers. She dolphin-ducks, and bucks, comes up wet-headed and lets herself go limp again.

It seems to her that the most delicious condition in the world is: *now, adrift.*

CHAPTER 5

Oracles

1958

He will ask her tonight. She *knows* this. The sky is full of auguries—a full-blown blossom on the magnolia at the corner of Grove and Bleeker, a shooting star last night over Washington Square—even the date, May 8, 1958, which in its European form would be a palindrome: 8-5-58. Also the anniversary of V-E day, as he has pointed out. He will disguise it with an ironic look and a negative construction: *Not that this is particularly sudden*, . . . and then it will be there, the future laid out before them.

He will meet her in front of Zabar's and they'll have supper with Mrs. Puig, even though that will rush them. (Why should they go to his mother's before a show if it's not a statement of intent?) The show is called *Nickels in May*, which must be a musical though she hasn't heard of it. She can see the stage: bare boards, young people in primary colors, a full-throated American belting out. Yes, and a young Negro chorine with a great bubble of black hair, like Kuli Moyala from his lab at Columbia, who wears bangles and batik robes of blood-browns. All the Negroes Simone has met till now have their hair ironed, but Kuli wears a band of beaded stuff around a sprouting of charred oak, so defiantly beautiful that Simone feels like a Miss Milquetoast in her presence.

She has actually eaten milk toast. She didn't believe it existed, but Mrs. Puig—she must learn to call her Hester now, or even *Mom?*—served it on a Sunday night, a bowl of warm milk with a slice of buttered white toast in it. An amazing thing. Simone had thought her years in England had showed her all there was for mush and bland.

That she hasn't heard of the musical is not surprising. It's Martin who knows about the quirky avant-garde. She nips back through Washington Square, sweating a little because the Kitto alone—*Form and Meaning in Drama*—weighs two pounds. Her brain, too, is a little heavy with all the ravings of Cassandra. She turns into Eighth Street, past Julia's Gems, not turning her head because if the ring is still there (the slender circle with the single black pearl) she doesn't want to know. And if it isn't there, what would it prove for certain?

She hadn't intended to marry. She had spent so much time in other people's squabbling families that she was only interested being a career girl. Now, here, in America, loneliness has not surprised her but the force of it has. The lack of purpose in a thought unshared, the pull of laziness when she lives in reference only to herself—all that was unexpected. Meanwhile everyone she knows is pairing off. Everyone is lifted on a tide toward marriage, children—and every other possible way of being is swept along.

Nor had she intended to be a teacher. She had wanted to be an actor, or at least to immerse herself in the life she believed actors had. Well, the classroom is a kind of stage. Martin teases her: *blood will out*. But wasn't it storytelling that had led her father to English literature, even if the subject was dressed up with High German and Old Norse? Whereas here she could study Norman Mailer if she chose. She has chosen Aeschylus.

She hurries down the half-flight to the Grove Street basement and lets herself in. She kicks off her pedal pushers and stands in her panties pouring a handful of seed in the cage where a Javanese Temple bird called Ginsberg scolds from side to side. The advantage of this one room, a half-story underground, is that if you adjust the blinds at an angle nobody can see in. The disadvantage is that car exhaust and the slightest breeze waft in the airborne detritus of New York. The guy she sublet from said, "You get more air below street level." Now she sees that the air in question contains ash, glass, concrete, carbon dioxide, lint, and pulverized dog doo. Everything she owns is overlaid with wasteland.

Not her clothes. She has tacked a burlap curtain over the cavity that serves as closet. Now she slings it over her shoulder to dig out the Merry Widow bra, a pair of pale stockings, the new drop-waisted linen on which she spent the weekend sewing and over twelve dollars, if you count the zipper.

She showers in the cubicle, leans into the Merry Widow (another extravagance, but also armor), and reaches back to hook all thirty-five miniature fish hooks from wing blade to base of spine. Putting it on lets you know what it feels like to have your hands tied behind you. But when the hooks are done, when she bends and settles her breasts into the underwires, she has a handspan of waist and lifted globes. It's hard to breathe.

The dress is pale bone Irish linen, bought from Art-Max discount fabrics on Thirty-Eighth. She has cut the top princess line and the skirt in six gores flaring from her hip joints. She has also laid out for linen pumps, which will probably not survive six blocks of New York streets, but she can't wear her stilettos with Martin; he's too short. She back-combs her hair—it takes on volume at once—and brushes the top layer smooth.

When she looks at herself . . . it'll do. It's good. Hair bouffant, eyes clear, stance solid on her own two feet. She looks to make sure she has a dime for the subway, considers the Ansco but leaves it behind. Martin doesn't like her taking pictures; he says it's crass. She slings a cardigan over her arm and drives home the key.

After two years of lame dates, aggressive jocks, conversations so stilted that she squandered her own patchy history just to have something to talk about, meeting Martin was transformative. He does not consider her a "lay." He likes to talk ideas. He wants to find the connective tissue between his subject and hers. They had exhausted most of B. F. Skinner and The New Criticism before he ever held her hand. He has a temper, yes. But she knows that's born of secret sadness.

In just this hour the air has changed color. *Twilight,* a word she loves, from the Old English *two-light; double light.* It is day and night at once, and New York energy rises in the clash of them. Mica in the concrete gives off sparks. Everyone is charging away from work or off to play, she not least, clattering down the subway stairs, breathing shallow against the metal stays.

She loves the urgency, the challenge. But she does not see herself and Martin living in the city. On the contrary, New Hampshire or Vermont, a small college town and a small cottage-y sort of house with a garden. She sees them in the kitchen, he with a dish towel in hand, holding forth on his latest experiments in Skinnerism while toddlers and a dog dawdle on the floor in the twilight. This makes her laugh.

She spots him a block away, sucking on a cigarette under the Z in *Zabar's*. Martin Carlo Puig runs everywhere, his body a fist of energy. But what comes off him when he's alone is a melancholy of that same intensity. Some people find him remote—Kuli Moyala calls him *Iceman*—but Simone understands his secret grief, and when the dark mood takes him she wants to thread into his sorrow and find the string to pull him out.

When Martin was seventeen, his father—having first made sure that Martin would arrive at his apartment at a given hour—had blown off the back of his head precisely in the white-carpeted vestibule. For Martin this memory, the cruelty of it, is an obsession, and for Simone absorbing it has become a way of life. Martin knows that she has scarcely any memory of her father. So she is as content to focus on Martin's loss as he is to let her.

Now, though, Martin merely grinds the butt under his heel. "Jesus. Gorgeous," he says. "We're not going to Sardi's, you know." But he himself, a dapper dresser, is in a blazer and a slice of oxblood tie. He has muscular dark hair, a fighter's body though he's a scholar in psychology.

Martin's Spanish great-grandfather married a Basque, and his grandfather traveled all the way up Europe and across to New England. The Mediterranean strain survives in him: the darkness, the fierce pride. He might as well be Greek, Simone thinks. *Hellenic.* His power thrills her, a man with authority enough to want a strong woman. A runner's thighs, and that interior dark space no one can invade.

"*M'sieur le Puig*," she says. He smells of nicotine. "How come we're meeting here?"

"I thought we'd get some decent coffee and a stinky cheese. I can't stand that stuff my Mom lays out. Maybe we could take some garlic and toss it in the soup."

"It would hurt her feelings."

"Her *feelings*? How would anybody know?"

His contempt for his mother causes her a flicker of unease, although she shares it, or because she shares it. She forms her face into a conspiratorial smile. They pick a brie, a bottle of Bordeaux. They will shop this way in the country, Simone foresees, always together, making an aesthetic out of sustenance.

Mrs. Puig has the glamorous address of 100 Riverside Drive. They cross Eighty-fifth for a minute to look at the Hudson in twilight, the shining sludge of it and the bone-bright rise of the Palisades across. There's a little chill, and she wills him to put his arm around her, but Martin is not susceptible to telepathy. In the mud at their feet a brown bird is pulling on a worm. Like a worm in a cartoon, the fat elastic stretches and snaps back, and the bird pulls again until the worm slips free. She says, "We lived on the river in Liege."

She remembers a balustrade of stone, the river narrower than the Hudson but also bright under the moon.

Martin replies, "As soon as we have money we'll go back there."

She says nothing. On the ground in front of them the bird has won this time; another time the worm, another time the mud. She cartwheels her cardigan over her shoulders and recites:

> The sea is there, and who shall drain its yield? It breeds
> Precious as silver, ever of itself renewed,
> The purple ooze wherein our garments shall be dipped.

Martin laughs. "You're not planning a swim, I hope?"

"It's Clytemnestra. She just means that purple dye comes from sea plants—anemones or something. But of course she's also planning to stab him in his robes."

"Ah, subtext." They turn back up the street and wave to the doorman and step into the bronze Deco elevator.

Mrs. Puig opens the door at once. "Martin-Simone?" She is a tiny woman like an antique windup toy, all grind and clatter. She's as much as sixty-five, Simone thinks. A smell of poached fish wafts from behind her—"Come, come"—and she manages to convey that they are wasting heat, although God knows it's too hot inside. She closes the door and offers each of them a paper cheek.

Vast, by New York standards, apartment 11E opens off both sides of a long hall. It's a turn-of-the-century building, but this apartment is furnished in a severe style it would be impossible to understand if you didn't know that Martin's father was a Bauhaus architect. He was one of the few Americans acknowledged in the European circle, though his reputation declined somewhat between the time he left Martin and his mother in '38 and his suicide in '49.

His widow now houses a collection of memorial chrome and canvas. The table is a concrete slab on pillars. The rugs are hard and plain. The only comfortable chair in the living room is a bent-pipe chaise you can't get up out of in a Merry Widow bra. Simone admires *form follows function* in a theoretical way, but it strikes her as dubious unless a chair serves the function of *comfortable to sit on*.

The friendliest piece of furniture is the blond cabinet housing the TV set. Crowded on top of it are family photographs: Martin as a boy in sailor suit, cowboy hat, graduation gown. Simone tries to recall such a picture of herself. Perhaps on the mantelpiece in Liege? Was there a mantelpiece in Liege?

The only picture on the walls is a photomontage called "Indische Tänzerin," *Indian Dancer*, though there is no dancer in it, and nothing Indian. It's of a woman's head with images severed and recombined: a French film actress as Joan of Arc, a fragment of African mask, a sand dune, a crown of knives and spoons. The actress's single eye is closed in grief or ecstasy. The mask's eye is open in the blind openness of stone. The parts don't fit together in any way that makes sense, and yet this cobbled-together thing is disturbingly itself. Its brokenness makes it whole.

"I love this piece," Simone says, because she does, and because Mrs. Puig always brightens. "I looked it up. Hoch made it the year I was born. I think she saw what was coming, how we'd have to put back the pieces." Simone touches the corner with the initials "H. H." and the year, *1930*.

"Give me Turner any day," Martin says.

"Hannah Höch was the only woman that the Dadaists were willing to accept among them!" Mrs. H. declares. "Of course, my husband never cared for the Dadaists. Too irrational. And I didn't often go against his tastes." Simone sees some complicated feeling behind her eyes: mischief? rage? "He liked *mesura*—that's Italian for proportional. He said it often, *mesura* this and *mesura* that."

"*Mesura* me . . ." Martin puts in.

She's confiding in me, Simone recognizes. Martin calls it a *momologue*.

"I bought it myself! Well, I saved up little bit here and there, and then I had my father's inheritance." She nods with satisfaction and turns toward the kitchen. Simone follows her, bemused. Martin follows her.

"It's nearly ready," says Mrs. Puig, hovering at the counter, "but these potatoes will *not* get done." Anxious as a way of life, she now wrings her hands, and Simone feels herself expand with good will and competence.

"Let me speak to them," she says. "They probably don't understand the assignment."

"No sweat," Martin says. "We don't have to be there till nine. I'm going to go check my mail."

That's odd. What sort of show doesn't start till nine?

The kitchen is done in some shiny white stuff like a clinic. Simone dons an apron, and the two of them fall easily into poking and draining together, even though Mrs. Puig follows Simone's least movement with a wipe-up cloth.

"How have you been . . . Hester?"

"I can't complain."

"You should have a big Porterhouse and a double ice cream sundae."

Mrs. Puig does not *get* teasing. "No, no. I'm not like you youngsters. Martin and his cast-iron constitution . . . !" She dishes up the fish, snowy meat on a fan of cartilage. And she launches into speech, a whirring of the mechanism behind the wind-up voice. "People have to work at it to find out what suits them. For years I followed Gaylord Hauser's regime, but my husband, now, it didn't suit him at all."

"It's a long time ago," Simone says gently. She has heard this before.

"He lost muscle," Mrs. Puig says. She pats the edges of the serving dish with the hot pads. "My husband was not a large man, but he had large needs. He liked to work with steel, concrete. Not that he lifted those himself, but he had to motivate his men. He used to say it was like being a football coach, you didn't have to tackle anybody, but you had to convince dumb guys to do it for you."

Simone laughs, although this has been said without humor, perhaps with reverence. Mrs. Puig shoves at the fish with the spatula. "My husband's voice could carry clear across the site. Although he hardly ever got the big jobs, not the really big ones. He'd lose the commission just by a hair's breadth, time after time.

"And then the Department of Transportation," she concludes. She must assume Simone already knows about this, because she makes no move to explain how it was a new government building in Albany where Mr. Puig was judged liable for a million-dollar overrun that began his professional slide.

"One thing my husband and I had in common," Mrs. Puig says. "We both wanted things to be perfect! But what was perfect for him was not always the same for me." She presses fingertips to cheekbone. "The things they said about him! In Albany, and after he died. I didn't recognize the person they were talking about. You understand? As if I'd been married to Jekyll and Hyde." Simone has a sudden insight into that marriage, the swarthy bender of pipes and caster of concrete, arms outflung—"I want things to be perfect!"—locked in with this little metal-spatter of a woman who is now tearing parsley heads and arranging the bits on each half-moon of potato.

"I was not meant to have these things happen to me," says Mrs. Puig (*Hester. Mom*). "I was meant to have a quiet life."

Simone sees the number of poached fish in the years ahead, one after another on platters, as if on a conveyor belt. She sees the hours spent in this kitchen, twisting ice cubes out of a metal tray, listening to the same complaints, decanting apologetically a gift cheese so ripe that Mrs. Puig's nostrils flare. She shakes this portent from her head.

"I'm so sorry," Simone says.

She is sorry. She remembers what Martin told her once: *in purely evolutionary terms, the only function of memory is prediction.* Her impulse was to protest this—*what about identity, history?*—but she can see that if you don't have any future to speak of, too much past just drags you down. Mrs. P. squares a tea towel on the tiles. Such a mousy way of being in the world. Simone makes a quick, implicit vow never to let her vision narrow. *The sea is there! And who shall drain its yield?*

"Well," sighs Mrs. Puig. "Well, that's all water over the dam."

"It seems to me," Simone says, "the gods of Olympus are your perfect example of intermittent reinforcement."

"Explain."

"Well, you never know if Athena or Venus or whoever is on your side."

They are showing off for Martin's mother. There's no harm in it. It's a form of making love. They can send little messages of appreciation, wit, exploring in this public way how their minds entwine, complement, diverge.

"You sacrifice your goat and get the seer to read the entrails, and you never know exactly why the god or goddess gives you the winds for your sails, or whether the same thing will get you the same result next time."

It's the banter that arouses her, and the hunger in his gaze. According to *Introduction to Psychoanalysis* she is sexually immature, so when they are actually in the act, she works at willing her orgasm back into her vagina, which would be a tribute to him (Martin, not Freud), but which usually only makes her anxious and stops her coming altogether. Then she fakes, which makes her feel corrupt. At the moment she is wary of the beets, their proximity to new linen. She picks at the fish.

"I think you're onto something," Martin says. "So naturally they have to keep carving up the goats."

Mrs. Puig wears a tentative smile, as if she understands maternal awe may be required.

"The only problem with your Greek analogy," Martin says, "is the seer. All that hocus pocus!"

"But the seer is the scientist! What is it *you* do but read the animals' organs after you've sacrificed them?"

Martin's mouth twitches with irritation, but he cocks his head and throws a hand up. "Touché."

It's not only showing off. They are also practicing, trying out dinner conversation against the time they will entertain colleagues at their own table. Simone leans far over her plate and pokes two small whole beets in her mouth. Thin red tang floods her jaw. She remembers that Martin's father shot himself on a white carpet. It comes to her—a preposterous notion—that Mrs. Puig has chosen this color scheme on purpose. She chews still bending over her plate and brings her napkin to her mouth. There's a small flower of brilliant vinegar on the napkin, but her dress is safe.

"Martin," Mrs. Puig asks suddenly, "do you have any use for those old *Hardy Boys*?"

Martin says, "I don't get the connection."

"What?"

"Between Hardy Boys and goats."

"I was only saying. I was going through some boxes, and I was thinking I might give them to the Goodwill."

"What's the matter with you? Those books are practically antiques. Besides." Here he lifts a grin to Simone that takes her breath away. "What if I have a boy of my own? You wouldn't want to deprive him, would you?"

Restlessness and joy war in her, a desire to be out of here. To be clattering along a Village street, belting out rhythms, Nickels in May!

"Have you been mucking around in my room again?"

"I try to keep it *clean*."

"Just leave it, can't you? I'll clear my stuff out when I have a house to put it in."

A house to put stuff in, a cottage with a peaked roof, his old tennis rackets and Hardy Boys in storage under the beams. What would she put there of her own, if any souvenir of her childhood had survived? All that comes to mind is the string bag her mother used to take to market before the war, a limp nothing-in-itself, but which would magically fill with paper packets, marzipan, beets with their tops still burgeoning.

Mrs. Puig has taken on her self-belittling air, her *don't-mind-me*. She has a mouthful of fish, and meticulously sets herself to chewing it. When she's done, she says, voice tight, "You say so, but that coin collection fell all over the closet floor last week."

"What are you talking about?"

"Those Buffalo-whatevers."

"My Indian heads?" says Martin.

"I think there must be rats in the space between the walls."

"There are no rats. It's vibrations from the pipes."

"You say. But Mrs. Delphine has a flea infestation."

"*Non sequitur,* Mother. What did you do with my coins?"

"She had to get the fumigation people in. They taped up all her doors."

"Mrs. Delphine has fleas because of that Pan-Asian yapper. What did you do with my coins?"

"It's just a little dog," Mrs. Puig appeals to Simone. "A Lhasa. Called Paramour."

Simone says, "Maybe Paramour got loose in the walls."

You can feel how unwanted a joke is, how wrong it sits in the souring atmosphere. There must be a scientific explanation for this. People thought radio waves were magic before they could explain them in mathematical terms. Someday they will find that anger waves, danger waves, dance in atomic particles in the air. They make the air around your eyes feel hot.

"How long do we have to allow to get to the Village?" Simone asks quickly.

"It's not in the Village, it's at a bar on Madison."

"Oh! I thought it was a musical!"

"Mike Nichols and Elaine May, the new social satire," he says irritably. "I thought you'd heard of them."

Lightly: "I count on you to keep me au courant." But she's disappointed. She'd been hoping for something rousing. Martin has the boiled look of somebody stifling anger.

"I thought it was Nickels *in* May!" she says, making a joke of herself. "Would you like me to get the coffee, Mrs. Puig?"

But it doesn't work. Mrs. Puig is rocking her fish knife on the tablecloth. Martin fixes his mother in his sights. "What did you do with the Flying Eagle?"

"I don't know. It took me half the afternoon to stick them back in those cardboard things."

The muscles go rigid in his maxilla, and the spasm takes up its place in Simone's diaphragm.

"What are *those cardboard things*? What about: *Numismatic Coin Folders*?"

"If you say so."

It hurts to see him sarcastic—because why, really, should his mother care about his coin collection?—though Simone knows he is operating on some hurt just out of sight.

"When was the last silver dollar minted?"

"It was your hobby, dear. I never claimed it was mine."

"Right. But that's not the point, is it? The point is, my *Father* gave me those coins."

Martin has a vindicated look from which Simone averts her eyes.

"This apartment," Mrs. Puig says in a strangled voice, "this apartment is a *monument* to your father."

"Right." He wheels back to Simone, so fiercely that her lungs clench. "Do you get a picture of what it was like growing up with this? I mean squeezing the life out of anything that gave you pleasure. Never allowed to come in contact with a germ or a lick of sugar or God-forbid a *dog*."

The mechanism of Mrs. Puig's body is slowing down. A cube of potato fails to reach her mouth, retraces its staccato rhythm to the plate.

Martin scrapes his chair back, a metal gouging sound, and wads his napkin down, striding off. Simone reaches out a hand to keep the napkin from unfurling into the beets. There appears, not anything so formed as a thought, rather a swipe of bright conviction: *I should run.* She can distinguish the place in her stomach where the chewed fish sits, and the vinegar. And with low clarity she hears her father's voice saying, "*Va t'en. Continue.*"

Go away. Go on.

Her breath comes short and burns her throat. She has never understood what people mean by "hearing voices," and she knows this voice is in her head. Still, it has body and heft. It is as recognizable as a voice on a telephone.

"Mrs. Puig," she says. "You mustn't mind. He doesn't mean it, he's under pressure. He barks at me too, when he's overtired."

"Oh, no." Mrs. Puig wipes her mouth and looks up with her withered smile. "You see," she says, "for my son you have to *be* somebody. And for him you *are* somebody. And I'm not."

Mrs. Puig has never astonished her before. Who would have guessed the little woman could take her own measure? Simone reaches forward and covers the sinewy hand. "Really . . . Hester. He's just overworked and overtired."

But she sits amazed—at the unsuspected self-knowledge. And the implicit compliment: *I am somebody.*

The glamour of Martin's social circle comes into her head: the bohemians who aren't married but have children; Kuli Moyala, who moves like Cassandra arrogant among the Greeks; Joyce Glassman, who seemed friendly and modest—but turned out to be Jack Kerouac's girlfriend: somebody, then.

Simone feels tender toward this stunted person who will be her mother-in-law. She leaves her hand for the moment over the age-spotted hand. She even dares a gentle stroke, which Mrs. Puig allows.

It will be all right with Martin. Satire is the thing to mend his mood. Nichols and May! They will laugh about it later. And about the essentials she is right. Clairvoyant, even. He will ask her tonight. He will be drained of anger, penitent.

I want everything to be perfect! She is washed over with well-being. She remembers the waif she was all those years in England, shopped from one family to another, always beholden to somebody else's benevolence. And she wonders how from such unpromising beginnings she herself has arrived at this richly blessed place: a woman with cleavage, and a thesis topic, and the love of a complicated man.

Transit: Lovelock, Nevada–San Francisco

1961

I was just about to start a ring job on a Chevy when I seen them coming—or either I heard them coughing over the alkali flats from Winnemucca. They was coaxing a '56 Dodge Custom Royale, two-tone green with the full fins and a ton of chrome, bad case of vapor lock.

It was Saturday. We'd been promised rain all week but there wasn't a scrap of cloud. I was down in the mouth from wrangling with Myrtle and Sue Lynn, the usual, and Sue Lynn was hiked up at the counter inside like she was hung up by her ponytail. She'd ought to have mopped the restrooms by now, but instead she was going over the account book looking for mistakes in my adding up. She's got those saddle shoes hooked on the stool rungs and about six foot of leg between that and her shorts that I told her not to wear in front of the customers. Twelve years old, that was fine. Now she's seventeen you don't want her sashaying around the truckers.

How they was lucky enough to make it in I don't know. Most any fool would've stopped—and froze up his fuel line doing it—but this one didn't have sense enough to panic. By the time they pulled in to the pumps the hood was snorting smoke. They got out gasping, both of them with their noses peeling, dog tired like all the first-time campers we get through here.

She said, "I'm so glad we made it. Have you got a ladies?" Foreign accent—Brit by the sound of it. Long-tall drinka water, skinny as a walking-stick.

I said loud enough for Sue Lynn to hear, "Cleanest Shell station in the U.S. of A., which is *darn clean,*" and the limey girl trots off. Slick's shorter than she is, trying to hide it wearing cowboy boots with his button-down. My money says this was his first car he ever owned. "Might be a problem in the carburetor," he says. He's not real sure where to pop the hood, squints at the dash and rubs his jaw. My granddaddy come from back east too, but if he hadn't known any more about his horse than this kid knew about his car, he'd be a bleached skull in the sand about now.

I propped up the hood and half a hell come blasting out. You get more mirage off a motor than off the highway in that weather; the dude's face went weewaw in it. "Or maybe we've got a leak in the radiator," he says and, would you believe, reaches for the cap. Got a good three fingers on it before I knocked his hand away, and then he screes up his face trying not to holler.

I said, "Tell you what, get yourself a co'cola, and by the time you've drunk it, it'll be cooled down enough to take a look." He went and stuck his hand down in the ice in the coke bin and held it there. I killed a few minutes wiping at his windows. A Mack truck come by and I filled it up with diesel, and then high octane for Hoss Rickett's Cadillac. Pretty soon the girl comes out freshed up.

I said, "Lemme guess, you're coming from Yellowstone, heading to Reno."

"Why, yes," she says like I said something clever. "And then San Francisco. My husband promised we'd go coast to coast for our honeymoon." Being stuck in the car with just the one person they tend to chatter. "We started out from New York City and we've been camping all the way, except in Wisconsin. That night it rained and we had to get a motel."

She had a bandana folded in a strip around her goldilocks. "And you were plenty glad for the rain," I said, and she laughs to admit it. "That's a heckuva honeymoon you're taking."

"Mmm," she says and runs her hands down her back, stretching. She had her shirttail out, but her Levis were stiff with newness. "My husband will be teaching at the State University of New York starting in September, and we thought, if not now, when?"

I knew that. I could have made odds on that at Felix's Casino. I said, "A professor, uh? By golly, he must be smart," and she bobs her head.

"He's in psychology," she says. I let myself give a guffaw, friendly, and he comes over with his hand clamped around a cold RC.

I called out, "Sue Lynn, could you come on out here and give us an opinion?" Sue Lynn untangled herself glumface, like she's grudging me a favor. The radiator cap was cooled down enough by this time I could get it open. Wasn't but a little spit of steam left in there. Another quarter mile they'd've cracked the engine block.

I said to Sue Lynn, "What do you think the problem is?" and she gives me a look and says, "Vapor lock and the radiator's run dry," and I said, "That's what I was thinking. I just wanted your opinion," and she narrows her baby blues at me. I said, "Sue Lynn is a better mechanic than I am," and the two of them made faces to show that was a marvel.

He said, "You don't think it's a leak?" and I said, "It's just evaporation in this weather. You'll need about twenty minutes cooloff and five gallons outta that hose; you'll be fine," and he went, "Whew!" They're always dumbfounded when you're honest.

I said to Sue Lynn, "This young fellow's a university professor from backeast."

"Martin," he said and sticks out his good hand, and the girl said, "Simone" and we said, "Roy" and "Sue Lynn," and I slapped the high-octane pump and said, "This here is Ethyl," and they laughed. The tourists love to tell how friendly folks are out West.

"I just hope you didn't hurt your hand taking off the radiator cap," I said, looking at Sue Lynn, and he says, "Nah," and shrugged big enough to slop some cola.

Sue Lynn ignored me. She'd got her I'm-gonna-tell-Momma expression, and she smiles to show them every crooked molar. "I'm planning to go up to the University at Reno myself in about a year," she said, and the two of them said how fine, good luck, what was she going to take.

"She's going to take about seven hundred and fifty a year," I said, "if she gets her way."

"If *Momma* and me get our way," Sue Lynn corrects me, steely. "I'm going to major in business. Some *other* business than gas stations."

They said that was fine, fine. But they weren't too dumb to be embarrassed. The girl whips out a little Ansco and snaps a picture of Sue Lynn and me leaning on their fins. She turns the camera catty-corner instead of squaring it up, as if there ain't enough crookedness in this world.

I told them, "Your antenna's broken, looks like."

The girl tucks away her camera. "It's the most amazing thing. We were camping up at Yellowstone in the National Park there?" It's a question, like I've never heard of Yellowstone. "We had some hamburger in the cooler, and I thought it was a bit off, so I meant to find a rubbish bin." She means a garbage can.

One thing I know, there is nothing like camping on air mattresses, no hot water, gnats in your pancakes and cooped up in a car all day to bring out your nothing-but-the truth. Here's this honeymoon pair a couple of thousand miles from home, she's making a bright-eyes story of it, he's got a death grip on the RC, and she's gravelling her saddle shoes around on the asphalt. It don't matter why he's sore. Once you start to grate on each other you might as well pack in the tourist attractions and the National Parks. I know.

"But we were driving along between Old Faithful and some of those mud bubbles? And we passed two little cubs all on their own."

"We were *told* not to feed the bears," he put in.

"Everybody was doing it," she said, to Sue Lynn, not to him. "So we stopped and I tossed out the hamburger. They just tore into the paper and batted at each other! Having a high old time."

At this point he takes over. "And out of nowhere the mother bear appeared, head and shoulders above the roof, looking for more. She just moved her paw aside . . ." He took the burnt hand off the bottle to show how casual the bear moved her paw, and he blanched. He was going to have trouble driving the next day or two. "That aerial bent like a stick and snapped off at the base. Only trouble we've had with this car between New York and now."

The girl was making a joke of herself. "I rolled the window up quick, I can tell you. And then I realized! That bear could put her paw right through it."

I said, "Well, it's a known fact a black bear will protect her cubs." It's also a known fact that easterners is the cream of tourists and tourists is the cream of dumb. I said deadpan, "I expect that's why the rangers tell you not to feed 'em."

Sue Lynn didn't say anything. She stomped back in to the books, and later when I was filling the radiator I saw her go in the ladies with the bucket and sponge. When she come out they were gone and I couldn't help rubbing it in a little. I said, "Well, that's what an education'll get you. That's what you get for being an educated jackass. That what you're after?"

Sue Lynn points the toilet sponge and swipes it east to west across the flats, from Last Chance Café to the laundromat. "You think that's any better a thing to want?"

I say, "Anyways it don't charge you seven hundred and fifty bucks per annum."

She says, "Maybe it don't bring in much more, neither."

I taste alkali when I see her Momma turning her that way. There's not a day goes by I don't remember that my Granddaddy come out meaning us to have a spread of Nebraska grass. It's not my fault if we kept getting pushed west and piddled down to these three pumps. When your kid wants to *better herself* you know what she has in mind to be better than.

So we stand there. I should smack her sass mouth but I won't give her the satisfaction. The professor and his Brit bride are twenty miles down the road to Reno, and we are right about where we were at sunup. I breathed in a whiff of gas. It took me dizzy, and for a minute I saw what maybe Sue Lynn sees, the desert a clean sweep from sky to sky the way it was in the beginning, and all our garbage sprouted and spat on it, the stucco and the neon, Teepee Motel, the truck stop, Hinkley's Diner, warts and scabs along the highway that is like a blue-black scar.

"Well, maybe it ain't enough for you," I say.

I turn my back and fill the bucket from the radiator hose. I wipe the squeegees, careful. She is panting, and I think maybe she's heard what she said, this time. I know I have lost her though. I've watched the odds up at Felix's too many years not to figure out how things are stacked. She'll go off to college, and she'll come back spouting smart, not bringing her friends because she don't want them to see what she comes from, and not staying long because she don't come from it any more. And I will be planted here with Myrtle and Ethyl for what's left of life, pissing regular into the tanks of tourists on their way to where the land leaves off.

I head indoors and commence to stack the Pennzoil, and she huffs off home. An eighteen-wheeler full of Hostess Twinkies pulls in to the diesel pump.

CHAPTER 6

Animal Crackers

1956/1963

Lazlo Aczél was born in a village called Csillag, which means "star," in the wine country south of Lake Balaton, about three hours from Budapest by horse cart, one by car, though there were no automobiles in Csillag when he was a child.

Lazlo's father Sandor was the chief vintner of the town, with five acres of vineyards, first turn at the communal wine press every autumn, and four labels he sold to restaurants in Budapest.

During World War Two, the inhabitants of Csillag occasionally heard a bomb off in the direction of Pécs, and everyone looked to the horizon. Most of their time was spent tending to the barrels or the vines according to the season, hoping the hens would lay and the grapes would ripen before the frost. But when their Russian liberators arrived, they pulled up the vines and ordered the entire village to plant corn. *Collectivization,* it was called.

That was one too many *behatolás* into their lives for Sandor Aczél. He moved his family to a ramshackle rental in the city and went to work handling horses at a Budapest distillery. Lazlo was twelve.

In Budapest under Stalin real information was hard to come by, and even as a boy Lazlo felt a slick of mistrust on everything. Clearly people were not free. But education was. Lazlo discovered science and subversion as a pre-adolescent and turned out to be good at both.

He was also good at languages. He and his friends Istvan and Imre learned English from a grammar that Imre's father had brought back from New York before the war, hiding under Istvan's stairwell with *Essential English* wrapped in a butcher paper. In these sessions the friends addressed each other as *Leo, Stephen,* and *Henry*. They all swore they would emigrate to America, though "Leo" was the only one who did—Istvan didn't make it out in '56, and Imre eventually became a party bureaucrat in Pécs, with a Russian wife and a small apartment full of large furniture.

In the '56 uprising the three of them demonstrated in front of Csepel steelworks and fervently believed that America would come to Hungary's rescue. When the Soviet tanks rolled in they got separated, and Lazlo went with a small militia across the Danube to Fisherman's Bastion, where they were fired on, and Istvan died, though Lazlo didn't know that until later. He did know by then, the fourth of November, that the Americans were not coming east, and it would be up to him to make his way the other direction. The Austrians hadn't closed the border, and the asylum seekers poured across, thousands on foot and by train, some even in cars or trucks, some barefoot, some bloody, all aghast at the mess they had left behind. Once across the border Lazlo caught a train and went to his great-aunt Ilona in Vienna, where he stayed for a couple of weeks alternately jumpy and comatose.

America was feeling remorseful by then and took in forty thousand of the refugees: minimal paperwork, choice of cities, job help. Leo met Anika at Intake in Camp Kilmer, finished his doctorate as a teaching assistant in Albuquerque and moved to Binghamton by the beginning of the sixties. Lizbett was born their last month in New Mexico.

Those were tender days. Anika was a fiercely protective mother, overtired by her attentive love for the demanding baby. When Leo saw mother and child, cheek to cheek on the edge of sleep, he felt a love for Anika that came from beyond his own capacity, from some ancient, shared well of such feeling. In Binghamton he tried to balance his work with fatherly duties, which was in some ways a poor fit for a Hungarian—his own father had played an indifferent role—but also seemed to arise out of the American atmosphere. As did the assumption that they would buy a house.

Which they did; a brick box that was so much more colorful and well-equipped than the tenements they had come from in Budapest that for a few weeks they walked from one room to another touching the walls. But a two-bedroom was all they could afford, and it was no more than a year before Leo began to feel he had no corner where he could spread out his work. He spent more time in his office, and then to make up for it took Lizbett out to give Anika her space too.

He was never anxious for his daughter. Anika might rage at him, as in her exhaustion she often did, but she would turn patient toward their sturdy offspring. It was Leo who, at the beginning of his second year as a teacher, feared his mood. Was he already, at twenty-seven, tiring of marriage, fatherhood, academia, even the cognitive powers of goldfish?

Martin and Simone arrived late for his first term in Binghamton, the Dodge crammed with books, a nine-month-old Irish red setter, a few plates and pans. Because landlords were suspicious of pets, the only furnished apartment they could find was one floor of a shingle-sided house on Greencroft Street a short walk from the shabby little Binghamton zoo. In the basement lived a Mr. Hershon, who grew tomatoes and gave them away to anybody who would take them. On the ground floor was an Italian family who dealt with many of Mr. Hershon's tomatoes, and earthy smells of garlic, oregano, and basil escaped upstairs through the vents. Martin and Simone had the top floor—"Cloud nine," Martin said. She said, "Cloud six, anyway." The rooms were small but there were three of them, not counting a kitchen big enough to eat in and a screened porch with outside stairs down to the driveway—an ideal situation for Che Guevara.

Che was good-natured, beautiful—that glossy setter red—and very stupid. He could not learn to come when called, and evenings when he had run away Martin would beat him with a tightly rolled *New York Times*—which Martin claimed did not hurt—while the dog howled, and Simone had occasion to reflect on the disaster she had made of her life.

No, not yet. This was the period in which she aligned the mugs on the shelves and scrubbed the floor on her hands and knees—a practice, Anika Aczél told her, that clearly branded her a European. In the kitchen, on the wall of the closet that held the water heater, was written in laundry marker:

Why does Michael always

Simone knew nothing of the former tenants. The words hung there like some outcry of Bluebeard's wives. *Why does Michael always . . . lash out at, shut me up when, think he has to . . . ?* She felt sorry for this unknown woman—sorry, along with a shiver of distaste. But then on some bad day with Martin she would find that she had opened the closet for no purpose, feeling both guilty and comforted, guessing at sisterhood. Or another day, when she had wine too early, she felt the woman still moving in the kitchen or descending the outside stairs. She remembered the doppelganger she had fantasized in England, a proto-Simone carrying on her life in Liege in parallel to her own.

Still, not yet. This was the period in which she walked in the little zoo while Martin beat the dog, breathing carefully over the dark weather in her stomach, and thought tenderly about Martin's childhood, how vulnerable he was, and how loving in his frequent days of self-doubt. The truth was that he needed her.

The zoo was no more than a couple of blocks long, with graveled paths and one peanut machine periodically on the blink. It had three or four species of monkey, and a molting camel; but most of the animals were common, if feral: deer, snakes in a terrarium, a family of ferrets. Red squirrels ran over the paths and busied themselves up the branches, in which a few drab birds also set about to withstand winter. It was impossible not to notice the contiguity of the free and the caged. Simone walked crunching the gravel, rehearsing the poignant paradox of Martin's character, carrying that inner chaos gingerly.

Sometimes she would run into Leo Aczél and his little girl, the girl intent and curious; the man slightly satirical and then every so often, suddenly, confiding. She liked his caterpillar eyebrows, the old-fashioned half-discs that made him look like a boy peering over his grandfather's spectacles.

Leo would push Lizbett around the Binghamton zoo on Saturdays, and on weekdays when his office hours ended midafternoon, because it got them out of the house while Anika was in the kitchen, and because parenting is boring. It seemed to Leo part of the biological imperative that toddlers should be terminally cute, or repetition would drive parents to infanticide.

The Ross Park Zoo had a sour-tempered camel, a toucan in an aviary, and a monkey house that included two genuine bonobos. Leo found himself searching the animals' eyes for signs of suspicion or disdain, and knew he was committing the sin of anthropomorphism. He remembered being taken by horse cart from Csillag to Budapest before the war, to the zoo on the Állatkerti körút, where the grandeur of the elephant and the giraffes had awed him. The zoo was destroyed in the war, and when it reopened was dilapidated, smelly and sad. In Budapest he had cursed the officialdom that let it continue in such disrepair, whereas now he nursed his boredom, wondering what had happened to all his fervor for improvement.

The wheels of the pushchair crunched and sank on the gravel. "What is that?" Leo would say at each station of each round. "Coyote." "And what is that?" "Monkey?" "What sort of monkey?" "N't bemember." More or less as one would do with a dementia patient, except that Lizbett was alert with promise, everything that he seemed so quickly to have lost. He watched her breath pulsing on the glass of the terrarium. He felt sorry for the zoo animals, most of whom were also immigrants isolated from their kind.

Leo and Anika agreed that Lizbett had, even before she was a year old, a regal style. The first time she stood, she let go of the coffee table with a look of triumph that said: *We told you so*. When she was delighted it was with loud-mouthed joy. When her mother yelled she would take cool interest in nearby upholstery or a copy of *The British Biomedical Bulletin*.

At home Leo read her a book called *ZOO* in which she could name all the animals, just as she could name the menagerie as they wandered, tossing peanuts—which was at that time encouraged. One afternoon he saw Lizbett—*saw* her—make the first connection of page to world.

"Camel," she said sitting in his lap, slapping a finger on the page. Then an hour later, "Camel," while the scowl and slobber swung down to the fence. Enlightenment dawned: oh, *this* is *that*. Leo taught goldfish to swim mazes for a living, and sometimes he imagined that they were experiencing that transcendent coupling. *Aha! Left at this corner!—Aha, this way to the flakes!* To encounter that moment was why he taught instead of making real money at Pfizer.

The zoo was free—to them, though obviously not to the toucan or the bonobos—with a slack chain that even after hours did not impede a stroller. But there was hardly anyone else there: a desultory attendant scattering hay, on Saturdays a few school kids. So it was a surprise that he kept running into Simone Puig, wife of Martin Puig who taught basic neuro in his department; an ambitious blowhard who was forever finding an excuse to cite his publications. The Puigs had no kids. They had a dog, but she didn't bring him to the zoo. She claimed to need fresh air, but she just looked cold. She always had a Polaroid camera hung around her neck, with which she took close-ups of a leaf or a puddle with oil-rainbows on it. If she aimed it at an animal it was likely to be at a single hoof, a nostril.

"I wanted a Speedex," she apologized, or complained, and then of photography, "I keep thinking I'll give it up. Who needs all these *snap*-shots?" She gave a diffident grin. "It must be a com*pul*sion."

He thought her pretty and peculiar, with her faraway eyes and her dun-colored scarf shrouding a Modigliani neck. He thought she must be Canadian, her accent barely tinged with BBC. He knew she taught night classes in Continuing Ed—not regular faculty because of the anti-nepotism laws—and that she and Anika had hit it off at a party "for wives and female faculty."

"This must be a giraffe," she said to Lizbett.

A shriek of derisive laughter. "No, a goat!"

with quick movements that seemed like hyper-vigilance even when they weren't. She was prey to sudden terrors and suspicions. When she and Leo met he wanted above all things to protect her. Her vulnerability moved him and turned him on.

She had different successive diagnoses: schizophrenia and adjustment disorder in Albuquerque, gross stress reaction in Binghamton, eventually it would be PTSD in Boston, which was more useful because there was less blame attached. Anika herself did not change much from their early years together, but Leo's expectations did. Or rather, there was an afternoon early in their Binghamton days—they were in Dr. Bahara's office and the good doctor was patiently explaining the treatment for stress reaction while Leo was looking at a clock behind the doctor's head, a gingerbread contraption with the air of a family antique. He was wondering how a medical man with his patently East Indian background had come by such a thing; and as the big hand clicked forward from thirty-six to thirty-seven, Leo understood (aha!) that everything had already happened. Anika was not going to "get better." This was what better was. Whoever she had been before she hid in that storage cupboard listening to the slaughter of her editors and her friends at *Szabad Nep*, this is who she was now. She was at that moment in Dr. B's office docile, her brow wrinkled in the desire to understand what magic he held out to her. But whatever he offered, later tonight or tomorrow a noise would startle her or a domestic injustice would assail her, and there would be a murder of dinner plates or a violence of spaghetti, followed by a torrent of *mea culpas*. He got it. They were these people now, she someone who was at the mercy of her own behavior, he a slightly disappointed academic who escaped his lab to pick up his daughter and escaped the house to go back to his goldfish maze and escaped on Saturdays and weekday afternoons to watch the toucan who also, perhaps, had rebelled in his time and expected more of his brightly colored life.

Little by little over the autumn Leo said some of this to Simone Puig in the Binghamton Zoo, *sotto voce* when Lizbett was absorbed with the animals. Not much of it, but enough to let her know that

Anika had been through a lot, so he was glad the two of them had hit it off and he would be—did he say *gratified?*—if Simone visited her.

Simone said, "Martin kicks the dog."

October in Binghamton the leaves were in riot, so bright that he wore sunglasses on the drive. There was no pressing reason for Leo to be in the lab on Saturday mornings, but he needed some short remnant of the week without disputatious colleagues or anxious students, demanding child, erratic wife. He came in "to pick up the mail," to "to check on my goldfish," mostly to sit and let their incessant oscillating empty his mind.

He also liked to visit Alice in Ned Orozco's octopus tank next door. He was jealous of Ned because he'd had the foresight to work with that phenomenally intelligent species. Alice, a California two-spot, was so smart that Ned had to screw down the mesh over the tank; she had squeezed out and scuttled into the broom closet, twice. It put his goldfish in kindergarten by comparison.

Alice now measured twenty-three inches from head to tip of tentacle, and was so curious that it was impossible to tell if she knew him or he just represented entertainment. He did not feed her—that would have been an unethical breach—but he did come by a few times a week so she might know him, and Saturdays he pulled a chair up to the tank and set his hand against the glass. This morning she darted across the water toward him, swiveled her left eye and stared at him for a moment, then slowly unfurled one tentacle and set it against the glass. You could see the suckers pulse, each an exploring fingertip against his own. He walked his hand upward; she climbed with her suckers. It was sexy. It reminded him of Pyramus and Thisbe, kept apart but hands pressed against the wall.

So absorbed was he this particular Saturday that he forgot Simone Puig was coming for lunch, and he got home earlier, probably, than Anika wanted him to. Nevertheless, when he saw Puig's ostentatiously finned Dodge in the drive, he could have gone elsewhere, but did not. He walked in on them in the living room, Lizbett in a bratty mood, shredding a paper napkin.

"Sorry," he said.

Simone looked over her shoulder at him, her hair haloed above her long neck, and he was struck with one quick note of arousal, like a drumstick on a snare. Jesus. Octopus and adultery, is that where he was in life?

"There is coffee on the table," Anika said. "You know Simone. Look at this, she is bringing pickles."

Indeed on the coffee table was a quart jar of drab green stuff.

"I want animal crackers!" Lizbett whined.

Anika said, "She is tired."

"We live above a gardener," Simone explained. "We don't know what to do with all the green tomatoes."

"She has brought Lizbett the animal cookies too," Anika said brightly, "but Lizbett has enough for the moment, not so, sweetie?"

"I want crackers!" Lizbett said, He heard in her the hysterical note of her mother's furies. But he must not think like that. Anika raged because she was damaged. Lizbett's was a toddler tantrum. She would never be damaged; *that* was where he stood.

Lizbett turned an angry eye on him, and he realized—had he not known this?—that he had not mentioned to Anika their zoo encounters with Simone.

"I'm afraid I've caused trouble," Simone said. She gave him a quizzical look. Lizbett, reaching up to tug on his jeans, mirrored the look. "They the animals at the zoo!" she said. Lizbett looked—sly. He saw that, like him, neither she nor Simone had mentioned the zoo; he'd swear to it.

Leo disengaged his daughter's fist. "Lizbett and I will read a story in her room."

"You don't let me animal crackers!" Lizbett accused.

She continued to fret though he read to her, aware of the women's voices beyond the walls, aware when the front door closed and the throaty exhaust of Puig's Dodge started up. By that time Lizbett had fallen into a plaintive sleep. But it wasn't until after midnight that they called the doctor, and after three when they learned she had a full-blown case of German measles.

It was the smell of pickling spice that first caused the roiling in her belly that led her to the doctor who administered the test that confirmed that she was seven weeks pregnant. And events unfolded as they did because she took a jar of the pickles to Anika Aczél, whose husband Leo was also on six thousand dollars. She had wanted to tell Anika about the pregnancy, tell someone besides Martin, who had greeted the news with hollow heartiness. Things turn, she thought later, on such tiny coincidences; and whenever she heard the phrase "turn on a dime" she thought of green tomatoes, and Anika Aczél's fretting toddler. The fretting, she remembered, had filled her with the wrong anxiety. *Can I handle this day after day?* she had asked herself.

But the next day Anika called to say that little Lizbett had German measles. She was so sorry. She thought she'd better let Simone know. Simone had had German measles, hadn't she?

Simone didn't know what she'd had. Didn't know whether she'd been breast or bottle fed, didn't know the medical history of her forebears, whether she could expect to die of heart failure or diabetes or colon cancer. She knew her mother had died of some liver ailment. Now she remembered having the mumps and the chicken pox, the names of *les oreillons* and *la varicelle*. The memory came unbidden: lying under a featherbed while her mother scraped at an apple's flesh with a flowery-handled knife: "*Voici un petit oiseaux. Mange pour la maman.*" But though the memory was clear it would not expand beyond the knife, the apple, the trope of the mother bird feeding the baby bird. And as for measles, German measles? She had no notion.

Dr. Hopkins thought they had better not take a chance and gave her a gamma globulin shot that (she thanked God, though she did not believe in God) was covered by the SUNY health insurance. And she went about preparing discussion questions on the *Odyssey*, for a class that was a pleasure to teach because, although her students did not know anything about the Greeks or poetry, they knew what it was to be traveling and not be able to get home.

But on the Tuesday one week to the day later, she felt the skin of her back burning and slipped her blouse off to see—twisting toward the mirror—a rash so general that it might be nothing. She dressed again and went back to finish up the breakfast dishes.

"Come on, General."

The air was crisp and lovely. She dared not take Che to the zoo. So Simone walked him around the neighborhood in the browning riot of fallen leaves. The tarred road curved among slightly ramshackle houses. Che pulled happily, nosing through the leaves. She tried not to obsess, but she thought she was woozy. She thought her bra grated on her skin. She thought her face was flushed, but how could you tell in this bracing cold?

By the time she got back the little pinheads of rash had begun to bracelet her wrist. She found that at some point she had accepted it. One moment she doubted herself for a hypochondriac, and the next she had begun to examine what she knew about the effect of German measles on a fetus. She pulled down the old *Everyman's Encyclopedia,* looked up *Rubella,* was referred to *Measles,* and skimmed with alarm through eruptions, catarrh, and dangers to the unborn. She imagined herself harnessed, not to a demanding child like Leo and Anika's, but one that was halting, haunting, needy.

She looked up to the tragic eyes of that great fool of a dog, slipped off one loafer and rubbed him along the fringe of his long neck. He groaned with pleasure and sprawled. Where her back came in contact with the chair a thin film of fever had set up.

Martin did not get home till after six. By that time she was handwringing feverish, on the edge of making herself foolish, doing something to regret.

"Didn't you get my message?" she demanded, shrill. "You're over an hour late."

This was not a good way to begin with Martin. Martin had quick responses: quick to laugh, to quip, to take offense. Although Simone was taller, when they walked together she had to scamper to keep up. Martin had a tennis player's body, springing in the thigh. He liked Scottish tweeds, Italian ties, sheepskin, any item of which it could be said it was "the best quality." He liked honors and publication. He had wanted her because she was tall, and Continental, and what he gave the name of "poised." He had inherited his father's brilliance and he needed hourly evidence that this was so.

"What's the matter with you? Calm down!"

She slipped her shirt off her shoulders and offered him her back, waiting for the spectacle to have its effect. Perhaps she had forgotten that she herself had not been convinced all at once?

"Oh, that's nothing."

She knew by now that she had mistaken his authority for strength. Much later she would tell the story to women in the process of lifting their consciousnesses; would roll her eyes and say, *Jesus, what an asshole,* and they would laugh. But at the moment it was as if her organs were in riot, her liver clamped in a fist and its store of poison leaking.

"Martin! Look at my wrist. Don't you get it? It's a danger to the baby!"

"Don't overreact."

And there too, looking back, she had known everything in spite of knowing nothing, hadn't she? The decision had already been made, before the statistics, before the options, even before the verdict of Dr. Hopkins.

Who said, "I feel I've failed you." He came back all the way to the clinic at seven o'clock. At one point he put his forehead in a palm. "It takes forty pints of plasma to make one shot," he said. "The chances are high that you'll get enough Rubella antibodies. I'm so sorry."

He wrote the fetal odds on a yellow pad, one after another: a ninety percent chance of a normal brain. An eighty percent chance of a normal heart. A sixty percent chance of eyesight. An even-steven chance of being able to hear.

"I had better odds than that, that the gamma globulin would work."

"True," he said. "Well," he said. "It is up to you, but I think you might want to take a look at this." He folded half a dozen pages into a manilla envelope. She saw, before the pages creased, the words, "Society for Human Abortion," and knew that he was trusting her with his freedom as well as his advice.

She drove home but sat for a few minutes at the entrance to the zoo, a hand on her belly, over the tentative body she had not begun to mourn and perhaps would never really mourn until the day twenty years hence when she would stand cracking eggshells over a pottery bowl, making an angel food cake for some inane academic function and, spilling one bad yoke bloody in its slime, would catch her breath for the whole spoiled dozen, saying: *I had no idea that would be the only one.*

But not yet. Now she only parked beside the rickety stairs and mounted, feeling, in addition to the sense of momentousness and grief, a surge of satisfaction, of triumph, even, in being right?

He met her in the kitchen. "Poor darling. You don't blame yourself I hope."

"Why would I blame myself?!"

"Don't snap at me! It's not *my* fault."

So they quarreled. But who hasn't had such a quarrel? Such quarrels get, if not unsaid, unmeant. When the blood-rush calms it is possible to see how this was not intended, this was said in anger, that regretted. He would meet her return flight from Mexico City with a bouquet of twenty roses. President Kennedy would be shot. They would carry on through the whole of winter in undulating truce.

"Isn't it awful about Simone Puig?" Melissa Kapshandy swung the blouses along the Salvation Army rack with a sound that Anika felt in her teeth. Anika would have been ashamed to buy her clothes at a charity shop. She was looking for an ironing board.

"What is awful? I have not been hearing from her now it is weeks." Lizbett stood among the toys, absorbed in watching a tug-of-war between two toddlers. The toddlers pulled on a yellow dump truck, each with a fist on a fender.

"Let go. This mine!"

"Mine!"

Melissa held up a blouse of slippery synthetic. She actually used it to shield them from the other customers. She whispered, "Had an abortion, apparently. Caught the German measles, poor thing. Not that I would have got rid of it myself."

Sometimes Anika had a foreshadowing of what she called *szörnyeteg*, the monster. It started with a perceived slight, a late arrival, a hedged promise—that sat as bile in her esophagus. If Lizbett was near she could deflect it. But this meant that it erupted nearly always at Leo, which meant that she would later be ashamed. Leo said the monster appeared when she was overtired, but when was she not overtired?

"I think she went down to Mexico for it," Melissa said, still whispering.

The longer the monster stayed in her throat, the more it would leak to her stomach, seeping into all her organs. Then she would know that she was going to spew it out, that she would blame and rant, even as she knew that later she would hang on Leo, who would forgive her and so prove himself superior. A small, sharp blurt came out of her; a safety valve.

"*When*?!"

Melissa started. "I dunno. Before Thanksgiving. Before, you know, Dallas."

There was no ironing board. She took Lizbett home and read from her new book, *Where the Wild Things Are*, translating from English to Magyar as she went, calling the wild things by their right name. Szörnyeteg. Which felt like an act of defiance—not of her monster, but of Leo, who said that Anika should not speak so much Hungarian. He didn't want Lizbett to "think of English as a second language." But what was English if not a second language? She, Anika, had learned it mainly to help her toward promotion at *Szabad Nep*, where she was on the very first rung of a career. She could speak English, but without nuance; she hadn't the right idioms, no certainty of tenses, no shades of meaning, which meant that she seemed less intelligent than she was.

Everything in this American life was a second language, really: the brick boxes of their "development," the narrow swaths of grass between them, the dull avocado shag in the living room as if they had killed the lawn by bringing it inside. The brass-wrapped feet of their coffee table reminded her of bullet casings on the floor.

She missed her father.

When she had brought up the *szörnyeteg* to Dr. Bahara, he had pointed out that she talked as if her feelings came from the outside, whereas they were within her. They were to be expected, given what she had experienced. Their work here in the sessions, he said, was not to unmake such feelings, but to give her the "tools" to deal with them. The term made her remember her father's electrical pliers, five of them, doll-sized, closed away into a box that held them in velvet negatives of their shapes.

Now she ate fish fingers and frozen green beans with Lizbett, read to her again, *Green Eggs and Ham*, every nonsense rhyme of which Anika could by now fluently read, but feeling at her daughter's level of comprehension. She kissed Lizbett and put her to bed. She left the beans on the stove, put the dishes in the sink and picked up the potted succulent from the table. But the fat leaves were browning and curling at the edges. She had watered it too much or not enough, she did not know which, a failure among failures. She set it in the sink, undecided. When a dog barked across the street her nerves clenched, they almost sang, a reaction she knew to be absurd. She was not afraid of dogs, and the sound had nothing to do with her actual fears. She tried Dr. Bahara's advice, sat and made m-m-m-m sounds till she could feel the vibrations in her cheeks and teeth. But this reminded her of the screeching of the hangers in the Salvation Army, and of the shaming news Melissa Kapshandy had brought her.

Leo was late, and by the time he arrived she was anxious with what she did not want to be anger, on the edge of doing something she would regret.

"You are nearly two hours late. I ate with Lizbett."

This was not a good way to begin with Leo, who dealt with all anger by drawing into himself. He had coarse, unruly eyebrows that she loved but that could pinch together so his eyes were hooded behind his glasses.

"I'm sorry. The meeting ran late, and then there were a couple of students bitching about their lab grades."

"We went to the Salvation Army but there was no ironing board."

"In English, honey. Please?"

He sat and slipped off his loafers, toe on heel, toe on heel. He said, "Go buy an ironing board at Sears." It was a complaint tucked inside a capitulation. He had told her the Sears bill was too high.

"They cost ten dollars."

"It will be all right."

"I got the table and four chairs for that!"

"It's all right, Anika."

He went to the kitchen in his stocking feet and poked in the freezer. She knew he was holding back his irritation. The holding back was a form of punishment. He closed the freezer and opened the other side, took two eggs from the carton, a pan from the cupboard. When the *szörnyeteg* had hold of her, everything became an expression of her guilt. His silent making of his own meal was a form of admonition.

"Something else is wrong," he said. "What is it?"

"You know always, don't you?"

"It's not hard."

"Oh, no, I'm a, what, a open book."

"Anika. What is it?"

"Simone Lerrante has not called in this month!"

"She's probably busy. Just call her." He was competent. A pat of butter, the flame just right. He cracked the eggs one after the other on the edge of the pan. They hissed and went white, opaque.

"Oh, everything is easy for you, because you don't know."

"What don't I know?"

"They don't talk about this in your labs?"

"About what?"

"She does not call because she lost a child and now she blames me."

"Is Lizbett all right?"

"Of course Lizbett is all right. Why you're trying to change the subject?"

The spatula, the eggs flipped. He scooped the leftover beans into the pan with the eggs to warm them; a sloppy, irritating thing a man would do, and slid all of it onto a plate. Then turned to her. "She lost a baby?"

"She had a, what, a terminate, to be rid of it."

"Why would she do that? Is there trouble in the marriage?"

"You never stay to the subject."

"Anika! Just tell me what happened!"

"You don't get it? She caught the German measles from Lizbett, and I called to tell her, and she was early in the pregnancy so she did it away with. And now she blames me."

"What makes you think that?!" Although he himself had the stricken look of someone caught in the act.

"Do you hear? Because she caught it from Lizbett and now I'm guilty not to tell her stay away—but I didn't know that the day she comes!"

He sat suddenly at the kitchen table. The plate clunked, but he made no move to eat. After a moment he said, "Anika. Her husband is a scientist. She knows it can't be anyone's fault." But his face was tight. Why did he pretend, when he felt exactly what she felt? "What makes you think she would blame you?"

"Because the otherwise she would call me! It's a kind of things women tell their friends. Now she is not longer my friend, she sits there to blame Lizbett, and me, and we did not know Lizbett was sick! It was not her fault and not my fault."

He said again in a tight and reasonable tone, "It's nobody's fault." Oh, she knew that reasonable tone. Though he did not eat.

"You do not know the ways things are for women!"

It was the reasonableness that drove her to fury, a way of putting her in the wrong that was the particular "tools" of men when they had none of the communion women had. He sat, reaching for the salt now, his restraint a form of blame.

The flower pot sat in the sink where she had set it earlier. Now its browning leaves seemed dead in any case, dead because of her incompetence. Even as she lifted the pot and flung it into the sink—something to make him pay attention!—where it broke with more thud than crash, she thought of Dr. Bahara pointing out that she spent her violence in ways that were easy to clean up. The sink, the back stoop, a washable wall. And she remembered that his saying this had filled her with shame, and her throat with the acid burn of her *szörnyeteg*.

For years thereafter it was in vogue to ask *Where were you when Kennedy was shot?* before it became the vogue to point out that everybody always asked where you were when Kennedy was shot. Leo would say, "I was in the lab, baby-sitting an octopus, and old Jacob, the janitor, came in with his mop, in tears." This was a good answer, just personal enough to set history in the context of the daily without laying claim to major drama. Meanwhile the colors of autumn faded to a fog-washed gray. As soon as Lizbett was well, he took her to the zoo half-hoping and half-fearing to encounter Simone, but Simone did not show up, and he told himself that it was too cold for her. He also suspected that she thought he had kept their meetings secret and now found him untrustworthy, even creepy. He continued to bundle Lizbett up in her puffy-suit, which Lizbett continued to enjoy, but then it was too cold for them, and he took her to his office where they played school instead. Lizbett was the Professor and Leo the bad-boy student in this game, which she found hilarious.

The holidays came, and Anika had the idea of buying a large doll at Salvation Army and dressing it in Hungarian costume for Lizbett. An accomplished seamstress, she made the dirndl skirt, laced vest, eyelet apron of the old culture. Lizbett liked it. But it was Anika who spent time fluffing the skirt, braiding the polyester hair.

The New Year passed and serious cold set in. The awkward timing of the semester meant that students came back facing exams; they hunched along the pavement with grim faces. The stacks of work-to-be-graded grew. One lunchtime in January Leo witnessed a civil breakdown in the person of Martin Puig, like him a junior member of the faculty research group called First Draft. A scant nine sat around a table in the common room, eating bag lunches while Halley Dromdere, a substantial Assoc. Prof. with blond waves, read her report on "Recent Findings Regarding Maladaptation in Neuroplasticity." Dr. Dromdere had a style that was convoluted and dry, and Leo couldn't concentrate on her argument, but watched Martin Puig, who sat with a face of concentrated apathy. Leo tried to imagine what Martin must feel at his loss, and wondered whether he knew where his wife had caught the rubella—and whether it would be appropriate, even courageous, to say something to him about it.

Was she all right? *Yes, really, he just took her by surprise.* He would have called but didn't know what to say, he felt responsible. *That's a strange notion for a biochemist; it was a virus.* Well, anyway, if there was anything that he or Anika. *Of course, of course; was Lizbett all right now?* Yes, fine, wearing them out wanting them to play with her new Lego.

Not enough. He said, "I didn't want to bother you, I thought it would be worse—"

"No, no, I understand. I didn't come to the zoo because—"

"Of course."

"No, I just thought it would be hard for Lizbett if she knew, or—"

"I know."

"I just came to get Martin's mail," she said, but apparently had not, because she now fetched papers from Puig's pigeonhole—"I had to come in anyway"—and set it next to the pile of her own, which she fanned out on the scarred tabletop with an ironic expression: term papers, syllabi, job openings. "It's called part-time."

They sat in metal chairs and looked for what else to say. The window threw the streetlights on them so that whenever he thought of it afterward he saw only luminous fragments, the rumple of his own corduroy sleeve, the blue circle of her scarf, the rectangle where glare lay across his book—a red paperback with a death's-head monk against a bombed-out city.

Talk came in shards as well. He held his cup in front of his mouth. She put a hand to her hair. He said, "I looked you up. You teach under your maiden name."

"It seemed politic, given the nepotism laws."

"*Lerrante.* Must be of French origin."

"Yes."

"Does it mean *wandering*? Like a knight errant?"

"You'd think so. But there's no such word."

"In French."

"In any language I know of. In English it seems to mean mistake. A maker of mistakes."

He laughed. "Everybody makes mistakes."

"So I'm told." Long slender fingers, and an air of melancholy diffidence.

He asked again, "Are you all right?" and having given one possible answer she gave the other, which was not to answer. He looked over the rim of his cup.

"Simone?"

She shook her head. "I'm a chopped and patched sort of person."

"Aren't we all."

"I used to think my memories were a faulty movie. Now I think they're more like a few dozen snapshots that I can't put together to make sense."

"Everyone's childhood memory is like that."

"I remember walking with my father in a field in the dark. I remember the grit seeping in my shoes. There's a great sense of abandonment, but I can't make out if I'm the abandoner or the abandonee."

He couldn't take this in. He agitated the book under his hand. A sliver of headlight beam flashed on the snow outside. "It's called eidetic memory."

"Sometimes I dream he's falling, or jumping, I'm not sure . . ."

Wanting to deflect or avoid and at the same time wanting to touch her hand: "What I remember is, when we moved to Budapest I had cleats on my heels because shoe repair was too expensive. But a roll of caps just cost a *forint*, and if you didn't have a cap gun you could shoot them off with the cleat. Bam! I got good at it. Bam!"

She smiled wanly, and he stuttered, "I'm s-sorry," hearing how like a man it was, that what he had to offer was a vocabulary word and a memory of gunpowder.

"*Eidetic*," she said. "I'll look it up." She blew her nose. "We start Macbeth next term, so I'm probably gearing up for the tragic view."

"Tomorrow and tomorrow."

"And tomorrow."

He splayed a hand on the green flyer on top of her mail and swiveled it to face her, said at random, still wanting to lighten the mood, "Here; here's a new career for you. '*Generalist in Comparative Literature Required.*' Jepson State College, Jepson, Missouri.'"

"Heaven forfend."

"'*A liberal arts college of the highest quality, in an idyllic rural setting. Candidate must be proficient in Classical, British and Continental prose, poetry and drama.*' It's tailor-made for you. No?"

She looked at him. "There is the question of my husband."

"Yes," Leo said.

He nudged the flyer back onto her pile and turned his book back and forth. *A Canticle for Leibowitz.* Post-apocalyptic stuff. Did lit teachers read speculative fiction? "All the same," he said, "you're wasted on the Ansco-Endicott crew."

"Maybe not." And, calming, she told him about a student of hers named Jimmy Grissom, who identified with the lame metallurgist of the gods. Her voice came through her sinuses; a red knob of a nose. Nevertheless she seemed to find ease in the telling, was careless of her eyes welling again, even grandly said, "It's how we read, dressing our failures in the skin of heroes."

"Mine was Gary Cooper."

"Jennifer Jones, me."

They laughed. He set his cup down, rested his chin in his hand. "Jimmy may not have learned about the Greeks, but he probably took what he needed. Probably we learn what we need in order to survive."

"And is that—probably—why we forget?"

He shifted, twirled his book. The front of his shirt was still wet. He relaxed back against his chair, and their conversation likewise settled.

"Martin says you do research with flatworms."

"No, I do goldfish now. I'm studying protein synthesis in long-term memory."

"I haven't a single notion of what that means."

"I'm teaching goldfish to swim water-mazes, and then I inject them with a protein inhibitor to see if they fail to learn it. If they do, there's a decent chance the enzyme is necessary to memory. It's not the *Odyssey*, but it's groundbreaking work in molecular terms."

"Do you believe it will teach us to live better?"

"I try not to believe anything at all. Which I grant you is a tall order for the son of Catholics."

"You and Martin are in agreement there. No miracles. No mystery."

He pulled at his forelock. "I'm very high on mystery, as a matter of fact. As I see it, a miracle happens when the laws of nature don't operate as usual. What's the big deal in that? The mystery is that they do. Why should a neuron grow its dendrites? Why should a synapse jump? Why should it do the same thing billions and billions of times every second in every creature? That's where the awe lies, and the power and the glory. Compared to that, raising the dead is a parlor trick." He spread his hands and saw his goldfish, suddenly, dutiful and doomed in their amniotic training tank. He was not going to point out that he killed them, though she would assume he did, to study the mystery of their little brains.

Which she must have done, because she said, "I know what it looked like. Not a goldfish. A tadpole at best."

He cupped his hand over hers. "No choice is easy."

"No," she agreed, although both of them knew that most choices are quite easy. They looked at each other. There was a moment of dead air.

"Anika is . . . very vulnerable," he said.

"So is Martin."

"No," he said, "Martin is insecure. It's a different thing." She did not seem insulted. She gazed at him, her eyes red-rimmed.

"Yes."

At which point it was enough. They could have mentioned obligations elsewhere and said good-bye. But did not. There was his coffee unfinished, and the silence over the lit snow. He pulled again at the Missouri notice, turned it over, and drew for her first a fat dagger of a flatworm, and then a neuron like an anemone or a skinny, burgeoning tree. He lectured her a little on the axon and its synaptic terminals, the dendrites studded with microscopic spines. She offered him Tertius Lydgate of *Middlemarch*, looking for a unified field theory in a novel before the end of the nineteenth century; and their tone became cordial, careful, slightly academic. It was nearly nine when she picked up her gear.

"Don't go," he said. Had he said this aloud? He stumbled on, "Do you know this book? *Canticle for Leibowitz*? It takes place in a future where there are still monks, but the sacred text is a shopping list left over from sometime right about now. It makes the point that, the point that, we don't ever know, really, what the effects of our actions are. We don't recognize the important things while they're happening." She nodded, assembling her things, and he went stupidly on. "Have you read this? Will you take it? I'd like you to have it. It's nothing much. But I'd, well, be . . ."

She didn't make any of the polite deprecations she might have made, but held out her two hands palm up; a child's gesture. "Thank you. I'd love to have it." She turned to go.

"Anika says you were born in Belgium."

"Yes."

"I'm sorry, I didn't realize you were European."

"Why does that make you sorry?"

"I think I assumed I had a harder past. It's a stupid thing to be superior about. Sometimes I do mistake myself for superior."

"It's a mistake I make myself."

"About me or you?"

"Both, probably."

They laughed. He asked, "Do you get back often?"

"I never go back."

"You're a full-on immigrant, then. As opposed to an emigrant."

"I don't see how you can be one without the other."

"No, but there's a moment the balance tips. Isn't there. The emigrant is looking back, and the immigrant is looking forward."

"I see what you mean."

"Or maybe you're an exile—*still* looking back."

"No," Simone said. "No, I'm a nomad. Just looking, thanks."

On Greencroft Street the slush had left the lawns edged with rot. She pulled into her driveway and sat for a moment listening to the dark. She put her palms against her face but there was no scent of him. She palmed the paperback, its malleable surface. Why had she not pocketed his handkerchief?

When she raised her eyes she met the wet, wagging specter of Che Guevara. This was not good. If he was out, he had been away. If he had been away, he would be punished. She got out and stood for a moment with her gloves tucked under her armpits, considering. Che bounded to her and began thumping his whole body into her thigh, stupid as a goldfish.

"Che, Che," she admonished. "Can't you *please* make it easy on yourself?" Her first thought was to take him by the collar and walk, anywhere, away. Then she remembered there was a spare leash in the back seat, and an inspiration formed. She felt for the leash and hooked it on his collar, wiped his flanks with a couple of Kleenex, then shouldered her bag and leaned up the stairs while he lunged ahead of her.

"We're home!" she called gaily. She crossed to the kitchen and shrugged herself out of her coat one arm at a time, keeping hold of the leather strap with the other. Martin appeared at the door with a rolled *Times* in one fist, his free hand worrying a rubber band up and down the cylinder. When he saw them he did an almost comic double-take.

"It's bitter out," Simone declared. "The campus is totally deserted. I mean, everyone is *outta* there."

He whacked the newspaper uncertainly in his palm. She was light-headed now—as if, she thought later, she knew that at some future time this would be funny, a setup for an episode of *Candid Camera*.

And it almost worked. Then—you could watch it dawn: "He didn't go to campus with you."

"It's much safer to take a dog after dark," she observed.

"He shot out when I went to take the garbage."

She unhooked the leash. "Well, he's in now."

As if to demonstrate this, Che bounded across to Martin and thumped his tail. Martin raised the newspaper, and Che shied, but continued to wag his hindquarters, tongue lolling and a-shine with slobber. Simone saw that he was playing the fool, waiting to be forgiven.

"Don't, Martin," she said steadily.

Martin pulled off the heavy rubber band and let the paper unfurl on the counter behind him. "Dumb mutt," he said—relenting?

Simone unknotted and folded her scarf. She sighed, set it on the table, turned back to see Martin stretching the rubber band between thumb and forefinger while he feinted it toward Che's face. Che tilted his head left and right as dogs do, trying to understand. He would not leave Martin's space. The rubber grew taut and long, extended to an amazing eight inches, ten, a foot. Just when it seemed it must break, it sprung free with an insignificant sound and struck Che across the eyes.

Though it did not seem so at the time—there was no thunderclap, not even internal resolve, but on the contrary a leaden curiosity, a sense of waiting in the heavy air—much later it would seem to her that this trivial snap, the sharp banality of this particular event, was the moment that her life "turned on a dime." She would handle—how many, several thousand, half a million?—rubber bands in the course of an academic life, and never once in the next thirty years would she stretch any manifestation of this innocent invention without seeing the band collapse, Che flinch and yelp, recoil, and stand his ground. Why such tenacity of memory, why such conviction (false, no doubt, since at the moment she was blank and numb) that this was the proof she needed, and that freed her? Martin had never beat her, never raped her; there were women enduring much worse, daily, momently, than either she or Che. It was not a question of what he had done, was doing, might in future do. This was who he *was*. She would not endure it. From this moment. It later seemed.

She went to the bathroom, where she stood looking into her composed face. When she next saw Martin she was settled in her chair, Che under her stockinged foot, Leo Aczél's paperback open on her lap. It was nearly ten. Martin came in with the scowl of a boy torn between remorse and "face," an expression that had won her before, because she knew what it was to feel dividedly in the wrong.

Simone looked down at the *Canticle for Leibowitz*. The sentence under her finger read, "*The robber that accosted Brother Francis was not in any obvious way one of the malformed.*" She remembered St. Augustine, whose whole life had pivoted on an accident of text. He had been weeping guilt over his riotous life when he heard a child chanting, "take and read;" and he opened the Bible to a passage that urged him to turn from sin to embrace the Lord. Martin said, "I guess I'll turn in early." Simone had stuck her finger deeper into the *Canticle*. Page 236. "*. . . right now, right here, right this very instant, maybe.*"

Va t'en. Continue.

"Let me ask you something," Simone said. She folded her green bookmark inside out: a dendrite on one side, Missouri on the other. "How can there be a behaviorist who beats his dog?"

Martin smiled uncertainly. "I stand before you, empirical evidence."

"I'm serious. You preach 'positive reinforcement'. You consider it 'negative' to withhold some kind of food treat from a rat."

He shrugged. "What is it your Whitman says? 'I am large, I contain multitudes.'" She waited. "Call it a paradox if it makes you feel better. One of your famous anomalies."

"How come you think it'll make your dog come home to you if you hit him?"

"*Beat, hit.* Simone, it's a *newspaper*. It's a rubber *band*. Any trainer will tell you it's the most efficacious way."

She put the bookmark in and closed her book. "All right," she said.

There was pigeon shit on the bench, white-purple in the florescent light. So Simone stood for a while at the fence while the camel bared his teeth and wound his head against the molting clumps of fur. There was a teeter-totter affixed to a clumsy shape like an amateur notion of a boulder, and when she went to sit she saw that it was indeed padlocked to the ground. Fake *rock*. What is the world made of? She straddled the fulcrum. The donkey was, she thought, depressed, dragging a hoof where it had worn away the grass. She had a notion that she pursued: in the early days of love, everything tender is nourishing, and to be angry is to be unselved with unhappiness. But when love sours, there comes a tipping point; the anger is a harbinger of self and strength. You welcome it. Then it's the sentimental feelings that undermine resolve.

Go away; go on.

She had not resolved. But for the moment she felt self-contained. She could imagine herself easily besting a shortlist, for example, of comp. lit. candidates in Missouri. Where better, after all—a moment of giddy optimism took hold of her—where better to begin anew, than plumb in the middle of America? Wasn't there some such thing as the Missouri Compromise? She would have to look it up.

She could probably also arrange the necessary deceptions—invent a convention to attend while she was being interviewed, spend the summer somewhere Martin wouldn't think to look for her. Instinctively she knew that she would have to hide for a time. She could not take a dog. She could see herself descending the wooden stairs with a single suitcase, her throat catching when she knelt to hug, and then abandon, Che.

This almost undid her. Somewhere a searchlight swept the sky, illuminating nothing but a wisp of cloud. A pigeon had died on the path just out of reach of the ocelot, and was being slowly stripped by insects too small to see.

She could go to Washington, say, where no one knew her; rent a cheap room for a month or two while she occupied herself with some research; bus from there to Missouri, untraceably. Later Martin would have accepted it, and there could be an amicable divorce.

Much later she would look back and know it was not a clever thing to do, to snatch at the first piece of green mimeo paper that came to hand. She might have thought it through, researched the job market, remembered that she meant to go to California. She might have looked before she leapt.

But then, would she have leapt?

Sitting there at the moment, she fantasized this part more or less as it would happen: at a faculty reception for some visiting academic potentate, she would encounter Leo Aczél by the punch bowl. She would want very much to tell him she was leaving, but she would not dare because her leaving depended on secrecy. So she would linger awkwardly, with an air of having more to say. Leo Aczél would also smile with bright evasion.

"I read your book," she would say. "It has made me think a good deal."

"Of the distant future."

"Yes, absolutely."

"And our false gods."

"And how a trivial matter can become the very thing that everything turns on, and changes us."

"That too."

This, at any rate, approximates the exchange they would have. She would offer to return the book and Leo would demur. He would wrap her in a friendly hug before she and Martin left, his jaw against her temple, the smell of his aftershave potent, the feel of his chest strangely and inflammably familiar.

She wouldn't see him again until little Lizbett was an assistant dean; till "MacIntosh" and "daisy wheel" and "windows" had revised their meanings; until a picture could be taken of a living brain in the act of learning.

Transit: District of Columbia–Columbia, MO

1964

They roll south and inland through the dark: Fredericksburg, Richmond, Charlottesville, Covington. It doesn't make sense that they should begin by going south, but they must do so to pick up Highway 64, which will take them west. The Greyhound stops every couple of hours so people can trickle dimes into the coke machines or sit at the counters to eat burgers. Some disappear and others take their place, youths with duffels, women with their gear in shopping bags, businessmen carrying scuffed brown satchels.

All summer she sat in the Library of Congress waiting for her life to begin again, studying the way the light pooled, doing research on her cuticles. Now she has no more self than a fruit pit spat out over the Virginias. She might as well have dressed out of Darla Moxham's old dress-up chest: a work shirt, her dirty hair under a scarf, schoolgirl flats, and a skirt in "permanent" pleats that balloon out over her bottom when she stands. The bus hurtles through Appalachian hardwood—poplar, maple, hickory. At dawn the haze swags like organdy among the branches. They descend toward Lewisburg past billboards touting *Lost World Caverns*. They stop for eggs and grits. Half a dozen passengers scatter into the alleys, and as many materialize to fill their still-warm seats. It is three years since the first Freedom ride, and federal law has ended segregation, but the black passengers sit mostly at the back.

An exception: At Beckley a boy gets on in a letter sweater, his Afro cropped, his neck thicker than his handsome head, swinging a disreputable radio by its handle. He swivels left and right with a readiness for challenge, then slings himself in the seat across from the driver. *To everything (turn, turn, turn)*, says the radio, *there is a season (turn, turn, turn)*. In Huntington he helps a black girl with her luggage—she in a yellow sundress like a bell. By the time they hit Kentucky the girl has moved across the aisle beside him. Her laughter rides above the hum of tires. *Blowin' in the wind.*

At Morehead they change drivers, taking on a rotund gnome who beams *how-do* at them and mops his head with a paper towel. At Owensville three ladies in pillbox hats, carrying each a small hard-sided suitcase, settle themselves with laughter. At Mount Sterling a portly man boards who lifts his leather vest, removes a pistol from his belt and wraps it in a shirt before stowing it on the shelf.

Letter-sweater and the black belle are a couple now. They murmur, the boy's head bent. *Kisses much sweeter than wine.* At Winchester a lumbering white giant in plaid flannel picks his way to the back. "Simmadun," he seems to murmur, "desiban at shee." The travelers consult each other with their eyes: *Did anybody understand him?* Simone tries to read, but lack of sleep has settled as a film on her eyes. The muscles of her back are knotted.

Hills shallower, trees more sparse, the landscape spreads itself under a sun so fierce that the air conditioning concedes defeat, and damp is trapped under Simone's shirt like a layer of long underwear. At Shelbyville they pull into a truck stop behind eighteen-wheelers and spill out into a little cloud of diesel fuel and gnats.

The café has two soda fountains that Simone takes for a sign of recent desegregation. The place is aclatter with lunch, the walls decked with paper hydrangeas and photographs of baseball teams. The smell of hot fat disinclines her, so she orders a coke and a moon pie. She stares at the map tacked to the window frame, which although they are in Indiana bears the logo *You Have Entered the Deep South*. Depth is represented as a cliff along the Mason-Dixon line. She feels the drop-off in her stomach.

There's a commotion. Simone looks up to see the white giant in his plaid shirt fling a chair at a plate glass window. It's a plastic scoop-molded kind of chair that bounces and clatters across the linoleum. Nevertheless passengers sprint toward the door while the man roars something garbled, "stuck the nongs," or "stuggernogs." Simone, half out of her chair too, can see his spit fly. The cashier is shouting into the telephone. The passengers fan out under the awning, embarrassed by their fear.

"Is he crazy?"

"What was he saying?"

"I don't know. I think a coupla truckers got him down."

The passengers climb aboard shaking their heads at each other, made a community by what they've seen. They grin, sheepish. The paunchy man in the leather vest asks, "Was he on drugs, or what?" This is somehow the wrong question. The black boy turns up his radio . . . *such a lot of world to see.*

"Was he one 'the truckers, or a local?"

"No, he was on the bus, before, there at the back!"

"They called the sheriff, though."

"Plain crazy, is what I'd say."

At this angle they can't see into the café, and gradually the talk subsides. They wait, as they have waited at every so-called rest stop for eighteen hours now. Simone bends to her book again.

Finally she feels the motor turn over. It's the intake of breath of a woman behind her that makes her look up to see the door begin to close and to hear the gasp of the hydraulics. The huge man who had thrown the chair is in the driver's seat. The plaid of his shirt strains over his shoulders. One hand is on the handle that operates the door, and he is trying to wrench it closed, cursing "Shittershee," while the mechanism strains and wheezes. In the door is wedged the furious little body of the driver. There is a stunned paralysis. Then the door flies open and the little driver lands like a pit bull. He grabs the huge man by his shirt, wheels him out of his chair, slams him against the windshield and flings him out the door. The man lands in the tarred parking lot, the driver straddling him, flailing at his hands. The passengers are half up, straining toward that side of the bus. The black boy is in the open door, and when the man makes a superhuman hump of himself to throw his attacker off, the boy grips the doorframe as if to leap. But falters. Looks wildly around. Does he dare make himself a hero by attacking a white man, however crazy? Leather-vest stands in the aisle. He lifts his palm, a gesture of authority and warning. The boy, his upper body still pitched forward, grips the frame and checks himself.

By now a pair of truckers have come to the driver's aid, and the plaid shirt is pinned to the asphalt like a struggling bug. Simone knows she was not breathing because she breathes again. The black boy crumples into his seat. Leather-vest stands a moment more and then he too sits. A sheriff's car squeals in from the highway. It takes four altogether to cuff the man and fold him, yelling his curses, down into the back seat. The car drives off, siren wailing. The heroes smooth their shirts.

This has taken three, four minutes. The passengers applaud. The driver checks his watch with a modest swagger. "I reckon we can make up the time between here and Louisville." The youth slumps over his radio. *For the times they are a-changin.*

Leather-vest leans across to the hatted ladies. "Uppity," he offers—a woman's word.

"Was he going to throw himself on that man?" asks one.

"You change the law," says Leather-vest, "and you asking for all *kind* of uppity."

The woman nods. "People never change."

Which must be so, Simone thinks; everybody says it. And yet surely people do nothing else but change. Children grow up into adulterers, scholars are corrupted by ambition, louts evolve into experts on Etruscan pottery. We are cobbled together like Polonius' drama—*historical-comical-tragical-pastoral.*

When dark falls they are still slicing through the southern tip of Indiana, twenty-six hours toward her destination. The bus is mostly quiet now, but you can hear the petulant note of the girl in the yellow dress. The boy is increasingly querulous; at Evansville he goes into the restaurant alone.

At St. Louis the two of them hoist their suitcases and stagger in opposite directions. The driver gathers his gear for another change of command. The fat man returns his gun to the belt underneath his vest, and mildly disappears into the night.

She sleeps a little. When she wakes they are crossing The Big Muddy from the edge of nowhere to the middle of nowhere. In the prairie flats she thinks for a moment it is snowing until she realizes this is the ejaculation of the cottonwood trees. The suffocating night air rings with cricket sound. At dawn they pass a porch where men sit like postcard art: boots on the railing, a yellow dog asleep on the floorboards.

She has come overland to limbo of her own free will.

At Columbia, Dean Sarah Maginnis of Jepson State College for the Liberal Arts puts forth a forthright hand and takes Simone's bag. She is here to drive the remaining eighty miles.

"Welcome to Mis'ry," Dean Maginnis says.

CHAPTER 7

Friendly Fire

1967

In a stand of poplar and sweetgum equidistant from Jefferson City and Springfield, Missouri, on a side road off Highway 54, lies an American fantasy of the gothic halls of learning. The local stone is amassed into fortresses with crenellated tops. Combed lawns surround a small lake, a maze of paths revealing at every turn a bell tower, a fountain or a stone bench under crabapple branches. This is the brainchild of one Jebadiah Jepson, who in the late nineteenth century bought up several thousand acres of Osage Valley that, after the construction of a hydro-electric dam, would encompass some two hundred miles of convoluted Lake of the Ozarks shoreline. Jepson sold this land off in lucrative parcels over a decade or two, but late in life philanthropy overtook him, and he pitched his fortune into this rough-rider version of an Ivy League imitation of the taste of medieval monks. The buildings sit like bulldogs behind their wrought iron fences. The bells ring out in hourly ululation. Jepson College Public Relations does not use the term "theme park," but more than one parent of a prospective student has said, "It's just like Disneyland." Approvingly.

Within walking distance of the campus sits a house that is a cross between a cabin and a cottage. Here are scrappy cypress, overtowering pine, and oak trees topped with shaggy branches; and here, landlocked in middle age in the middle class in middle America, lives a woman who has come to a dark wood.

Simone Lerrante is part of a new and growing group on the American campus: a divorcée, which means that academia is for her both a second choice and a second chance.

She has done everything right. She has embraced the concepts of "liberation," and "career girl." She has navigated her divorce, if not amicably, at least without needing to deal with any person other than her lawyer. She has relinquished any claim to alimony. She now answers to the designations of "Miss" and "Teach" and "Prof." Five days a week she peddles Chaucer and Keats and James to young people who out of quirk or failure elsewhere have chosen this educational retreat; and also to the aspirational foreign students on which Jepson depends for its financial health.

She has become peculiar in precisely the way she understands lonely people to be peculiar. She drinks milk out of cartons, works in front of a log fire in her underwear and slices a block of mozzarella with dental floss. She has covered one wall of her bathroom with fragments from her own photographs in a novice effort to collage a woman's face. She has bought sunglasses that she wears in every weather. She has bought a '59 Volkswagon Bug in which she flees to the lake, Glaize Branch, Osage Branch. She wheels along black roads between cliffs of the same grey stone that built Jepson, tire treads whining. She listens to local radio, alert to the "Show Me" state slogan indicating nothing so much as the distrust of language, which is all that she, tentatively, impurely, trusts.

She dwells now on the doubleness of English words, which too often seem to point to leaden truth; for example, she strives to be *selfless* for her students' sake, but in reality she is without a self. Everything she might once have wanted—the theatre, scholarship, love, marriage, motherhood—seem to have receded beyond the Ozark woods. She still takes pictures, usually at such close quarters that they look like something other than they are. She can access her British and American memories (relentlessly, unbidden, the eyes of the dog Che on the morning she walked away); but of her childhood in Belgium she retains mere scraps, like newsprint rising from a fire: grasp them and they smear in the palm.

When she sleeps badly, which is often, these wisps float incessantly inside her eyelids. *Wasn't there a rabbit covered in painted flowers?—attached somehow to the name "Lotte," right? There was a cobalt blue perfume bottle, and Maman in a bed—no, a cot. Her face? Nothing but a smear. There was a harlequin window—blue and gold—that opened out over a river? A young man, tipping over a balustrade into it?*

Having no personhood, Simone has failed to reciprocate invitations, so she has only superficial acquaintance among her faculty peers. On the other hand, Jepson has stringent Service requirements, and so, feeling most at home among those who feel least at home, she has become faculty advisor (den mother, therapist) to the high-tuition-paying students of The International Club.

The foreign students are a solace. She likes their awkward efforts to fit into American culture. No doubt they are also drawn to her because her quasi-British articulation is easier to understand than a Missouri drawl. She also observes that by and large her foreign charges have a comfortable relation to their own bodies that the American students do not. There is Obi Onyefulu from Biafra, already the survivor of a war, squatting wherever he can meet the earth; Despina Christakos from Greece who drapes herself in whichever is the nearest chair; the Singh twins Jewel and Jade who can twist their hair into a repertoire of buns and braids while taking notes one-handed. Maria Elena de la Iglesias, Spanish by birth but British by education, endears herself to Simone by entering class demanding, "Where's the loo?" The most unfamiliar names are the ones she remembers most easily: Arghil, Yao, Erjabet, Daichi, Valerian, Zelide. When they leave they write to her and she to them. She has a drawer full of onionskin envelopes and international postage.

It is through her mentoring that, at the end of the third year, she acquires a friend. She is given a Service Prize—one of those awards for which, at the cost of a framed certificate and a ceremony, the administration hopes to buy a few paragraphs in *The Columbia Tribune* or the *Springfield News Leader*. Service Prizes come in pairs, and the second goes to Harriet Glaucia in Modern Languages, who oversees the Film Society and the Happy Campers Outdoor Club (They probably don't know she also runs the off-campus Socialist League). Harriet sits behind Simone at the ill-attended function, and when Dean Maginnis reads out their praises, she leans forward.

"If we're so special, we should get together."

"Come and have lunch with me," Simone says. Then for twenty hours of disagreeable panic she cannot remember how to sauté mushrooms. But the omelet is plump and fragrant, Harriet Glaucia is garrulous and droll, and easily as that, she has a friend.

Harriet—Hetty to her friends—is tall, dark, with wide gestures and supple torso bones. In a period of campus mania for big hair, she exposes a nape clipped halfway up her head and a small, perfectly formed skull. Talking, raucous, she rubs her fingers through the brush top as if she would scrub off her pelt. Because she teaches French she assumes kinship with the resident Walloon, and they take to snatching coffee at the campus hangout, the Mecca. Hetty is generally dismissive of men but makes an exception for her boyfriend Gary Gross in Gary, Indiana, a union organizer who has made himself an expert in lead paint. That is his real name. Gary and Hetty prefer their long-distance-but-exclusive arrangement because it leaves them time for their careers. According to Hetty, after sex and a shower, Gary of Gary wants his pubes dried with a hair dryer. Hetty complies. "I give him his blow job," she says.

Hetty is probing as well as confessional. "Why are you not sleeping?" she might demand.

"What makes you think I'm not sleeping?"

"Red eyes. Body language."

"We call it semiotics now."

"Why am I not surprised?"

She wants to know what Simone remembers of her childhood, and why there isn't more of it. She thinks it bizarre that Simone hasn't ever gone back to fill in the Belgian blanks.

"What should I go back to? This is the last stop for refugees. There must be thousands of European Jews who haven't been back to check out what's left of their old lives either."

Hetty says, "But you're not a Jew."

"No, I'm an anomaly even there."

Hetty might sit barefoot on Simone's floor with one foot propped on the other knee, her long undersole flexing like a fish. "How do you know your father's not alive?"

"If he was alive he would have come for me in England."

"Hmmm. When you were a child did you wish he was dead?"

"Of course not."

"That's never 'of course,' of course."

Simone thinks the foot would make a good snapshot, but her new Pentax thirty-five millimeter is in the study, a hall away. She knows where this line of questioning is heading.

"I wasn't molested, Hetty."

"Why not? It's more common than you think, trauma and not remembering."

"What can I tell you? I have to go on what I feel, and it doesn't feel true."

Hetty's real interests are political. She is a poster maker, an organizer of sit-ins. She is always running to Springfield to confer with a Socialist League counterpart at Drury, or setting up a support group for Jepson's half dozen blacks, or taking off for the weekend to proselytize the Happy Campers in ecology.

Inevitably, she involves Simone and her Internationals in the teach-ins and sit-ins that take place even at Jepson. Weekends when Hetty is heading off to see Gary in Indiana, she co-opts Simone to ferry the protesters to Columbia or Springfield or the capitol at Jefferson City. They crowd her little Bug with the sweet reek of marijuana and a scrub-cheeked enthusiasm for taking on the gray eminences of the world. "Get Dow *now*!" they chant. "Hey, Hey, LBJ . . ."

Simone has been to teach-ins on Vietnam: the history, the war, the lies, the draft, the death. She has felt the heat of protesters energized by speeches and each other. She believes in everything they stand for—she is for peace, yes, she is against napalm, yes, she thinks love should be rather freer than it is. But sometimes among the demonstrators she hears a note that is itself almost military. She learns that one weekend someone broke into the registrar's office, pissed in the wastebaskets and poured bleach in the filing cabinets. Then she remembers what Virginia Woolf said, that women should do nothing at all about war. They should remain indifferent.

It is late in the academic year when one of the Iranians, Farouz Alipour, comes to Simone during her office hours. Farouz has volunteered in the English Language Lab this semester, patient and exact with the under-prepared, and has been offered a rare adjunct position to continue here next year. He aspires to translate Persian poetry into English. Farouz is formal in a way that can come off as arrogant to his tutees, but is impeccable as to the grammar they most need. Now he sits scratching at his scruffy beard. He pulls a paper from his back pocket and sets it on the desk.

'I was summoned to the Office of the Dean."

"Which Dean?"

"Dean Seitz."

Dean of Faculties, then. The Uber-Dean. "Yes, all right . . . ?"

Farouz wears a short-sleeved shirt of some silky weave that falls concave against the dejected curve of his torso. He wears a plain white *kufi* like a pillbox hat.

"They inform me that I must shave my beard or lose my position of next year."

"Why? Did they give you a reason?"

"Because I will be teaching freshmen."

"You've been teaching freshmen for the last six months. You're very good at it. That's why they hired you."

"Yes, but now I do so with a contract. Which leaves me subject to the rules."

"Farouz, that's stupid. You have a constitutional right to your beard. It's freedom of religion. Leave it to me."

Furious, she goes first to Hetty, precisely because she knows that Hetty will fuel her anger. The two of them bend heads at the Mecca and strategize. Hetty says the Young Socialists will storm Hutchins' office. They will occupy Old Main.

"Wait, first I'll go to Maginnis. She'll be our ally."

"You can count on your Internationals?"

"Sure. Well, some will worry about expulsion."

"The papers will love it if we get arrested."

"They wouldn't go that far—would they . . . ?"

"Assholes," Hetty says.

Simone heads to Dean Maginnis's office, waits on a hard chair through the last fifteen minutes of some meeting or other, then is ushered into the spotless Sacristy of The Liberal Arts. Dean Maginnis's books are alphabetized along three walls. The Dean rises from her desk to extend her hand, mild-mannered and reasonable ("For a dean," Hetty says). She is as an ally always composed, who now listens to Farouz's story with a cheek against her hand.

"As if the freshmen are harmed by a little facial hair!" Simone blurts.

She knows she should have made an appointment and prepared a measured argument instead of this theatrical sputter. She is suddenly aware that her little toe has slipped out of its sandal strap.

"There is nothing in the Quran that says Farouz must wear a beard," the Dean says. Simone is caught off guard that the Dean knows anything about the Quran, which she herself does not.

"There's nothing in the Bible that says the Pope should wear a crown!" she retorts. But something is happening between her head and the tidy book-filled room in front of her. Stage fright, is it? A breach in reality. She feels as if there is a plate of wavy glass between herself and the reasonable Dean, who reasonably nods and pulls down something—not a Quran but a tome in a blue jacket, with a title not big enough to read.

"Apparently," says the Dean, an index finger between the pages but making no effort to seek out anything that might help her argument, "apparently Mohammed approved of the beard because it's 'manly.' It was a form of instant recognition among the superior sex." An ironic smile, woman to woman.

"There are lots of worse things . . . worse practices." Simone can't think of any. Mormon underwear? She isn't going there. She grips her knees and thinks she may faint. It is too ridiculous. Why is she here? In this chair. Why is she here in the Ozarks of Missouri?

"No doubt," says the Dean. "But Jepson has a dress code. Your young scholar has an alternative, and, apparently, he has a choice to make."

Simone is wearing some skirt too heavy for the weather, a coarse Guatemalan weave. She suddenly remembers Miss McKenzie back at Cambridge, the fall of gabardine over her knee, its dull sheen in the firelight, and herself the arrogant, whole-life-before-her girl who held forth on the aesthetic transformation of Keats's "disagreeables." Such promise! And what does she know of promises, except that they are broken? She is ashamed of her judgment of that old don, who spent her dowdy life in, however, a real university, in real intellectual rigor.

She grips her knees. "If Farouz's job is taken away . . ." she says, fumbling, "he may be drafted! If he is, I will. . . . It's a Constitutional—Freedom of . . . the students will occupy Administration!"

"And then you will be fired. And then I will resign in your defense. And then there will be three of us out of a job."

Simone sits stunned. These are surely outlandish consequences, which she never considered. That Farouz could be fired in any case, and that the gentle Dean . . .

"Harriet Glaucia is ready to bring out the Socialist League!"

"Harriet Glaucia has tenure," the Dean points out.

Simone feels the seductive pull of the easier choice, the quicksand of true dilemma, in which anything you do will be deeply wrong. She is in truth powerless. Yet if she crumbles now, she will fail not only Farouz but Hetty, who has the necessary conviction for such a fight. She does not care about her own job . . . does she? The sudden specter of bundling up her meager belongings, heading out again to start over, again, again . . . *Go away. Go on . . .*

"Give it a day, Simone. Let Farouz think through what he wants to do. Think through what you want to do."

She dreams of a boat, the dream suffused with the knowledge of abandonment. Her shoes are full of sand, the hull leaking water that slowly turns the sand to mud. She wakes afraid. It is 2 a.m. She drinks a double brandy that sits in her stomach like a hot stone. She throws on Levis, sneakers, a shabby top, and gets in the car. Just outside the Jepson gates, between the campus and the mishmash of bungalows, sits a cemetery with a monument to the Jepson County dead of World War II. It is too dark to see more than the outline now, granite against the black sky, but she is familiar with it—some forty etched names, Joneses and Purdys, Millers and Hoffmans (some of them German, then, gone back to fight their cousins), and some of them dead at the Battle of the Scheldt. She sits on the road in the dark and tries to absorb the fact that these men traversed the sea to lose their lives in the patched-together country of her birth. But her spirit does not rise. She cannot in retrospect grieve for them any more than the roadkill she encounters in the next hour—a possum, an armadillo; it is possible she mourns the fox.

She drives. She follows the whine of the treads saying, "Home, home, go on, go home," but this has no particular meaning, an onomatopoeia constructed of a sigh and a moan. "Om, om," the hippies chant, cross-legged on the green; pure want displaced as meditation.

She circles aimlessly toward Kansas City, down toward Springfield and Branson, listening to Synod brimstone on the radio, and she-done-left-me blues. As the sky begins to lighten she passes sleeping dogs, plowed fields, idle harvesters. She speeds up hills river-cut with gorges. The woods will suddenly ruck, then open into meadow and farmland—as if the English countryside has been picked up by a corner, flapped and shaken, landing crumpled in this other continent.

On one hilltop curve steeper than others, she catches a tire in the sandy shoulder and spins out toward the cliff; sees the drop come toward her, foresees the car arcing into the canyon as clean as a Technicolor shot, and knows that she is dead. Then at cliff edge the tread takes hold and spins her back toward a hill of weeds that stop the Bug with a soft shock. The door opens, complaining. The front bumper is rearranged and one headlight lies sprinkled in the grass. She hurts where a kneecap hit the dash, but the rest of her is fine. The car backs neatly and drives on, still functional.

Sunup, she crosses back into Ozark country, where rosy fingers of Homeric dawn thrust through the cumulus, dramatically to illuminate a billboard advertising Jesus in hippy beard and hair. She registers her stomach's gnawing and pulls into a curio-store-cum-diner.

The coffee is strong, the easy-over hot and golden. Failure of nerve is never as certain at dawn as in the shank of the night. She stretches, testing, feeling maybe more footloose than unmoored. Maybe she looks footloose in the rising light.

The trucker who comes to sit with her is leather-tanned, with deep laugh lines etched in paler skin beside his sky-blue eyes. He wears a blue baseball cap that he doffs and sets on the banquette. "You mind if I ease down here?" He has tumbling flaxen hair, a moustache of the same sun-bleached luxuriance, a wiry body no taller nor thicker than her own. He speaks with a staccato mixture of braggadocio and self-deprecation. He is strange to Missouri, usually doing the New Mexico-Montana run, but he has a refrigerated load that was deflected here "back east." He has an ex-wife down in Albuquerque and a boy of six. He has the arcane hobby of falconry, with all its paraphernalia of feudal times; he opens his wallet and shows her a picture of himself wearing the gauntlet, the tethered and hooded red hawk on his wrist. He has a habit, he says, of driving nights and sleeping days, which suits him fine. He has his motel room already, just a couple of miles up 54.

"I've never been in a big rig," she volunteers.

"No," he says solemnly, "no, you bring your car. You'll feel freer that way, that you can take off when you like."

She admires him for that. She is aroused, and still some combination of shaken and nonchalant, still bleary and newly coffee-hyped. She tries to look as if she does this all the time. She lets him pay for the breakfast. She lets him buy her a raccoon carved out of black walnut, "Made in Missouri," which he presents with a flourish, and she follows him up the highway to a stucco motel where the doors open straight from the asphalt and the carpet smells of diesel oil.

He comes the minute he enters her. He sighs, "Sorry" and rolls over on the ribbed bedspread and falls asleep. The nightstand clock registers not quite 8 a.m. Her Levis are around one ankle, one of her sneakers under the bed. She buttons her blouse. She understands that, her car being right outside, he has no need, now, to interrupt his sleep.

Transit: Atlanta–St. Louis

1971

She flew to Atlanta to give her paper: "Unforsaken: The Search for the Father and the Self in Margaret Atwood's *Surfacing*." She wore vintage crepe over bellbottoms and performed by rote, though certain of Atwood's phrases continued to burp up in her for the three days of the conference ("*I have to recant, give up the old belief that I am powerless . . .*"). She ate an *enchirito* with a bibliographer of George Gissing. She sat through a session on "Grant Writing Dos and Don'ts." She did with a translator and didn't with an academic dean ("*Love without fear, sex without risk, that's what they wanted, and . . . they almost pulled it off.*"). She attended a panel on the inadequacy of Doris Lessing's feminism and another on "Heidegger vs. Sartre: What Is a Self?" She got drunk with a Dickens scholar and went to bed with a Floridian fundraiser ("*In a way it was a relief, to be exempt from feeling.*"). She went to the airport to catch her plane.

Onto the seat next to her in the boarding area someone had shed a glossy *Elle* with a four-inch gash of cleavage on the cover. Back and forth in front of her, people were crossing and recrossing the concourse, airport, country. Stuck in motion. It was eleven o'clock in the morning and she was still buzzing slightly with hangover ("*Pleasure and pain are side by side they said, but most of the brain is neutral; nerveless, like fat.*"). She opened the magazine on a full page of belly button and zipper. Thought levitated like a photographic trick on the field of stomach flesh. On the flat bronze around the navel the words edited themselves: *Pleasure and pain are neutral, like fat.*

Her flight was delayed and she was offered a coke and crackers in the Frequent Flyer Lounge. There, she went to the ladies', peeling a cloth towel from a stack and seeing beside her in the mirror the imperious smile of a woman pinstriped, manicured, beringed.

"Delayed, or cancelled?" the woman asked, in a voice sonorous with money.

"Delayed . . . they *say*."

"Isn't that the truth! They like to let you down in increments."

"Though you'd rather they cancel than fly with a mechanical problem."

"Well, but the mechanics! How does one know what their training is?"

This exchange appeared to Simone as a prototype, word for banal word appearing in latrines across the world, an international chorus of The Flyers' Lament. In the mirror the woman was giving her a funny look, and she realized that she had been systematically wiping the granite sink with her towel: *orphan, home help. (The old belief that I am powerless.)*

Back in the waiting area, she watched a man of some girth surreptitiously clean his teeth. A young woman dozed over a paperback of *Death in Venice.* An elderly fellow in coveralls came up to the Delta desk, carrying a clipboard and a cardboard box. He set the box on the floor and handed the clipboard over the counter to the blonde in the uniform. She signed. He nudged the box with his foot. On the side of the box it said: *Crylor Freezer Pak: Human Heart For Transplant. This Side Up.*

CHAPTER 8

Time Lapse

1975

Harriet Glaucia pulled into the Jepson lot and tucked her new Corvette (metallic blue, five-speed, 350 V-8, woodgrain dash, tilt steering) between the Dean's reserved space and a bed of yellow mums. This was illegal, but she only got ticketed one time out of seven, and if she left home early enough to find a space she would spend thirty-six hours per term at it, which, figuring her time at twenty bucks an hour, meant she was forty dollars ahead just paying the tickets. This was the kind of statistic Hetty liked to calculate when she was facing a stack of sophomore essays on *No Exit*. Also, she was in love with the car, its blunt ass and its sleek rooflines, and it pleased her to shove Nuke Riddick's nose in it when he came out to drive some grizzled benefactor around campus. Nuke still had a Malibu, for Chrissake.

Keep moving. Crucial to keep moving, because Gary Gross was taking off from Indiana about now, maybe this minute, and forever. Heading for North Dakota without her. Her choice.

She was cutting it fine considering the lecture started at five over in McClatchy and she had to pick up Simone first, plus Simone would have forgotten about it, which might be a bit delicate because Simone didn't like to admit she forgot such things.

The trunk of Gary's Camaro would be lashed down over boxes and tote bags—he was such a loser at packing—with dishes swaddled in dirty clothes, his precious grill tilted over in the back seat, snow boots obstructing his rear view. Don't think about any of that. Keep moving.

She cut across the quad under the old oaks and sprinted up the steps of English-Philosophy, shifting Heidegger from one arm to the other. The corridors had beveled-glass fanlights above the office doors, but the paint was peeling and some of the lino was loose.

Today she wanted Simone with her. Not that she didn't genuinely want to hear what Dr. Professor Olivia A. Purdy had to say. She did. A home-grown feminist historian with two groundbreaking books: *Stubborn Roots: Patriarchy from Scripture to Cinema*—and this new one, *Why Britannia Is a Woman*. But after the lecture Hetty didn't want to be alone, wanted to hear what Simone had to say over wine and pizza, because even (especially) if the event was a drag, the post-mortem would make them laugh.

She could have forgiven him the popcorn girl (the *literal popcorn girl* out of the Magic Mall 20 complex), if he hadn't tried to blame it on her, how she was too far away, he got horny, and—looking all bright like it just occurred to him—anyway he had *enough love for both of you*. Did he *hear* himself, fahchrissake?

Simone's office door was closed, and when Hetty knocked there were shuffling sounds, the squeak of a drawer closing before Simone called, "Yes? Come in."

She was chin deep in books, one piled open on another, her hair wild, wearing a severe jacket over a slinky op-art skirt with an uneven hem. "Hi, Hetty, dear," she said. But skittered a glance around instead of looking her in the eye. No doubt there was a pint of Jack in the drawer, not that Hetty'd begrudge it.

"What's up in the world?" asked Hetty.

"I don't know about the *world*. In Florida it looks like the ERA is dead."

"I meant, how about your world?"

Simone shoved her hair out of her eyes. "God help me. I've got Barthelme at ten tomorrow and I don't have the faintest effing idea what it's about."

"What course is *that*?"

"Contemporary Lit. For which I am not cut out. I stop at Joyce."

Hetty lounged in the doorframe and shifted Heidegger again. She'd tried to get Gary to read *Ulysses* once. He got fifty pages in. He said, "What use is it?" It was annoying she should think of this just now, but it was also *empowering*—a word she'd encountered at the Women's Caucus, and one she needed. She loved Joyce. If Gary hadn't the patience for it, screw him.

"What's to know?" Hetty said. "The kids drag their father's corpse around. It's a metaphor."

"Duh."

"In Beckett they put him in the trash can."

"Dear old existentialism."

"I'd trade you Barthelme for phenomenology."

Simone's office was like some Dickensian bookshop, dun-colored tomes threatening to fall from their perch on the windowsill. But the thing that caught your eye was a photomontage on the wall, a woman's head made out of knives and forks, a photo, a broken mask—that managed to be at once dated and disconcerting. The odd thing about it was that it had been bequeathed to Simone by her ex-mother-in-law, per an actual item in her will. This mother-in-law had apparently inherited a dog in the divorce and meant to thank her for it—something like that. "I didn't appreciate her," Simone said of this mother-in-law. "But she knew what I was getting into and she didn't blame me when I got out." Hetty suspected the picture was valuable.

"Pack up, though. The Purdy lecture starts in ten minutes."

"Oh, Hetty, I don't think I can go. I've got half *The Dead Father* yet to read."

"Now, Simone."

Simone sighed, hooked her bag over her shoulder and jammed a clipboard into it. "I'll look a fool tomorrow."

"You know so much more than they do," Hetty reminded her. "It was you who told me that."

And they were off, down the stairs and back the way she had come, past the Corvette she had driven to Gary, Indiana half a dozen times (Don't think about it), and double-time to a bridge over a shallow stream.

He'd be driving too fast because he was mad at being alone. Was he alone? Yes, of course: she would *not* get crazy. Fifteen above speed limit on the Interstates, and then thinking the Dakotas were just an invitation to gun it. "Don't kill me, please!" she'd say, and he: "I have to get around this truck, don't I?!" (*Her* book would be called *Rides: The Patriarchy from Zero to Sixty*).

"I'll tell you what I've figured out," said Hetty as they crossed the bridge. "When I'm under-prepared, it's better to spend the last fifteen minutes on mascara. I can wing it when I know my eyes look good." Simone smirked.

He'd been lead-footing it on County B when he yelled at her: "I'm saying I want kids, the whole caboodle. I'm fucking proposing, don't you get that?" That made her laugh. She got it. Not: *Let's talk this over; I've had an offer.* Not: *I really want this, babe, but I can't do it without you.* No. Just: *I'm doing this. Are you coming?*

"Also, a good trick is, put your sunglasses on so you can enter taking them off. You wheel in a few minutes late like you could care less."

"*That'll* be hard to fake." Simone said ruefully. "What's going on among the Francophones?"

"The usual. Well, an interesting conundrum came up talking about *Man's Fate*."

"Let's have it."

"Is a coincidence a coincidence if nobody knows about it?"

"Such as."

"Such as, your cousin that you've never met sits next to you at some dinner party, but the subject of family doesn't come up and you never know it's him."

"Things like that happen all the time," Simone said. "They just don't mean anything."

"Or two soldiers kill each other that were born on the same day, but they never know it because they're dead."

"Then I don't suppose it matters to them one way or the other."

McClatchy Hall was Chem-Physics, but Humanities used it for lectures because the auditorium was raked and Chem could afford overhead projectors. The place was packed, which was a good sign. The mostly female audience was bunched toward the back, so they found side seats on the third row, and had barely settled when Maginnis got up to do the introduction, *especial-pride / one-of-our-own / product-of-Ozark-country / amazingly-young / internationally-regarded etc. etc.*

North Dakota. Christ. Who moves to North Dakota? *A chance to get in on the ground floor,* more geology, more fieldwork, *a change of direction* in his job. Change of direction! If he wanted a change of direction, how about West? How about South? "Horizontal hydraulic fracturing," he'd said. "Fracking," he called it. Frack you, Mister.

Dr. Purdy, when she got to the podium, was kind of—what was Simone's word?—*unprepossessing,* really. Medium height, on the soft-stout side, sensible cotton suit and Cuban-heel pumps. Hetty had imagined her different: flowing hair with a Sontag streak, maybe. Whereas Purdy warmed up with thank-you's and a lame joke ("At Sedalia School we thought there was only one cuss word: Oh, zark!")

Oh, but he was magic at the start. He'd walked in to a party in Madison, business with a geology minor (geology was his real love; that part was true). Walked in and she'd said to Maureen, "*Who* is *that?!*" He made straight for her too; beeline. "My name is Gary Gross. Do you dance?" Before that first evening was over he'd said "Where would you like to go?" And she'd said, "Where did you have in mind?" And he'd said, "I'm thinking Venice. We should see the Piazza San Marco before it drowns, no?" Oh, he was magic then.

Not that they ever got to Venice.

Purdy had a good voice: low and full, grainy with fine-grained sand, confiding and confident as she went into an origin story. Born into a Lutheran enclave not far from here, her mother a school nurse who'd expected to be a housewife, her father had died in the Second World War when Purdy was an infant, and was awarded the Silver Star for volunteering with a suicidal mission over the ice fields of Greenland. She never saw him. He never saw her. But it was because of her father that she became interested in history; and because she felt the weight of his absence her whole childhood long, she went seeking the experience of the host country where he spent his last days. And because of that, she had discovered the heroism of the wives and mothers celebrated in *Why Britannia Is a Woman.*

"Sartre said there is no world apart from the external world," Purdy proclaimed. Wait—didn't Heidegger say that first? Now she was outlining the weekly rations of an adult in 1943—the sliver of soap, the two ounces of butter, two ounces of cheese, two ounces of tea, the one fresh egg. Up until 1950, Purdy said, "There was no world apart from scarcity."

In 1950 Hetty was playing jacks at Buckeye Elementary and Gary Gross was a scab-kneed kid in Linn, Wisconsin. And now he was leaving her, heading west on—what was the number of that highway? Eighty. He would have left late, the union organizer being so disorganized. How is it she always loved that about him at the same time as she knew she couldn't live with his mess?

In the war, Purdy was saying, at the local level it was the men who did the patrolling in hard hats, but women who organized them. In heavy industry men held the front offices but the women were running the punch presses, setting the rivets, wiring the radios.

Gary would start out twice as far east as she was south, so if she started now and drove ten, even fifteen miles an hour slower than he did, she would cross his path at just about Omaha. She could see herself on the highway verge pretending to hitchhike, the Camaro approaching, Gary with his dumbfounded face on, and then the slow-spreading joy, like a last scene in a film romance.

The doughty women of England took care of the *Kindertransport*, yes, the food and childcare that had always been their lot, but also the weaponry, the records, the communications—"Men ran the war," Purdy said, "but women ran the country—and sometimes the Resistance as well."

Oh, good, she was going to show a film. It's always easier to give yourself over to a film than to a lecture. Even with TV you'd watch dumb stuff you wouldn't put up with in a book. She had a fondness for heist movies, for example, but couldn't get much past the dead body in a detective novel.

Of course there was a glitch in the audio-visual booth, and of course Maginnis got up to see to it, and of course Simone whispered,

"Yes, we'll need a woman," just a second before Purdy said essentially the same thing, and a couple minutes later the screen came down and a red-headed anchor appeared, some glamorous Brit announcing one of those earnest BBC documentaries that got replayed every few years. This was a sixties piece, Hetty could tell by the fuzzy film stock—and the Mary Quant miniskirt of the anchor-glam, who promised "Interviews with the forgotten *Women of World War Two*." Okay. Why not?

On the screen a matronly type, walking a path along the edge of a cliff, cross-cut with footage of Channel chop. "Mrs. Winona Farnsworth," said the voiceover, "took part in one of the most daring joint ventures with the Belgian Resistance."

Belgian. Hetty glanced sideways toward Simone, whose face caught the sunlight from the screen, and Hetty registered how much her colleague had aged in the less than ten years they'd known each other. Sometimes you didn't see it happening in somebody you knew until an odd angle showed up the fine mesh of blood vessels, the tiny sags. Hetty was seized with a premonition that this was her future, this fading and thinning, the anachronistic outfit, the crow's feet, and—what? Nothing more. She folded this thought in on itself. She stuffed it in the trash can of her mind. No way. She was nothing like Simone. She'd picked career over marriage of her own free will, an act of liberation, not a fallback position. She had interests. She had dark hair and tougher skin.

"Such as," said the TV, "I'd never worn a pair of trousers, and what I couldn't get used to was the twill going swish between my thighs." The old woman, standing now on a cobbled street in front of a dock, wore white crimped hair and a girdle under a dress with a flower print. Behind her bobbed the masts of small boats, seabirds swooping in and out of frame. The film was overlit. There was a cut to a beach under a chalk cliff, gulls riding an updraft over churning surf, and then the woman again, saying, "Don't show me saying thighs, will you?"

Hettie flashed a grin aside, but Simone was engrossed and didn't see it. The woman on the TV gestured toward the dock, sobering. "it's the children stick in your mind—a wee tiddler with its eyes wide open and its mouth tight shut . . ."

She *told* him she didn't want kids. She'd had enough *family* to last her a lifetime. She should have picked up on it when he told her that she had good child-bearing hips. She swatted him when he said that, but she should've picked up on it. A not-joke joke.

The camera began following the woman on a tour of greasy trawlers and rusted pilings, the woman squinting into the sun and saying. ". . . one boy landed skew off the dock and broke his shin, so the bone stub rolled under the skin like a tongue in a cheek."

When it came down to it, he had lied to her. Not so much about the blond fox (well, that too) but about their mutually chosen life. For all that time he had said, *go, do your thing, we'll still be a couple. We'll just suck it up*. And that's what he was sucking. Forget that. Pay attention.

"It was that same trip we were expecting a father and daughter that didn't show up, and we about pushed off without them. We'd heard dogs, and you never knew the meaning of dogs . . ."

A funny thing—she'd become aware of Simone again; something muscular. A tensing where their arms touched. Truth is, Hetty had a soft spot for Simone, who was a cross between a perfectionist and a flower child, a schoolmarm with her logic all precise and her emotions like a nuke dump in the North Dakota desert. What would it be like to run into Liberation just as you hit middle age?

". . . there's this girl, maybe ten or twelve, gawky little tyke, slogging straight into the water up to her coat hem."

Early in their friendship there had been an awkward hiatus between them. But it had worked out all right. Everybody kept their job and Farouz had kept his beard (running the Language Lab now, teaching Persian poetry in English to the Iranians), and Hetty'd been magnanimous in triumph, and Simone penitent, and they'd eventually come to an agreement (as women do) that cowardice was just another name for empathizing with the other side.

"Sandiford swung his arm signaling her to go round the dock and fetched her down with her shoes full of water. She'd got one hand done up in a fist against her collar bone. Skinny as rail she was, and those scupper eyes. And her coat too small, though it was posh—velvet collar and that."

She could have told Simone about Gary. But there are some things you have to get through on will and grit. If somebody started *sympathizing* you'd deflate down to a little rubber balloon scrap.

"I wrapped her up, and she says po-faced, 'My father arrives not. I arrive alone.' She says, 'My fa-zher.' I knew better than to ask."

Hetty was startled by something pulling at her thigh, and she looked down to see Simone clutching at her skirt so it dragged against Hetty's slacks as well. The print on the cloth, Op-Art black and white squares, curled under her fist and then slowly uncurled as Simone let go. Over the woman's voice the screen began a montage of refugees, women with a hard case in one hand and a toddler on the other, close-ups of the eyes of children, staring; girls in little collars, boys in little pea jackets. One boy rubbed an eye, his wrist bone protruding from too short a sleeve. *Like a tongue in a cheek.*

"But you lot want me to show you frightened in the telling. And I'm not, you see. You can't be afraid of the past, can you?"

On Simone's thigh the pattern squeezed and turned—mesmerizing—which was the point of Op-Art, right? It was supposed to make your eyes go wonky. Simone's hand clenched and unclenched. She was distressed about *something*. Hetty concentrated on the film, trying to see what had upset her friend so much. But there was nothing in particular; it was an ordinary talking-heads sort of documentary, intercut for atmosphere. It was touching but hardly *riveting*.

"What I remember is," the woman was saying, "we had a little paraffin stove, and usually when you got out far enough to rope the motors into life, they were all glad to settle down over a cuppa."

She was square, this woman, her blue-white hair curled to her skull. The set of her mouth had that British Empire look, determined she could muddle through. ". . . skinny one didn't leave the stern maybe eight hours of rough crossing, looking back where we'd come from in the dark." Simone was having trouble catching her breath. Her mouth grabbed at the air the way her fist grabbed at the cloth—no, that hand was still now, with a death-grip on the thigh.

"She held that one hand tight, and I thought she had some money in there, maybe, or a bit of jewelry, something she'd been told to keep from harm."

There was something wrong with the way Simone held herself tilted toward the screen. Was her friend hyperventilating? Having a panic attack? Hetty wasn't quite sure what a panic attack looked like. But it was possible.

"I remember I tucked the blanket tighter around her and held it there, which she let me, and for most of the way we just stood till it was lightening a little down by the horizon."

Hetty reached across to lay a hand on Simone's arm, whispering, "Are you okay?" But all she got back was, "Shh-sh!" Which did not necessarily mean she was okay. Was her face rigid on this side? Was the arm in fact paralyzed? How could you know?

". . . sagged against me, and bit by bit her hand relaxed over the top of the blanket. There was nothing in it. Not a thing."

Now Simone had her fists at her heart. They pressed with enough force that her stomach pillowed around them, something you did not ever see on Simone's lean frame.

"I suppose I hoped she'd remember me now and again," said the woman. From Simone a sharp intake of breath. A heart attack? Hetty had taken a first-aid course at UW, so she knew how to do the pump-and-breathe if it came to that. But how would she know if it came to that?

". . . that greasy little trawler in the black wake, like a clot being washed from a wound," said the old woman, and the screen went blank. Then Hetty realized that if she'd been going to do anything, she should have done it sooner; the film would have been at least a partial cover for the fuss. Maginnis would *not* thank her for disrupting an occasion like this, but nobody'd thank her for sitting here frozen if Simone was really ill.

"Are you ill?" she whispered, but Simone just gave her a hard glance—or a glare, more like, or as if she did not see Hetty at all. What if Simone actually *was* ill, and she was failing to get help for fear of making a scene in the middle of a lecture that was exactly about strong and decisive women?! She should act *now*.

"That was not as extreme an example as you might think," Purdy was saying, "and the workaday attitude toward danger and death is one I encountered over and over again in my research."

Hetty was not superstitious, but she was alert to certain words. Now *danger and death* turned over in her mind.

Meanwhile Simone curled in on herself, her body shuddering as if she might be crying without tears. And Hetty still did not know what to do. If she intruded again Simone would rebuff her again. If she went for help she'd have to climb all the way up past Maginnis and those girls, and it would still totally upend the lecture. Why couldn't they have had seats farther back?

Purdy was going on and on: this example of female courage, that organization run entirely by women. The audience loved it, but Hetty was distracted and undecided, every one of her muscles tight while Simone bent in on herself, quite still but somehow little by little no longer dangerously still, until little by little, with no effort on her part, as the lecture droned in the background, Hetty began to feel the danger seep away and spread harmlessly in the stale auditorium air. Her senses remained alert. She heard a pen drop and roll behind her, and the hinge of the chair as someone bent to pick it up. She could feel the heat of Simone's shoulder. And the voice of Olivia Purdy diffused so that she heard it not as individual words but as a surf washing over the audience of mostly-girls, and felt the undertow of their attention, sitting each in their fold-down seats with their particular burdens: this absconding father, that addicted mother, last weekend's heartbreak, the future lumbering toward them with its promises and threats. She felt the surf of Purdy's voice and the pull of their responding plea: *Tell me my strength. Give me to me.*

Hetty loved them all.

The lecture ended with a flourish of which she could hear the cadence but not the sense, and Purdy was given a standing ovation, at which Simone seemed to come to herself somewhat. She even gave Hetty an apologetic smile, and they continued to sit for another half hour through the questions, and the boasts that were posed as questions, and the challenges that were posed as questions, and afterward while the girls thronged the podium to touch the plump hand of the celebrity.

They were still sitting as Maginnis broke up the knot of girls and led Dr. Professor Olivia Purdy up the steps, not acknowledging either of them (in case they'd want to be asked to dinner, Hetty thought; which she emphatically did not). When the auditorium was empty she still let a few beats fall before she asked, "What happened?" and Simone turned on her the round eyes of the child refugees.

"I know the coat."

Hetty held her tongue.

"That woman in the film, she was, that little girl . . ."

Hetty waited for Simone to get it out.

"I remember the velvet collar—purple velvet. And pocket welts to match." Slurring a little, still, as if she had in fact suffered some physical trauma. "I remember the boy's broken shin."

Hetty waited.

"And the woman with her blanket. It was army wool, rough. I don't mean I *recognized* her. But I remember."

"You remember the woman in the film."

"Yes."

"You mean her, herself? *That* woman?"

"She was younger."

"But you mean—that girl she was talking about, that was you?"

"It was. I do."

Hetty knew enough not to contradict this unlikely statement. She knew that something had happened to Simone, and that it might take some time to come to terms with it.

"There were a lot of refugees in that war," Hetty said. And then, "Do you want to talk about it?"

"No. I'm sorry."

"It could help. . . ." Hetty hesitated, but Simone shook her head.

"I'm sorry, Hetty. Maybe later. Not yet."

Hetty nodded. "Maybe we should get to Purdy and find out something about that woman."

"No. Purdy doesn't know that woman, it's just somebody in a documentary to her, same as to you."

Hetty picked her bag up off the floor, and the heavy Heidegger. "Do you still want pizza?" she asked. "A glass of wine will help, no? Or two?"

"No. I'm sorry, Hetty, no."

"Or shall I drive you home? You could leave your car here and I'd bring you back tomorrow."

But this seemed to agitate her. "No, no. I can drive. I'm sorry. I just need to be alone." And then she said, in perfect imitation of the woman on the film, "*My fa-zher arrives not. I arrive alone.*" There was something about it that made Hetty wary, and eager to humor her. Or to "handle" her, was it?

"I'll follow you and make sure you get there."

"Yes, all right." And at last the two of them rose and headed up the steps, over the bridge and toward the parking lot.

Hetty did not for a minute think that Simone was the one, out of all the thousands of kids secreted out of Europe in World War Two, who was remembered in a BBC documentary twenty-five years later. By her own admission, Simone's memory of her childhood was scant. It was probably Hetty's own fault for having mentioned coincidence. She'd put it in Simone's mind, and when the woman in the film stirred up that period, Simone just naturally took it to heart. She was overwrought, Simone. She was heading into the school year—winter!—with not an ounce of sass to see her through.

Whereas Hetty—Hetty was *empowered*. She was safe now. She had gone an hour and fifteen minutes without a single thought of Gary Gross.

Transit: Around and Around

1976

The merry-go-round at Skelton Park has been oiled for summer and responds to a running push. Simone turns it fast, faster. She steps onto the running board and flings herself back on the drum. Around.

The drum is eight feet across, pie-sliced into six by the iron bars she now holds to steady herself against a careening sky. She feels the wood against her thighs. Trees ring half the sky and the moon swipes the circle closed. Around. Around.

When the revolutions slow she drags a sandal to slow it further until it stops. She picks up her thermos and hoists it to her mouth. The thermos is—was—full of bourbon. She sets it back carefully on the ground.

As a rule now, the first drink makes her cheerful. The second makes everything sharp, pristine. It used to be that the third set reality askew, but it no longer does that, so she comes to Skelton Park at the edge of the lake. Here the dirt, both packed and powdery, eddies around her ankles as she runs. It's a scruffy playground—full of kids and mothers in the day, but they have long since gone home. Tonight there's one other person, a man on a bench twenty yards away. He's no threat to her; just a harmless wino. She raises the water bottle, sets it down, repeats the routine: push, run, fall back. Around.

The tops of the trees ring an emptiness. Dizzy now, she brings the habits of the classroom to the fragments in her mind: *Problematize the obvious. Interrogate the text.*

First is the gritty soil that settled in her shoes. But now there is also the woman in her flowered dress walking along the English quai. And this woman—the same, but other—is also a bulk against her back, enveloping her in rough blanket wool. The boy with the broken shin. The lavender coat with velvet flaps.

Drink, push, run, step up, fling back. The drum might be the head of a giant bolt, winding itself into the earth toward the Underworld.

There were furrows in the dirt. There were seagulls in the furrows, but how can that be when it was night? There were no trees. Maybe the sound of dogs? Papa trudging beside her, both tall and bent. And then the soil has turned to mud and her coat hem flaps cold against her thighs. The man in the boat gestures with his arm that she should climb the dock.

But when she peers into the space between the soil in her shoes and the mud in her shoes—a disconnect between the furrows and the boat—her mind flees to the irrelevant: the angel food cake she has promised for the International Students' picnic; the shooting last week of a student in Soweto.

Drink, push, run, fling. Around, around.

Who knows why sometimes thought is inaccessible and the synapse declines to jump? Even Leo Aczél did not pretend to know. Who knows why, after dogged and fruitless effort, "out of the blue" the hidden suddenly leaps and reveals itself? Here is the field and its furrows and they are crossing it; here is her father, tall and stooped. She sees that she thinks of him as elderly, but also that he is younger than she is now.

The years collapse. It is cold and the armholes of her coat bind too tight. She reflects, bitterly, that if her mother had not died she would have had a coat to fit. The field is wormy with the smell of new-turned earth, and overhead a moonless black bowl of a sky that she has thought of as God's creation—because she has lived surrounded with Catholic schoolgirls, and their influence is strong.

Moonless dark, and yet a pair of horses' rumps catch the starlight. She can feel the dirt sift into her lace-up shoes. They are not close enough to smell the sea but it can't be far. They cross with difficulty, furrow after furrow, and come to a little hummock of scrub along a drop-off, after which the land becomes marshy in the direction of the Channel. They know this part of the coast is patrolled, so there's bound to be some element of luck in it, but they have seen no one and heard only the one dog far off.

What she remembers is the sound of a high branch cracking, though there is not a breath of wind and no trees for acres in either direction. The sound comes just at the edge, so that as she jumps Papa also partly jumps and partly falls and they land against the sandy shelf under the ridge, which then leaves them mostly or at least partially concealed from the field.

The bullet has hit him in the back—and she has since heard that the point of entry is small and the exit wound more shattered, but if that is so it is concealed now by his overcoat, in which the hole is so small that she does not at first believe in it. But presently it begins to soak and darken.

They hear shouting and a dog then, but it does not seem very near, and she hopes they can make it across the marshy part to the lighthouse that is their rendezvous.

But Papa says both "Go away," and, "Go on."—both "*Va'ton*" and "*Continue.*" In what must, to her, be the voice of absolute authority. Because otherwise why would she do so?

"*Tu peut rien servir ici,*" he says.

She puts her hand out—it must be to close the hole.

But he says again, "Go. Go on. You can't be any use *here.*"

The drum has wound to a stop. Simone lies still in the stillness. There is a moon, which that night there was not. Now she watches the little gray-on-gray clouds scudding, and what comes to her is the face of a screaming child that passes across the moon and out of sight, past every window of the departing train.

"He'll be laughing by the time we're out of the station," the mother says.

The baby knows otherwise. This is the grief that never ends.

CHAPTER 9

White Space

1977

What am I doing here? I should have parked around the corner; any number of people know my car. Anyone passing by can see my faculty tag. And there's a five-foot marijuana plant on the porch where any meandering patrol car could see it: *cop spots pot in pot. I do not want my mind to do this.* But I won't go back now. I won't be seen to turn chicken.

It's an ordinary block of dilapidated student houses, seventies bungalows, tacky screen doors, wrought-iron grill with an iron bird perched on an iron tendril. The door swings.

"Hello."

"*Hello.*"

The strains of *Dock of the Bay*. Why do they say the *strains*? *Music is the sieve of stress? It strains the strains? Stop this.* I taste the bourbon deep down in my throat. I need a refill.

He is so blond. And taller than I remembered, even though I last saw him not five hours ago in the chair beside my desk. His eyes are spaced out, tuned out, dropout eyes; he has the bone structure of Adonis and the expression of a spaniel. I am his Advisor. I advise him to find a barber. I advise myself to turn and go back to the car.

He says, "Hey, Teach."

"Don't call me that."

"Simone. Simone."

He says *sea-moan*.

His hair is long and matted. Not “dreadlocks,” just dreadful, down past his nape and uncombed for much too long. I could cut it for him. Not what he wants from me. No matter: give me a pair of scissors and I could be his Delilah.

“I didn’t know if you would come.” But cocky smile, his lanky frame slouched in the doorframe. What coed ever turned him down? I am his new challenge; he has never tried an Adviser.

Be advised.

Inside, a table full of leaves of grass, some limp and pale, some dried to a brittle brown.

“Would you like a drink?” He hands me a heavy-bottomed glass that I take, and take a swallow. He has a joint ready, which he hands me, reaching with a wrist furred and banded with a—Jesus, Rolex? I take a drag and hold it in. I had forgotten that he comes from money, this Kenilworth Adamson Lowenthal. *What kind of parents choose three dactyls for a name?* Answer: a moneyed pair. And here is their *heir apparent* with his *hair apparent*. No.

Otis is *sitting on the dock of the bay, wasting time*. The hi-fi covers a whole wall, and facing it an Eames chair where no doubt he writes his term papers, cradled in a few thousand dollars’ worth of bent plywood. Above the fish tank is an Escher print—the one of the flying geese—in a museum-quality frame.

I touch the rough wood of the frame and he says, “Distressed ebony.” He adds, “Naturally distressed,” which I infer is the most expensive kind. He twists the button of the standing lamp and now there’s only black light from the bedroom and blue light from the fish tank. I accept another toke and watch the fish.

They are flat-bodied, silvery and heavy-jawed. Their teeth slot into each other perfectly. They hardly move.

“These were shipped from Argentina, genus *Serrasalmus*, family *Characidae*,” he says. “My father sent them.”

“Piranhas,” he explains.

Who has such a father? Is that what sent this lovely boy running from California to this tacky rental and a third rate *college of the liberal arts?*

"What brought you to Jepson?" I ask in tea-drinking teacherly tone.

"I wanted to try the heartland," he says. "What brought you here?"

"I wanted to go to California," I say, "and only got halfway," and laugh, and drink. I hear his *heartland* and I hear *hurtland* and I hate this habit of my mind, these slippery words that wander into the word next door.

We toke and watch the fish in their super-aerated double-filtered blue-lit tank. They float instead of swim, dead-eyed and placid. If I put my hand in they would strip it to the bone.

There was Leo Aczél who gently murdered goldfish to understand the way they learned. Where is Leo?

He says, "Fuck my father." And "I want to get a ray."

The time has started to stretch, and the words stretch with it. *I want to get a ray, I want to get away, I want to get a way.* He leans to me and buries his blue eyes against the sinew of my neck. I feel his blue eyes bore. His matted hair clumped at my jaw, I breathe the scent of dust and musk. We knew I came for this. The Escher geese are flying two directions, black and white, tail slotted into tail. I take another drag and hold it in.

He says, "My fuckin' father. You know what you should do? You should teach a course in infanticide." I peer at him. "There's a wealth of material: *Oedipus, Medea . . .*"

"*Agamemnon,*" I observe.

"Sure. *Romeo and Juliet. David Copperfield.*"

"*What Maisie Knew.*"

"*Catcher in the Rye. Rabbit Run.*"

I say, "A semester of infanticide . . ." and am astounded at this insight. My glass in hand, the joint in his, the fish regard me silver-eyed. This Kenilworth could talk in the halls. I could be dismissed. But that is not what will happen. I will get away with it. He breathes against my collarbone and nibbles at my ear. He rears and looks at me, making sure that he may proceed. I close my eyes.

He scoots back onto the Eames and eases me to the footstool. "Another drink? Is bourbon and water okay?"

"Okay." Forget the water. Am I naturally distressed? Is that the most expensive kind?

I see his golden arm upend the golden bottle. The glass comes at me slowly, and I slowly raise my eyes. The geese slot into each other tail to tail. I see what Escher wants you to know: this picture is nothing but ink on paper, a patterned trick.

But consider: I have perspective because my eyes are inches apart. Say they were three feet apart, I would see perspective more profoundly. I would see around a goose to side feathers and underbelly and the curve of the body to the other side. Since these are not real geese, maybe I could see behind the skin of ink; it would hang forward off the paper, and in that space I would see the sky. I lie back, certain of my insight's profundity.

He cuts the powder on the glass table. He rolls a twenty-dollar bill. I'm game, God knows, but suddenly I'm hit with stage fright because I've never tried. I'm not afraid of chemicals or even self-disgust, but only of being clumsy with a line of coke.

It's easy: use the money like a straw and sniff.

Gently I let myself down to the magic carpet, dried-blood red. This beautiful boy with his matted hair and hip-hanging jeans slides down beside me so my face rests against his golden belly. This is what I blame male colleagues for: for taking advantage of the fucked-up fragile young. Well, *they* feed on fresh flesh; why shouldn't I? Is that what liberation is? I shove that thought away: not now, not now. There will be time enough to be sick-to-my-stomach sick-at-heart. Now *give me the beat, boys, and soothe my soul.*

The floorboards have dustballs in the cracks. I sight along the furrows and remember the stooping figure of my father, the black dust sifted in my shoes.

"Infanticide was not my father's crime," I say.

"What was your father's crime, then?"

"No. I mean the crime was mine. He was dying and I left him to die alone."

"Everybody dies alone."

"They don't! That's lazy talk. I could have stayed with him."

"Hush. Hush." He is pulling me after him knees and elbows on the floor so we can stumble and fall up into this bed where we roll and pull and tug and are naked now in black light in the smell of bodies and old pot.

What for? What help? What can we hope from it? It is only the ritual dance, the what-we-choose or don't-know-any-better, the pointless slap of flesh on flesh. He reaches out to light the candle and his face flares out, white mask, red mouth and jaw elongating into Batman's Joker. I flail and freeze, but he settles back above me, drop-out eyes and cocker-spaniel cock too limp to find me.

It is not I he harms. It is not I from whom he is in danger, who is his own distress, as I am mine. We are here to dig ourselves a little deeper. *Drift away*. He finds me, parts me, slots into me and here we fly, tail into tail, away from each other in black light.

And after that, white space.

Transit: Twickenham, Middlesex–Jepson, MO

1981

Hampton House, NHS Trust
Middlesex TW12, U.K.
18 March 1981

Dear Professor Lerrante,

I am writing this from the night desk of Hampton House, having earlier cleared with Matron that it would be appropriate to answer your letter to Mrs. Farnsworth. I have ample time because the Home is usually quiet from 10 at night to 6 a.m., though they must by law have a nurse on duty, and prefer a male in case of heavy lifting—and so in me they have so to speak two for the price of one.

I am pretty well bedazzled by your detective work—from the BBC—to the director of the piece—to Mrs. Farnsworth's old address—to the Teddington rectory—to here!—especially in view of the fact that her children don't seem to be able to find their way down Waldegram Road on visiting days.

I know Mrs. Farnsworth very well, she being one who tends to sleep in the day and wake at night, and likes to talk while I sit stroking her forearm, one direction only, like a cat; a thing my mother also liked when I was a child.

Mrs. Farnsworth's room is on the Alzheimer's wing, although the diagnosis in these cases is never absolute, and I myself would put her in the general dementia category. She is capable of an acerbic tongue, and in any case has moments clear enough to know: that she had four children of which one died in fifth form, and the two boys are unmarried and given to cricket umpiring on a minor scale, while the girl lives with husband and two daughters near Streatham Common. Which is not much and yet as much as many of us know about our families.

But for the main query in your letter, I must disappoint you. She does not remember you. I would like to tell you otherwise and might do so if I didn't know how a well-intentioned lie can embroil one in ever more elaborate deception. I read your letter to her several times, and several times asked her about the lighthouse, the boy who broke his leg, the girl in the velvet-collared coat. But she did not respond to any of this, nor, indeed, any reference to the war—I thought it possible she perked up at the mention of a "trawler."

However, there is something of a clue in her photographs. Though Mrs. F. is in the stage we call "dwindling"—that *is* an accurate description—still she has intermittent bouts of lucidity. If she is especially restless, I get her up into the wingchair, and we play a memory game. She has dozens of photographs stacked any-old-how in a bureau drawer with the antimacassars that they removed from her chair because she chews on them. Some of these photos I can myself identify and others not—her parents are clear enough in their wedding finery, and the children in Teddington with their scabby knees, but there is a hodgepodge of others with not a mark of identification. I like to show her the photos and ask who the people are, and I pencil the names on the back and then test her again to see if she says the same. Often she does and sometimes she does not. It is very like the game my mother played with me when I was small and slow at reading (although I assure you I have since become an avid *lecteur*). Sometimes Mrs. F. can come up with the names of aunts or cousins. Sometimes she knows no one, including me. On those occasions like as not she will reach down making a digging motion with cupped fingers, a look of effort on her face, and I think, oh, lord, that is *exactly* how it is when you can't come up with something but know it's *in* there.

In any case, among the five-by-sevens is a picture of a fishing boat, with Mrs. Farnsworth (in her thirties?) posing with a cleric and a swaggering old salt in hip boots. When I showed her this picture, she smiled and said, "Duck." I laughed and said, "It's not a duck, though he's ready for the water," but this displeased her. I pointed to the cleric and asked who it was, but she could come up with no more than "vicar." "Of course it's a vicar," I said to her. "Don't you remember the name of your vicar?" and felt bad because she hung her head. I penciled "Duck" on the back but she has not since responded to this, though once she reached out and pressed her fingers there.

What is remarkable: you know, I think, that she was postmistress at the news agent on Teddington High Street for thirty years—by contrast with the pictures of her children (who never come to jog her memory), I can hold up an old stamp, and she will say "Clown Series, 1954," or "The Queen's Fortieth Birthday" or "Annals of Air Travel." It touches me that this small competence and its pleasure remain to her. After a half-hour or so at these games she is spent and ready to go back to bed, and I tuck her in and sit with her till she falls asleep.

That isn't all. Sometimes she hangs onto my hand, and I call her "Mum" and she calls me "Ray," which is not my name, but near enough. I stroke her arm, elbow to wrist the way she wants, and say I'm sorry I disappointed her, but it was not my choice to make; it's the way I was born. And she forgives me—"There, there, now," and it's a little fantasy of my own to think that's a thing no mother forgets how to say. Sometimes when I make to leave she pleads, "Do you have to go?"—and it's hard, though I know by the time I'm back at nurses' station she'll have forgotten all about me.

Well, this is not the letter I meant to write, but though my news must disappoint you, it may be some consolation to know that your search has made a difference in her life, inasmuch as those who care for her here now know she was once a genuine heroine. And it occurs to me that, as she told the BBC she hoped you would remember her kindly, by your letter you have done so. So were it not for this brain disorder we call old age, she would wish you a long and productive life; and it is not usurping on my part to convey such a wish.

I hope too that it will offer some recompense that she is held in affection by

Yours sincerely,
Ralph Thomas Holman, R.N.

P.S. Since you ask after photographs I am enclosing the picture of "Duck" and "Vicar" with Mrs. Farnsworth in front of the boat, because it might mean something to you. If not, you may toss it without guilt, knowing that it would in the fullness of time meet no other fate from her louts of sons.

CHAPTER 10

Newcomer

1983

Kai Jesse Maginnis could not do crowds, so he came late to his mother's funeral. Even so, he was drawn into the "receiving line" by his sister Selina, who was forty to his twenty-nine, in charge as usual. It was September, but summer would not let go. Selina was wearing some boxy gray thing with darker braid around it, and he could hear her stockings swish. At least he could stand back to the wall as the mourners filed in, and he told himself that if he held onto his own brand of grief, he could swallow down the fear.

This worked, more or less. *Things I cannot change,* he chanted silently every time he said, "Thank you very much," which set up a rhythm in his head (*THINGS i CAN-not CHANGE; THANK you VER-y MUCH*). He concentrated on each person as they passed so as not to see them swelling the crowd inside.

But when it was over there were a few hundred bodies in old Gibbons Hall with its gaudy ceiling and its Persian carpet the size of a tennis court. The AC stirred tepid air. Even Selina knew he could not sit with his back to a mourning horde. And she'd proposed that he could sit against the wall just inside the doors. It would look as if it was his job to greet latecomers. Selina said.

He could do it. A year ago he couldn't have done it, but now he thought he could. She'd lent him one of Riley's jackets. A bit too short, a bit too generous in the girth, it flapped open against his T when he sat on the soft-bottomed chair.

The Vice Chancellor was presiding, and then the tributes began with Mom's old friend Patty Plummer, in from New Jersey. Kai remembered being frightened of Patty P. when he was six, her booming voice and her black toque. She didn't boom now. She was as stooped and as white-haired as Sarah Maginnis had been in the last near-comatose days. Patty P. droned on unsteadily about the friendships of women, and Kai tuned out, hoping he would be tuned out for the whole hour, which would be full of admiration for his mother and was supposed to accomplish something called "closure" for the family for whom he was a humiliation. The methodical woman who would be praised was not the mother he knew, who was a weeper and a pleader, who suffocated him in hugs, who drove him to rehabs and debased herself for him even as she debased him with her sticky, undead love.

The familiar tremor set up in between his stomach and his lungs. *Break my mind, break my mind* began in his head, so he picked somewhere to concentrate, a woman on the aisle halfway down, whom he had seen before though he could not remember where. It was her stance he recognized, slumped and then straightening with a little head-toss, somebody trying to keep it together. She was dressed in mismatched blacks, one sandaled ankle awkward in the aisle. Now it clicked: she was the newcomer last Friday at the AA meeting, one he had already picked for an academic, so it was not surprising to see her here, though whether she would stick to the program he could not tell.

He couldn't remember the woman's name. Something with an S— not Selina—he would have remembered that. He remembered that she only asked one question, "How do you know when you're ready?" and that she got the usual mishmash of answers, at which Del made his rattle-eyes, swiveling eyeballs side to side.

The woman took a white chip, he remembered, but newcomers mostly did that.

Kai had not shared at that meeting Friday because his mother was dying and his confusion did not resolve itself into words. He knew you had to get to "rigorous personal honesty" and he knew the truth—the

NVA units coming from the North on Ho Chi Min Trail, but locals, farmers by day and guerrillas by night. They crouched and jerked their heads at the slightest sound, like him. They stopped and froze exactly as he did. Once he saw a face tight with fear in the green gloom, and knew he mirrored its rigidity.

Not four months before he had flown in over the jungle in the Huey workhorse—it was a helicopter war—with the sun rising, lighting up the Se San River like a golden snake. Now he had come to love Rico and Matt and Grady and even Striker, and even when they were only sitting in the long grass sharing a damp joint he thought he was attached to something you could give the name of Honor.

In that eternity of four hours up that tree he figured out the war made no fucking sense.

Now he must have dozed in the branches, or zoned out, because some had already arrived. And now it was too late to climb down and pretend to be coming from the parking lot. Selina would rip into him for having missed the casket lowering, but it was nothing to what she would do if he crashed into it out of a tree. *Things I cannot change,* he said to himself, and made instant peace with it. Let her chew him out; let her throw him out of the house. That's what Mom should have done all those years ago.

Here Selina came along the path, heels digging into the grass. Her hands hovered over the heads of twelve-year-old Riley the Second, who had the sulks, and ten-year-old Robert snuffling with what was either grief or a summer cold. Here came the two stout cousins, then Patty P., a handful of administrators and former students—and, surprisingly, the somewhat disheveled woman from last week's meeting, who sat herself down on the last row with a hesitant, uninvited air.

A sound behind him: a black hearse on the road, and now, sliding out of it, the glossy blue casket. Six men surrounded the contraption and rolled it toward them, headed by Riley sweating against his collar.

There had been a shitstorm about that. Surely he could help to carry his mother's *body,* Selina said. Not even carry, *roll.* Just *roll* it, along with Riley and four of Mom's old friends.

"It's not that I can't; it's that I can't know whether I can or not," Kai said. "I can't tell you for sure what time I'll be barfing or have the shakes."

"After all she did for you," Selina said.

The six—no, eight—men sweating in suits rolled the casket right to the grave, where a couple of them somehow slid the whole caboodle across the grave and whisked the contraption out. The casket remained only a quarter descended, festooned with fleur-de-lis, laden with a gross or so of white roses in a pyramidal spray, ready at any moment to collapse ten thousand dollars worth of metal into the hole while the two flunkies rolled the contraption back to the road. Waterproof, the casket was. What was the point of that?—he'd asked his sister, who stared him down with an exasperation that would have penetrated its steel.

Did he owe Selina some amends? No doubt. He was working on it. The trouble was that at every encounter her contempt got stirred into his remorse until he couldn't tell one from the other. When he was a child his sister's acidity had been a grief, but now it was only acid. He shifted against the prickling in his calf.

This ceremony was short. A concealed speaker poured forth "Amazing Grace." A minister (a minister! For his Mother!) stood over the casket and intoned:

> The LORD upholds all who fall and lifts up all who are bowed down . . .
> The LORD is near to all who call on him, to all who call on him in truth.
> He fulfills the desires of those who fear him; he hears their cry and saves them.

This verse had so little to do with Sarah Maginnis that Selina might have chosen it in pure vindictiveness—or—wait. Had *Mom* chosen it, to send a final plea to him? And would she have understood that these words expressed what all the Anonymous signed up for, the people now scrambling after that so-called salvation?

By some mechanical miracle the casket lowered itself into the hole. For a long ten minutes his mother's intimates and administrative kin rounded the grave, tossing in handfuls of dirt—all but the woman on the back row, the newcomer, who still sat, while Kai discovered that his ass ached and his left calf was tingling. He had done this before, though. He knew how to shift noiselessly from side to side, hunch his shoulders to stretch the blades, endure this minute, and then endure this one, and the next.

And in fact the mourners left more quickly than they had come. Another minute and he could come down and sprinkle a little dirt, try to feel something, if not "closure," at least something in the neighborhood of loss.

Except that the woman on the back row still sat, bent over now, fists limp on the dry grass, head between her knees.

He waited, resentful.

She sat.

He decided to come down. He slid from his branch. She did not look up.

Kai dropped from the crotch of the tree and strode to the urn on its stand beside the grave. He took a handful of dirt and sprinkled it on the already dirty roses. And felt nothing. No shame. No fear. No peace. He lifted the urn and upended it into the grave, where the dark earth fell with a thud. And he felt what a waste of money was in that hole.

The newcomer looked up at that. "I'm sorry," she said. "I should leave . . ."

But a lifetime of Maginnnis upbringing made him say, "Not at all. You take your time." There was also the issue of her being a newcomer, which he did not take lightly. He walked to where she hunched over her knees and said, "I recognized you, from the Friday meeting."

Her eyes widened, caught. Not dead eyes, though, like some of them. Not bloodshot, so she probably hadn't been drinking recently.

"I knew a few of the people there," she admitted, "from the college."

"It's always a bit of a shock. But what d'you think *they're* there for?"

She laughed a back-of-the-throat laugh, acknowledging. She had a certain funky class, he thought. Like his mother maybe.

"You must have been good friends," he said indicating the grave.

"Not really. She was the first person I met when I came here, and she was kind to me. Did you know her well?"

"She was my mother."

"Oh, God, I'm so sorry! I should leave, I didn't hear your name at . . . oh."

"Yeah, that's the drill among the Anonymous."

He'd embarrassed her, though he hadn't meant to. Saying so little for so long had turned it into a habit, so when he spoke up he blundered. He turned a chair around and straddled it.

"I'm Kai," he said.

"I'm Simone. Hi, Kai." She laughed, that same in-the-throat not-funny laugh. What did he expect? It was a funeral. "That's an unusual name," she said.

"Not really. It means *fire* in Scottish." He thought he should leave now; Selina would be expecting him. He also thought he should stay and make friendly with the newcomer. She fanned herself with the funeral program, his mother's face on the front of it whipping back and forth in her hand.

"*Maginnis Fire,*" she said.

"Turns out it means a lot of different things, depending what language you're using: *King of kings,* or *vegetables,* or *victory,* or *chicken.*"

"You made that up." Now she did have a laugh in those sad eyes.

"Swear to God. There's a bunch of others I forget."

"I'm sorry. I never thought about her having children!"

"She liked to keep us separate from her job."

This was the wrong thing again, implying a coldness in his mother that couldn't have been farther from the truth. He pressed on. "What brought you to the meeting?"

"Oh." She tossed her head. "It's complicated."

"Start with something simple then."

"Okay." She set the card aside. "I got a letter from somebody I don't know, who takes care of a woman who doesn't remember me. But once upon a time this woman risked a lot to save my life, and it seemed as if, you know, I owed it to her to give that another try."

"Saving your life?"

"Mmmm." Wry, her smile.

"Yeah, that sounds about right. Nobody gets to the program unless they're FUBAR—*Fucked Up Beyond All Recognition.*"

"I know what it means. The students use it."

"So. That your situation?"

She sighed, and thought about this for long enough that he remembered again Selina would be furious. But you don't rush somebody stumbling around at the edges of getting honest. Let her speak up in her own time, that was what he'd learned.

"I had a terrible experience as a child, and I seem to have dealt with it by wiping out my memory."

"Lucky you."

"No, because without your memory you don't know who you are. I have, you know, struggled." She spread her hands open and lifted them, bouncing in slow motion to show the weight on them, which could have been a watermelon or one of the old M14s with the long wood stock.

"That doesn't sound like your fault though."

"Well, but—I'm not proud of this. My father was killed in the war—the other war—when I was eleven."

"The Good War."

"Right." She got the irony. "I was there. And he told me to walk away, and I . . . I did. I got on a boat and was rescued while he . . . died, a, a, alone. And I still don't know if—you know—if I committed an unforgiveable act of selfishness, or if that's what he really wanted me to do."

"Oh, that's what he wanted," Kai said.

"I turned and walked away from him, to the sea."

"That's what he wanted, no doubt about it. I can tell you what parents'll go through to get their kids to outlive them. My god. I couldn't *get* my mother to give up on me! And I never worked at anything so hard in my life. She held on like a dog on a sock." He had said this in

AA enough times that the meaning had been wrung out of it, like a shaggy-dog story where the punch line doesn't land. But he pushed on. "One time I was so pissed off at her I put up a tent in the front yard. I made a spectacle of it to shame her with the neighbors—gear and mattress, camp stove, the works. I was so tanked I pulled the tent over on the Bunsen burner. Thing went up like a grease rag, and I couldn't think of a thing to do but piss down my leg. And yell at *her*. But I'll be fucked if she'd give up on me. I beg your pardon."

He always said, *I'll be fucked* and he aways said, *beg your pardon*. But this woman turned her gaze on him, not bothering with his apology.

"How long have you been sober?"

"I don't call it sober." Kai said. "I call it dry, going on ten months, ever since my mother gave up on herself. No, that's backwards. She gave up on herself when I got sober. I'd been keeping her alive by fucking up. I was her *project*."

He hadn't said this at a meeting, not these words, exactly. The trouble was, once he got started he wanted to spill it all, like the last Gentleman Jack down the drain. If he did, he'd be fine for a while, but it might make for nightmares later on.

She was waiting, interested.

"Once in Vietnam I saw a woman take a cloth—some old shirt, I think—and wrap her baby in it—swaddle, is it? A tight package. There were Vietcong tunnels all over that village, and she takes this kid and shoves it down the mouth of a tunnel and pulls a straw mat over the opening and sits on the mat and looks me in the eye."

"What did you do?"

"They were VC all over that area. The whole village was booby-trapped."

"Okay."

"I shot her."

The woman—Simone—flinched, and he had the hot reaction: let her be in that village if she thought she dared. But she lifted her head at once. He was struck, how she looked straight at him even if she judged him; even if she had her own demons and must have told a lot of lies, like all of them.

"You were following orders," she said with an edge.

"I was scared shitless," he said, and after a minute she relented and relaxed.

"I'm sorry." She didn't say what for and he didn't ask her.

And that was enough of it. Rigorous personal honesty, yes, but you need to stop the spill before it would scare her away. He didn't need to tell about the pumpkins (though he had shared that once in Group, and would again): how, in Houston, when he was seven or eight, Jimmy Morales' dad had told them to take the rotting pumpkins and put them in the garbage can out back. The Moraleses lived up over their store on the second story, bedrooms on the third, with stairs up to a flat roof overlooking the alley. Instead of taking the pumpkins around back, he and Jimmy lugged them up the three flights of stairs, each at least ten pounds, and going soft, so they carried them up three trips apiece; and when they got them all to the roof they competed aiming for the corner fence post three stories down. Which as it turned out didn't matter. When they missed, the tarmac had the same effect: a pulp explosion, noisy and splattery as two eight-year-olds could desire.

But Mr. Morales was enraged. Kai had grown up without a father and he had never been shouted at like that. Kai thought he was going to be beaten with the bat he knew Mr. Morales kept behind the counter. But in the end he and Jimmy were just made to clean it up, every scrap, shoveling the slime, picking up the soft chunks and the slippery white seeds and the stinking moss stuff, out of the tarmac and between the fence posts and even off the black garbage bags already out there. He was not allowed to call his mother until they were done. He knew she would be panicky and mad in her shaming, scary way. He was made to stay there with Jimmy till the alley was hosed and the fence wiped clean and even the shovels themselves were rubbed down.

When Kai woke screaming, what he smelled was not jungle but rotting pumpkin. Sometimes Mr. Morales was in the dream, sometimes not. Jimmy was never in the dream. It was only Kai forced to clean up the woman's exploded head, the pulp and the hair and the slippery white brains, every morsel out of the grass and the spongy alien ground and the reed mat covering the tunnel where the baby was.

He needed to move now, to get out of here, with the grave and its stupid canopy and its dirty flowers. He was sweating. He said, "There will be food back at the house."

She shrugged, her smile tight. "And drinks," she said.

"Right."

"I don't want to be around alcohol right now."

"That's right. Good for you."

If he didn't show up at the house for Selina's wake, having skipped out of the funeral and the gravesite service too, she might make good on her threat to sell the house out from under him. Anyway, maybe he didn't care one way or the other whether this newcomer made it. Maybe he just liked being the hero, doing good to congratulate himself as the gospel-delivering "Friend of Bill W."

Or maybe this was the only way available to him, to make amends to a corpse.

He said, "I think there's a four o'clock meeting at Columbia Methodist."

She said, "I'll follow you."

CHAPTER 11

Deconstruction

1987

Hetty says, "My mother used to have . . ." and pirouettes her fork in her collard greens, and I have no idea, none, how the sentence will end. The Mecca is famous for its greens and its black-eyed peas. Hetty opens her mouth and puts a forkful in that capacious pocket. She licks a speck of bacon off her smile.

I think: *What is it that mothers used to have? What sort of object or feature or tendency? What do people say over lunch that their mothers used to have?*

". . . a pair of falsies," Hetty says, and laughs a soggy mouthful to which she claps a paper napkin.

Nan sits under the great satin cowl of her hair, the part as white as a seam down the middle. We are here for Nan, who has been betrayed by a man in some apocalyptically new way, as only a late twentieth-century feminist can be betrayed, though her googly-blue eyes hold the usual stricken look.

Hetty says, "The molded foam kind? With the little nipples, just one pair. She'd take 'em out of her bathing suit and stick 'em wet in her bra."

"People didn't buy things by the half-dozen then," I say.

Nan taps her fork on the rim of her plate abstractedly. Nan has been working for four years on the postmodern theorist Paul de Man. She has been a passionate advocate, a disciple. Next week she was supposed to read a paper in Tuscaloosa, Alabama at the biggest-deal

Deconstructionist Conference ever to hit the States, headlining the academic hotshot Jacques Derrida. That her paper was accepted was a pedagogical miracle, the take-off point of a promising career.

But in advance of the conference Derrida has sent out photocopies of some newly discovered articles, written by de Man in occupied Belgium during the Second World War. In these articles de Man betrays a convoluted antisemitism, and the magazine they appeared in means that he was collaborating with the Nazis. Now the conference is likely to be about nothing but de Man's disgrace.

Trying to cheer Nan up, I say things like, "We don't understand the pressure people were under."

Hetty says things like, "B-b's on a bread board, my mom. I used to have to go with her to shop for linger-ee. I'd have to sit there under her armpit while she stuffed her foamies in."

I say, "I was *there*, and I don't have any idea what I would have done in his shoes." This is not exactly true. I was too young for responsibility, but as I remember more and more of that time, I do know that I lived in an atmosphere of grave integrity hard to imagine at The Mecca in Jepson, Missouri in 1987.

Nan stares and swallows, picks at the thick red pudding of her nail polish. Nan is twenty-seven and Hetty is forty-two and I am fifty-seven; an even fifteen years between each pair of us. They don't always invite me to lunch with them, and I can only assume that Hetty remembers my father died a hero of the Belgian Resistance.

"Simone," says Hetty. "Are you using that Tiger Sauce, or what?"

Nan was born in Pismo Beach, California, at the end of the postwar boom. She has the muscular sleekness of surf and steak, the expectations of the period of Awful Affluence. She cut her critical teeth at Berkeley on the rigorous French feminists and came to Missouri because Modern Languages needed either Deconstruction or Queer Theory. Most of the old guard were relieved to get by with a tawny Californian. The universities were in a buyers' market then, and Nan was lucky to be hired, just as I was lucky twenty-three years ago, although in those days you didn't need a specialty. Being European was a qualification all on its own.

I could press my claim—that it was I who lived under the occupation, I who lived within a few tens of kilometers of the journal *Le Soir* in which de Man laid out his antisemitic speculations, I whose father was murdered fleeing from the Nazis.

But I don't want to talk about my father. It might make de Man look worse by contrast. Nan, though she may be a mere camp follower of the fads of thought, rings true in grief. I wouldn't trust her politics, but I trust her suffering. Her skin has the parboiled look of mortal shock, like Bosch's bugs.

For another thing, what snags in my mind is Hetty's lilting phrase: *my mother used to have*. I try to imagine that phrase falling from my mouth. What would come next?

"No teenage girl should have to watch her mother try on bras," says Hetty, while blue-eyed Nan and her black-eyed peas sit staring lidless at each other.

My mother used to have a doeskin nail buffer, ebony-handled, with which she would sit by the French doors onto the balcony, swiping her nails back and forth, humming a jazzy tune. She tilted her head to one side because a woman buffing her nails must survey her hand. Sunlight or rainlight splashed at her from the window, on the gloss of her blond marcel, the perfect brushstroke of her jaw. The windows were squares of stained glass, blue and amber. These checkered her face according to the way she turned, leaded lines dissecting her cheeks, her throat. Outside the sun or the rain fell on the Meuse. Our apartment had only one bedroom (at night my cot was opened in this spot under the window) because that was our choice: to live in a small space with a lovely river view, where my father could walk to his work at the university. "*Fenêtre sur la Meuse*," my father would pronounce, looking out over the water and the façades on the far bank, "Window on the Meuse," as if the view needed a title. My father, thin and straight as a staff himself, would take the long-handled hook and open the transom latch just so far. Later, in the absolutely unforeseeable future, I came to spend much time with him. But at the period I am speaking of, he spent hours away in his office, and until I went to school I was home with my mother all the livelong day.

My mother used to have the life of a generic *femme de ménage*, academic subspecies: she spent her day cooking potatoes and mussels and brown bread. She would never have put lacquer on her fingernails. Still, she had an ostrich puff, a perfume bottle in cobalt blue, an oval mirror between the cherry uprights of the vanity. She dipped her ostrich puff in a box of loose powder and patted her nose and brow. She tilted her head and looked into nowhere. I seem to remember that I was not to disturb her at her *toilette*, but this is not something she would have said, so either I am making it up in my memory or else what I remember is that I made it up at the time.

"Everybody in my family lied," says Hetty. Her wide mouth makes a shrug. Hetty is tall and angular like me, but dark, and unlike me she moves easily, stirring the space around her. She has American gestures, open-handed, who-gives-a-damn, whereas mine are constricted and restrained, and have been mistaken as both stand-offish and mysterious.

"They lied all the time, on principle. My mother told people we had a Van Gogh hanging in the living room. The neighbors used to come to look. It was the sunflowers, one of those prints on textured cardboard?"

Nan has not spoken since the iced tea pitcher was plunked down. Ordinarily she would be bopping along with surfer-girl enthusiasm about how language does not really *refer* to anything and we are never really talking about what we are talking about because the fact of our talking about it merely points to its being absent. Now for the first time today she hazards a sip of tea. "It changes the nature of so much he said."

She means de Man's antisemitism. "Well, of course," I say. "But in a poignant way. He was too weak for the terrible times." Nan lifts her tragic gaze from the peas. I have been here before. This is *Mistreated Woman Excusing Suffering Man*. This is *Chick with Broken Jaw Pleading His Sad Childhood*.

However, I agree, more or less. "I wouldn't want to be held responsible for everything I believed when I was twenty-two."

Hetty says, "Forget those Deconstruction guys. All they're ever saying is learning can't be fun."

But Nan is not ready for this. I have sat with many a broken heart and I know that no good can come of badmouthing the heartbreaker. One half of the fractured organ is still attached to him by sinew; no matter how blatant his sins you will only alienate her by rehearsing them. That Nan never laid eyes on Paul de Man is beside the point. That all she ever encountered was a rarified mind in opaque prose, as if it were not the new clothes that were imaginary, but the Emperor, is beside the point. One day—not because he betrayed the Jews but because in doing so he betrayed her—Nan will blow him off like dandruff. Not today.

Hetty has taken up the *Jepson Weekly Torch*. She turns to the horoscope. "My mother lied about her sign," she pursues. "She was a Gemini but she claimed she was a Virgo. Virgo! Virgos are meticulous. My mother couldn't hit the laundry basket with a dirty sheet."

"I'm a Cancer," Nan admits mournfully.

I pick up on this in Hetty's style. "Why do you think Cancer is a crab? I looked it up but it doesn't help. Both the constellation and the disease come from Old English *canker,* but it doesn't say why. *Ulceration, spreading sore.* Because the blotches looked like a crab, do you suppose?"

Hetty rolls her eyes—affectionately, I think—to indicate that I am forever *looking things up*. "Did you ever read *Tropic of Cancer*? Most boring book in the universe. It could put you off sex for life." She continues without transition, "The horoscope in this newspaper is a crock. Not," she adds "that that proves there's no truth in astrology."

"No," I say. I can tell by the way my mouth feels that I have gotten on my high horse. "*That* doesn't prove it. There are plenty of things to prove astrology's a crock."

Hetty pouts. "You can't discount the influence of the stars."

"Watch me."

"How about the moon and tides, then?"

"The moon and tides are a scientifically observable phenomenon."

"What does it say for Cancer?" Nan asks, and Hetty runs her finger down to find the crab.

My mother used to have a best friend in the dormer at the top of the house, Lotte something, an infectious giggler. The house was four stories tall, with only one apartment on each floor. We would mount the stairs nearly every morning, nearly every afternoon, Mama with her language book and buffer, me with my shoebox of paper dolls or my wood puzzle. Lotte's apartment had slanted attic sides, and her window was much smaller than ours, but its view was over the roofs across the river, tiled and shingled, tessellated like a turtle's back.

Lotte's husband was a clerk of some sort for the city of Liege. He kept records of streets or sewers, he filed municipal works. This information has no more authority than a guess. I don't remember what he looked like. I remember that I loved to go up to Lotte's because she had cupboards full of kitsch—a rabbit painted in wildflowers, a teapot shaped like a goose that spewed the tea out its beak. She had a waffle iron suspended from a fleur-de-lis hook on the wall, and ranged on a shelf a whole set of dishes formed to represent vegetables and fruits: a cabbage plate, an apple creamer, a water pitcher in the shape of a radicchio.

We must have been going to Lotte's before my memory began, perhaps I lay on her floor in swaddling clothes. Until you are three or four other people's memories are in charge of your existence, and when those people vanish that much of you disappears with them.

Still, like eyesight memory has a periphery. My mother used to have an angular, modern way of moving and a man's laugh to Lotte's tinkle. The two of them smoked and drank coffee in the morning, tea in the afternoon. They mended stockings and buffed their nails. At some point they began to study English, but whether this was an act of political defiance, or merely cool like the jazzy tunes, I do not know.

Lotte was something of a linguist, anyway. There, then, this was not considered unusual. She spoke her native Ghentenaar, high Netherlandish, German and a round-voweled mellifluous French. Perhaps it was Lotte's idea to add another trophy to her shelf of languages. "My dress is blue," they would say, writing slowly, each in a bound notebook. This was the first English I ever learned. "My dress is blue." Then there would be gales of laughter, I suppose because the dress that either of them happened to be wearing was blue or because it was not. "My dress is blue."

Lotte was short and luscious, my mother tall and elegant, like a chocolate puff paired with an Erté. They danced sometimes to no accompaniment but their humming. I bent the tabs of the paper dresses carefully over the paper doll shoulders, a short dark one and a tall pale one, and set them dancing. I was allowed weak tea in the painted goose, from which I served the dolls at the footstool while my mother buffed her nails and Lotte chattered in four languages.

My mother used to have a Tarot pack she spread out on the table. I know that to lay out *love* was good, and *death* bad, and *a journey* ambiguous. I know that the point was to control the future by uncovering it. I know *death* had a skull for a face and a scythe taller than himself. The eyes of *love* were sorrowful and sly. Big deal. If I'd never seen a Tarot pack I could guess as much as that. I think that *death* put in its appearance increasingly as the jackboot crossed Europe and my mother's health began to fail. I also think that such a memory partakes of the same insidious process that drives people to the Tarot pack and the horoscope: to make coincidence a cause.

Hetty says, "My mother was New Age before there was Old Age. Palms, crystals. The first time I walked in on her with a guy she told me he was teaching her aromatherapy."

The immediate dilemma is whether Nan should go to Tuscaloosa in spite of de Man's being outed. Hetty is all for it, on the principle of don't-let-the-bastards-get-you-down.

"'Cancer,'" she reads. "'Plug into a task, get the job done and mull over a decision. Go within yourself for answers, and be sure of yourself, despite others' challenging points of view.'"

"Oh," sighs Nan with a searching look. "Read it again?"

I interrupt. "What's Virgo?"

Hetty tracks down with her finger. "'Though the unexpected occurs and behavior is erratic, you get a sense of caring. Be understanding, but don't let another's quirks cause you a problem.'"

"There," I say to Nan. "That sounds just as good. I think you should plump for Virgo, like Hetty's mother."

"You don't get to pick your own sign," says Hetty.

"Why not? Why give in to astrological hegemony?"

"That's the point, it's *in the stars*."

Mabel clears the plates. Her name is really Mabel, etched in plastic on her bosom. She really says, "Get'ch anything else, Sugars?" and I see incipient panic on Nan's skin. What the hell, I don't have office hours till two. I say, "I'm going to have a sundae. Fudge with coconut, please, Mabel, hold the cherry." Hetty gapes a little, because I am not known for ordering dessert, but by the time her mouth is fully open she has got a sense of caring.

"Is there poppy seed cake? I think Nan needs a dose of opium."

Mabel guffaws and swipes clean the oak top, the sugar shaker and the mini-juke. The Mecca is what passes in Missouri for antique, forties booths and a pressed tin ceiling. Safe for the length of dessert, Nan shrinks back into the oak and lifts her stricken eyes. She ventures a quotation in the key of doomed, the lover remembering the tender words of the beloved.

"'The dialectic of self-destruction and self-invention that characterizes the ironic mind is an endless process that leads to no synthesis.'"

Hetty doesn't have a thing to say to that.

My mother used to have a string bag of magical capacity. Like a womb, it scrunched up to nearly nothing in her jacket pocket, and then expanded to contain the meats and fruits of days. In the early years there was a market on the *quai* just two short streets from our front door, where plums and celeriac and the perfect little globes of ripe tomatoes were set out in slanted boxes. There were trugs of the dirty delicate root called *salsify*, and artichokes no bigger than you could hold in a fist, which we bought by the dozen. There was a fish cart with slabs of halibut, skate with flat dead eyes, a bucket full of squirming river eel that the fishmonger would pick out, admiring, and chop on his board where they writhed. There was a stall hung with *saucisson* as if with meat chandeliers, manned by a mountainous proprietor in a bloody apron, who, while my mother stood projecting a skeptical air, would draw a mammoth knife across a salami and hand down to me a salty sliver so thin I could see his fingers through it. The string bag would start the morning limp on my mother's arm, and then begin to puff out with packets of greased wrap and newsprint, root vegetables on the bottom, squashable ones on top, till it was distended with its meal. Last stop the sweet stall: three *petit fours* or three macaroons in a little paper cone that my mother tucked in the top of the bulging bag—and for me a marzipan, according to the season mouse- or chick- or flower-shaped. I would walk the short way home with my hand in hers, tilting on the cobblestones, the grain of sweet almond between my teeth.

My mother used to have dinner parties, or perhaps *soirées*, because someone sometimes sang, or read from a manuscript, or held forth in a poetic way. Lotte was not present at such occasions. Sometimes she would help my mother pare and chop in the afternoon, but by evening she was gone and the door swung for people palpably different in some indefinable way. I was not then aware of the divide between the intellectual and the petty bureaucrat. Nor between the gentile and the Jew.

These evenings the little flat became more cramped, the table pulled out into the center of the living space, the books and magazines stacked in piles, the cushions bunched in the corners on the floor. My mother would serve lobster bisque from a huge tureen, *anguille au vert*—the bright white cylinders of eel meat steaming on a spinach bed—and *rable de lièvre* larded with strips of smoked bacon back. My father sat perfectly still, a beaming benevolence. I would not have said that he failed to help my mother but that he did not distract from her radiance. Professor Vanderleven would squeal culinary compliments and dribble spinach on his tie. Dr. Sarraute would speak in his voice both at ease and booming. A topic would be proposed in the smell of coffee with just a hint of chicory. The room became dense with energy and smoke; my father would crack open the stained-glass transom. I see a woman all angles with her dark hair sliced along her jaw, a short bespectacled man with a beard as fuzzy as his mohair vest; I see a waiflike boy, palely intense, with a flower of a woman on his arm. I see that my memory is a string bag, tucked in a pocket all these years, but expandable as I fill it with these scraps and packets, these candied violets.

I was allowed to stay up, to set the bowls of bisque carefully on the tablecloth, then to huddle on a cushion in the corner until I began to drowse, then to be put to bed in my parents' room on the high four-poster under a duvet. My sleep was laced with laughter and urgent argument. When I woke I would be in my own cot under the window in a room in shambles, the dishes piled with shells and bones, the air sweet with the aftersmell of lobster, cognac and cigar.

I don't remember when scarcity began. Perhaps because sugar outlasted meat, I didn't notice. At some point the parties stopped. At some point we began eating omelettes for dinner instead of Sunday brunch. At some point the profusion of the market stalls thinned out; there were roots but no leafy vegetables, and then such potatoes as there were came small and wizened. The smell of coffee turned more bitter with chicory. Salami disappeared and we ate blood sausage for a time, which I hated because it had little cubes of rubbery lard in it, but which I later longed for when there was no meat at all. My mother and I went to market earlier, to encounter a mood no longer festive but dour and strained. After a time there were no sweets, and then no fish, no milk, no apples, and then no market. Where the stalls had been, uniformed soldiers patrolled in twos and threes, as if to prevent an invasion of hostile foodstuffs.

My mother began to leave me at home while she foraged in the outskirts, into the back streets where there might be black market vegetables, and then into the country hoping for eggs or cheese. At first I was told that Lotte would be upstairs if I needed her. Then Lotte and her husband went away, and the apartment at the top of the house was closed, and when my mother could not get back by curfew I was by myself in the dark, and sometimes when my father did not get back either, alone all night. By this time I was ten. Where was my father? I have no memory of it.

My mother used to have a red flush on the bone point of each cheek when she bent to tell me that she was going out to look for food. This was in the mornings as she was sending me off to school. She wrapped her arms around me, smelling of toilet water called "4711"—not that I remember the name or the scent but that I have since seen the same bedizened gold and turquoise bottle for sale in department stores in New York; unlike my mother the maker of toilet water apparently outlived the war.

"I won't be here when you get back but I'll try to be here with something delicious"—*très appétissant*—"by suppertime." I would stand skeptical and cool, as I had watched her stand in front of the sausage man.

After school I would dawdle, though I had been told not to. The playground gave down a few steps to a cafe where a few old men sat with their beer or schnapps. There, then, no one would have supposed this proximity of bar to school was a corrupting influence. The men were wholly self-absorbed, or waved vaguely as I headed along the quai toward home. Where was my father? I would let myself in, up the dim stairwell, into the empty flat, and if the weather was warm I would kneel out on the balcony, sink sideways onto a haunch and press my face against the medallion at the center of the grille. If not, I would pull the curtains over the French doors and watch through a slit beside the jamb. It was boring, but I had been bored a lot, like any child. Most of Lotte and my mother's conversation bored me, her cooking bored me, the buffing of her nails. I had been free to distract myself with my toys, inhabit whatever fantasy I chose. Now I discovered the place that boredom intersects with loneliness. I watched the quai, the water, the cobblestones in the direction from which she might come. There was little movement in the streets, and even that ceased at dark. As the curfew hour approached and I knew that I would spend the night alone, I would drag my cot to its place, making nonchalant gestures for nobody's benefit. Then I went back to my post.

Such loneliness is immobilizing. Time stretches out on a monotonous thread, a suspension between madness and self-containment. I thought I heard that note again, much later, in the chant of "Ommmmmmm," which I was told brought peace but in which I could hear only the humming emptiness of those nights of waiting, waiting. I watched the ripples on the surface of the river. Nothing else stirred. If a cat passed, that was an event—although, one night, late enough that I had begun to doze, I heard a scuffle and running feet in the street below, and two youngish men in the rolled sleeves and drab waistcoats of the petty bourgeois flung themselves belly-foremost against the balustrade of the riverbank. One climbed and made to dive. The other, who was heavyset, had just got a foot up when they were both downed in a ripple of staccato rifle shot. Blood burst from them over the cobblestones. The first pitched headfirst into his dive, and the indifference of the future rolled over him. The other caught there on the stone, one leg up and one leg down, his head concealed on the river side. A pair of soldiers no bigger and no older than their prey ran up to him, caught the heavyset man by his waistcoat on a bayonet and tipped him over. Then the soldiers ran on, not the way they had come but as if they had been briefly deflected from a more important mission, forward, in the direction of the disused market.

That was my first sight of violence, wiped from my mind later, together with my father's death. But I remember that for months those several seconds used to flash on the inside of my eyelids. Somehow I held that image as the paradigm of victimhood. I notice now that I do not know this was the case. For all I know the two young men were caught committing some atrocity in the next street. Why, for example, if they were Resistance, did the soldiers not check the pockets of the second man?

I went to bed. I lay awake for most of the night with my arms straight at my sides, and still I was asleep when at lift of curfew my mother came back. She held me and asked me what I had seen. Later she went down with a bucket and brush to scrub the balustrade. "We must find another way," she said. But what other way was there? She had to find food. My father? had to do whatever he was doing.

So I waited again perhaps three or four times a week, and was more afraid, and still the fear was not as all-consuming as the loneliness. I think now that if I had known my mother was to die, I should have made better use of those waiting evenings; and yet all the same I think I was in training unbeknownst. In training for my life without her and, to a certain extent, in training for my life.

Monty Hodge, on his way to another table, stops thigh to elbow with Nan, sets down his gumbo and leans on a fist beside her poppy cake.

"Nan, dear," he says. "I heard about de Man. Are you all right?"

Mont has a broad, naturally consoling face and a beard like excelsior. Now that everybody is downsizing to short back and sides, he has decided to do hair (any radical alteration of the hirsute level can be recognized as part of the divorce syndrome). A straw mane emanates from his head, backlit and gently fanned by The Mecca's ceiling fixtures.

Nan seems to consider this. Is she all right? She tests the looping fall of her own hair with a tentative hand. She focuses on the indelible wound. What is it about the hulking deep-voiced blanket of a man's sympathy that carries so much more weight than a woman friend's? Nan splays a hand beside the fist beside the poppy cake.

"I haven't taken it in yet," she admits.

"I haven't processed it," she amends.

"I'll be okay," she assesses bravely.

Monty says, "Good girl." He's a nice guy, Mont, just divorce-prone and currently, dangerously, recovering. By the time he has opened his fist and rolled it over to squeeze Nan's manicure, I can see the double rebound, the romance, the wedding, the *sturm und drang*, the breakup, the alimony. In the surface of the gumbo a cross-section of okra surfaces, a perfect flower in a pool of slime.

However, neither Hetty nor Nan seems inclined to ask Mont to join us, for which I am grateful—I might say impressed.

He says, "Good girl," again. "If you want to talk about it—any time. I'm not an expert, but I have dabbled around the edges of postmodernism . . ."

Amen to that. Monty turns the smothery blast of his goodness on me now.

"You were there, my God."

"I was a little girl," I say.

"It must have been at the same time de Man was writing for *Le Soir*, though, no?"

"I don't have much memory of the war."

"You must have some."

"Some."

"What a fantastic life you've led!"

Why does this have to come from Monty Hodge, philanthropist philanderer of Eng. Lit? It would have been nice if Hetty mentioned it, for instance.

"I've led a pretty ordinary life," I say, "if you count the number of Europeans that got bumped out and ended up in"—I bite my tongue on *third rate*—"American colleges . . ."

"But my God, look how much you had to endure!"

". . . or the number of divorcés that are burned out on their jobs," I finish, pointed.

Monty picks up his gumbo, aims his index finger at me, grins, and carries on toward a farther booth. Nan looks after him.

My mother used to have something alien in her liver. *Elle avait quelque chose au foie*. Now, I lived in a house of words, where my father, taciturn, nevertheless insisted on the minutest attention to language. In French the word for liver, *le foie*, masculine, is next door to feminine *la foi*, for faith. I have thought long and hard on this. I certainly knew the difference between faith and liver, but I was also almost certainly aware of incipient pun. As a child might think, in English, *a liver is one who lives*, so in Liege, I thought: *ma mère a quelque chose à la foi*, my mother has something wrong with her faith.

It was necessary to get a paper of some kind from an official of some kind in order to go to the doctor. We went to the bureau of authority, which was nothing but the vestibule of a house that had been commandeered from someone richer than we were. There was a bureaucrat—can I really remember that he had a moustache the shape of Hitler's own?—and there was a disagreement. My mother insisted that we go to this doctor, and the squat man in the moustache insisted that we go to that. My mother became indignant and I saw that she was tearful but concealing it behind a rigid mouth. She was offered a paper which she at first refused.

The man said, "This is the doctor our own soldiers see, Madame." My mother said, "I am not one of your soldiers, Sir." But she took the paper, with its stamps and flourishes.

I think now that the paper was a permission she did not use, because she went to Dr. Sarraute to whom we had always gone, in a clinic downstream and away from the river, in a neighborhood full of pompous houses. My mother went to this clinic perhaps three times a week, always late in the afternoon and by unfamiliar, circuitous routes, which gave me the impression that she was not supposed to go there. At first she tried to get me to stay home, but I pleaded with her: if I could not go with her for food at least I could go for the "*traitements*." We arrived, as I say, by diverse back ways, but always entered by the same side door, down a corridor and across a small courtyard with a fountain on which a naked boy poured water from a cornucopia, both the boy and the horn green with mold.

Sometimes the doctor was with someone else, and then we would sit in the courtyard until he signaled from the window, and inside he would be locking the front door. The waiting room was a square, plain place in spite of the grandeur of the neighborhood, with folding chairs set up as if for a classroom. Dr. Sarraute was an engulfing, bearded man. He would take my hand in both of his, in which it would disappear halfway up the forearm. His fingers were colossal. Once he had painted my throat with stinking purple stuff, and I thought it was his fingers that made me gag. The very benevolence of his tone made me shrink from him because I knew my mother would disappear with that hugeness behind a curtain and through a door beyond which I was never invited.

I was used to waiting by this time, and I had chosen to be there, but perhaps for that very reason I waited with bad grace. What had been desolation at the apartment window was pent up and petulant in the clinic. I don't remember what the floor was made of but I remember the grit of it under my worn soles. The chairs were of slatted wood, designed, it seemed, to poke at your bones. There, then, it had not occurred to anyone to leave magazines as an amusement for the relatives of the ill. I could have gone into the courtyard where the moldering boy poured his unending supply of water on a ring of stone—I had not been told not to—but the yard was not like the outdoors at all. Nothing grew except a few clumps of nettles and the fur of moss on one side of everything. Besides, there was a window onto the room where my mother had disappeared, and although the shade was drawn I found it vaguely threatening to be within sight of that window. I suffered from a sense of something being covered up, in which I was implicated, as if it was I, and not whatever procedure went on behind the shade, that was furtive and unclean.

What sort of shame was that, compounded of weeds and ether, the dank corruption of the little courtyard? My mother, too, when she emerged, was flushed and flustered, overcheery, smelling of sweat and chemicals. The doctor held her hand reassuringly in his great hand and offered me a sugar cube, long after sugar cubes had vanished from any legitimate source.

My mother used to have a brittle, mechanical manner after her *traitements*, hurrying through the twilight to beat the curfew, skipping up the steps with energy I did not believe she had. How could she have *something in the liver* if she had more energy than I? In those days supper was always minimal, but ordinarily my mother invented ways of disguising its meagerness. On clinic evenings she set a dish of potatoes in front of us, or a single egg stretched out with a bit of flour. My father would listen gravely to her telling what this or that had been predicted, what action or substance had been prescribed, the doctor's current view of the something wrong.

My mother used to have a cot under the blue and amber window. It was my cot. I slept now on the daybed which was filled with horsehair and scratched through my thin sheet. My father no longer spent hours at the office, he came and went sporadically, which was the way I went to school. I seem to remember that Lotte returned for a time, but this memory is washed-out like the rug under the window, which I now watched so long that its ruined colors were burnt into my eyes.

Sometimes I looked out along the cobblestones and the river, but there was no point in it because the person I looked for was behind me in my own bed, mostly sleeping. Soft-fleshed Dr. Sarraute came once when my father was not there, and having put his hand to my mother's forehead, which seemed intrinsically appropriate, then strangely put my mother's limp hand to *his* forehead and held it there for a long time. My long-drawn-out note of loneliness was gone and in its place came an anger of spurts and starts, the place that boredom intersects with blame. I remember the feeling in the muscles of my mouth, distaste, recoil. I was on my high horse.

My father, it was, who went for food now, mostly potatoes, sprouts, a few withered beans. There was no more oil to sauté—butter was a memory—so we boiled whatever we had, like the English, and ate it from the pot. My father was attendant but distracted. Sometimes he went out at night and left me alone with her, who needed silence and no longer could attend to what I needed. When she was awake she had a forced smile, faraway eyes. People told me—who?—Lotte perhaps?—certainly my father—that if I were very quiet and attentive to my mother, she would get better. I think now that there was never any chance of her getting better, and that it occurred to no one how long or how hotly I would resent that lie.

So I became the mother of my mother, keeping a cup of fresh water by her cot, ritually rubbing her forehead. I brought the toilet water in its gold and turquoise curlicues and dabbed her temples—but this, I think, was because I could still smell the alien combination of microbe and drug. I freely confess that in the whole period of which I am speaking, I had no interest but self-interest, not in the dead flipped in the river nor the heavy-booted boys that patrolled the quai, not the government in exile nor the deserted schools. Hunger itself was a dull constant in a dull anger. Of course I knew there was a war, but what I mainly understood was simply that something just beyond my sight could always take something more away.

My mother used to have a body and a spirit, flesh and sinew and nerves and bone. My mother had desire and bitterness and sex. She had underwear and toenails. She had attitude and irony. She had longing and, at the core of things, like every creature on this earth, concealment. My mother used to have a secret that was not burned with a letter or hidden in faded ribbons or whispered to her friend Lotte but concealed at depth, readying in the nerves or veins, the misfiring signals of mortality.

No teenage girl should have to watch her mother try on bras.

"Well, Nan," says Hetty, hunkering down to it over coffee. "I don't see any reason you should be ashamed. You didn't do anything."

I say, "She was duped. You always feel ashamed of being duped."

"Well, okay. But what did he really do? What did he say, de Man?"

"It's not clear yet," Nan says in a small voice. "There are only half a dozen of the articles translated, out of more than ninety. But he talks about 'Jewish decadence.' He says something about a 'Jewish problem.'"

"Ouch," Hetty says. "Is it possible he was doing, like, underground? You know, I mean, ironic code?"

"Well, and of course," says Nan eagerly, "there's the possibility that the articles deconstruct themselves. Maybe they don't say what they seem to say."

"You mean if you go on down to Tuscaloosa, maybe the theorists will be able to theorize them away," I say.

"Well, Simone, it's not like you to argue that she shouldn't find out," Hetty admonishes me. "You're the research fanatic." I hold my tongue. "What do these guys believe anyway? That language itself is a tool of the power structure."

"The hegemony," says Nan.

"Of which we are a part," I say. "As employees of an educational institution."

"And that all stories self-destruct."

"All narrative," Nan corrects her dully.

"Just look at it, like, he's a writer whose narrative self-destructed. He's his own best proof. If he didn't turn out to be a Hun of some kind, he'd contradict what he was preaching all along."

"That's sophistical," I say.

"Sure. Listen, sophistry is underrated. Growing up with liars is great training for comp lit. Anyway, everybody's being outed as some kind of pervert. Writers, politicians. Kennedy to start. T. S. Eliot, Ezra Pound, F. D. R., Philip *Larkin*, fahcrissake. Who's next? Truman prob'ly. The prick stops here or something."

And now, a dozen beats late, Hetty pulls the upside-down bowl of her spoon out of her mouth and aims it at me. "Wasn't your dad some kind of hero in the Resistance?"

"I don't know for sure," I say. "I was eleven when he died. But what I pieced together is that a colleague of his named Vanderleven—I do remember him because he was a slob—made some sort of a speech defending Jews. 'Positive Influences of Judaism on the Literature of Ideas'—something foolhardy like that. I don't know if he was Jewish himself, but my guess is not. My guess is that he'd've been underground by that time if he was."

I say I have pieced it together but even as I say this, I know that piecing is not what I have done. Rather this conviction grew or seeped or accreted in me like mold on stone, to become at some time I can no longer remember my Article of Faith.

"In any case, they came and asked my father to denounce Vanderleven, and my father wouldn't. I know the kind of objection he would make. He'd say that he could only denounce slovenly scholarship, and Vanderleven's seemed to be impeccable."

Nan begins to sob, and I realize with alarm that I have just done what I told myself I wouldn't do, bragged about my father. Instantly, I begin to backtrack. "But look, I don't know. For all I know my father was just as duplicitous as de Man, or just as weak. For all I know he was murdered by the Resistance, or by mistake. What I'm saying, Nan, I don't know."

So I stumble on, undone by a hood of hair and callow grief, offering up the dearest convictions of my life. At the same time I am thinking about the proximity of Brussels to Liege, wondering how many months our little market may have crossed with the distribution of *Le Soir* before the food gave out. I wonder if any of the newsprint in my mother's string bag was from that source, whether de Man's perfidy once wrapped a hunk of cod or a phallus of *saucisson d'Ardennes.*

My mother used to have a plain stone in the municipal cemetery downriver beyond the Palais des Congres and the Parc de la Boverie. I wanted her in the marble mausoleums of Saint-Martin, where tinted pictures of the dead were ringed with flowers, and whole families were stacked in stone drawers under pediments in the Grecian style. Some had weeping angels, gilded crosses, windows to display relic bones. My father explained to me that these were Christian graves, which would dishonor and displease my mother, who eschewed all forms of organized religion. She had been estranged from her family for these convictions, my father said. Chastened, I complained no more. But I wanted ribbons on her grave. Now it occurs to me that, after all, she did lay out the Tarot cards. She had something the matter with her faith, perhaps. *Elle avait quelque chose à la foi.*

After my mother died my father stopped going to the university. My school had been closed by that time in any case. There, then, a man had no expectation of having to raise a child, and I think he tried his best. It must have been frustrating and diminishing, after those eager young scholars, to have no charge but an awkward ten-year-old girl. He was unalterably kind, but he had not the knack of it. I was oppressed by his unrelieved attention. I longed for him to be there but ignoring me the way my mother had, leaving me to my fantasies of Pinocchio or my paper dolls.

He set me to parsing and composition; he adjured me gravely that I must never let a point of curiosity go by, because curiosity, like a muscle, will atrophy if unexercised. Therefore he taught me to haul down the great *Dictionary of Etymology* and the *Rhetoric.* He taught me English, and for this I used my mother's own notebook, a cover of shiny marbled stuff, bound down one side. I copied the sentences she had copied—*My dress is blue*—and moved beyond her in the grammar book, as if, having first become her caretaker I was now, literally, taking up her life.

My mother used to have the space between my stomach and my lungs. For a long time the pressure of her absence lodged there, bloated like a string bag full of holes and scarcity. My father devoted himself to me. Yet I notice now that until my mother died he had continued at the university, where to continue must have meant, to a certain extent, to accept the context of the German occupation, just as to write in a newspaper sanctioned by the occupation meant to accept that context. Just as to visit that moldy courtyard meant to accept the context of decay and death.

My mother used to have mourners who dropped by the flat and sat with blue and amber squares of rainlight on their faces. I remember Vanderleven sitting there. What chiefly interested me about Professor Vanderleven was, still, his prodigious fat, the way his lower lip protruded so you could see the shiny inside of it when he talked. After he had praised my mother and wept over her *anguille au vert*, my father sent me, unusually, into the bedroom that he had shared with her and which was now his, stripped of her scents and puffs, alien and austere. I heard the voices from where I sat on the low stool under the window into the shaft, an urgent pleading on the professor's part, and on my father's a tone that was calm but firm. Vanderleven continued tearful. What was he saying? I remember the urgency of it, the strangeness of being exiled to my father's room. I remember that their voices were raised, but whether in anger or anxiety or excitement I do not know.

It was not long after—a few days, that week, a few weeks?—before my father said that we must leave, and that I could take nothing but my birth papers, which I must sew into the hem of my skirt.

And is that all? Is that the whole of the remembered text? And where, then, did I get the notion that my father died for truth and

Professor Vanderleven? What do I know, as knowledge? "Positive Influences of Judaism on the Literature of Ideas"? Out of what art flick of the fifties did I make up such a thing out of whole cloth? Who was dark and *saftig*, clever Lotte; and why was my mother's best friend not allowed to join my father's colleagues at their soirées? Why was the dormer apartment abandoned in the middle of the war?

And why do I suppose that my father, who lost the freedom of his profession, and then his job and at the same time his wife, had any interest in the threat of ideological contagion in the world? How do I know that when we ran, we were running from the Nazis and not from my mother's grave, from the oppressive memories of that apartment, from Vanderleven, from the war itself?

When I think of these events they appear as a sort of historic prelude to my life, more and more distant, derealized, abstract, and foreign. Inversely, the "real" events, the effective and indelible history, was already taking place, there, then—a thunderous prelude to a lighter and less serious theme: America, New York, Missouri, academia. What I live is a posthistoric afterlife.

"Don't go," I say to Nan with some vehemence, so that I register Hetty's recoil, a little flicker of exasperation in the corner of her wide mouth: *Simone is off on one of her tangents.*

"Make a clean break with all of them," I advise. "Why let yourself in for all that pain? They'll only wallow in it. You'll get a Ramada Inn full of breast-beaters and apologists."

"How can you say that?" Hetty almost yells. "You're the one that's always insisting on the facts and the follow-through. Screw 'em, Nan. You've gotta know the worst."

My mother used to have a secret behind her eyes, some secret that could not be understood by a ten-year-old girl and cannot be revisited by a fifty-seven-year-old woman who, nevertheless, by this time must have a certain generic knowledge of the secrets that a woman might parcel up behind her eyes: *my husband is cold and dry, I drink to endure my life, I am having an affair, my husband is weak and fearful, is collaborating with the enemy.*

"Don't go where pain is," I tell Nan.

"Buy yourself a pair of killer boots," says Hetty, "and go kick academic ass."

"Just walk away from it. Let it go." Nan is still weeping into a disintegrating wad of paper napkin. I drop my eyes. I note inanely that—among the constants of civilization—my dress is blue.

Transit: Jepson, MO–Hanover, NH

1988

Prof. Simone Lerrante
Dept. of English, Jepson College
475 Tupelo Blvd.
Jepson, MO 65857
Sept. 21, 1988

Dr. Leo Aczél
Department of Neurology
Dartmouth College
Hanover, NH 03755

Dear Leo—

Yes, here I am. Yes, anyone in the world can be found with determination and a good library—I have done some such sleuthing of my own—but it did not occur to me to track *you* down, welcome as your letter is.

I'm so sorry about the loss of your Anika. No, she never mentioned the legacy of her family, and I never saw the first sign of instability in her—of course I did not know her well. We were faculty wives thrown together by accident, grasping for friendship. But I do know that in college it was the golden girls who dropped into madness and suicide. I don't know why this is so except that they tried so hard, they broke brilliant through the fear that bound them. One of these, a lovely girl named Heather, went to an asylum and survived through unspeakable anguish and came out and made herself into a Queen's Counsel in Carmarthenshire. Another, Dody Ventura, committed suicide. I don't know why the one, or why the other.

You ask for a brief catchup, but the medium seems ill-equipped. No, I have not remarried. No, I never had a child. Of course I have been through traumas personal and political, and if we had an afternoon I could tell those stories, but when I look back it doesn't seem they would say much about my life. When I look back, I see myself spat out of the war's mouth, propelled in an arc over the channel and the Atlantic to mid-America. There are worse places to be than middle America, and no doubt many of those I loved ended up in them, only I do not think it is a very good choice of place for me.

I am grateful to Missouri for sweet William, red fox, black tupelo, and bigmouth bass; a lake named Taneycomo; a few (perhaps too few) friends. The invention of the twentieth century that has most improved my life is a pesticide for fleas, which allows the freedom of the house to my cat Byatt, third in a line of feline feminists. I try to live in the present but I seem to live most in the past tense of fiction. Perhaps this represents some sort of escape from life, but it is my life.

Such as it is, that is my news. I would love to hear from you again.

S

Simone Lerrante
57 Poplar
Jepson, MO 65802
Oct. 7, 1988

Dr. Leo Aczél
158 Old Lyme Rd.
Hanover, NH 03755

Dearest Leo—

Re your conference in Brussels: Thanks so much for the suggestion. You flatter me—by which I mean I am impressed by your Center for the Study of Aging, and by the scope of your proposed conference. "Senior Class"! An encouraging theme (basically old-dog-new-tricks), suggesting that the aged synapses continue to pursue new life. But when you suggest that I might speak about what the old have to offer to the young, I fear that I may have misled you into thinking me reconciled.

I am not. I'm a pallid burnout, buoyed up on the sea of irritation by a few good (usually alien) students, at whose later lives I have learned not to look too closely since so many have done terrible things or had terrible things done to them. I did not pursue teaching because I cared for youth but because I cared for books, and teaching seemed the best way of securing them at the center of my days. The young in the aggregate I find no more wonderful than their elders, presenting in about the same proportion louts and lotharios, hustlers, dullards, tourists of academe. There are precious few I care about, though those few are very precious. I have, tenuously these latter years, defended certain dead white males on the grounds that to be dead is the fate of us all, and white my fate, and maleness in any case unchosen. Most of us have little choice as to where we land. You can learn that from the acorns clattering on my brick path.

So, though, no; I am not interested in how my late-life learning can serve youth, how fine a model, source of inspiration, repository of knowledge, wise woman, sage I might be for the edification of the young. Been there! Done that! I'm sure it is always a disappointment to be old. But it is a shock to feel so unfinished, so in process, so an experiment still in the works. I am not done yet. I have not been *exercised.* I have not drawn breath to the bottom of my lungs' capacity, I have not run to the end of the oak-canopied path, I have not seen enough species of parrot in their histrionic coloration. I have not been sufficiently mothered, fathered, friended, loved. I am still on the verge, dissatisfied, still yearning. I am not ready to be relegated to a resource!

So I cannot tell your conference the "value" of the elderly. I would like to be there. But you see that I would only rage.

Oct. 18, 1988

Dear Leo,

Well, yes, I could say all that.

No, there is nothing to prevent me from coming.

Give me a few days to think about it.

Love, Simone

FIVE

Home Help

CHAPTER 12

And Be One Traveler

1989

7 JUNE
Waterloo Station, London

I have seen Darla in her Sussex garden, peonies spilling into the asparagus beds. She is mother of three, all grown, the youngest just up at Cambridge. She is still beautiful in a blowsy British way. She had her hair piled under a straw hat. She said of ending her career, "Oh, the theatre seemed too much trouble. They warn you it's a hard life, but you think they mean it's full of glamorous tears and heartbreak. It's just *hard*. Difficult people, terrible hours, grungy provincial hotels. And I wasn't so very good at it—that was just puffery; a bright young thing is good for a few paragraphs. Anyway, that was before I had Oliver!" She lavished cream on a scone. "Not that I was much cop at motherhood!" I wondered if *her* mother would have said the same.

She, Anna Moxham, apparently is still alive. Having left Moxham in the sixties, she is finishing out her days in a Yorkshire nursing home, addicted to a cocktail of painkillers and tranquillizers. Whether she recognizes Darla is a moot question. "She puts on a great *face* of knowing me, very chuffed. But whether she knows it's me or just knows she's supposed to, I can't tell. Perhaps no more can she."

Darla is not at all dissatisfied with her life. A pad in London, a country house. Her husband is a tile contractor. There is apparently unprecedented interest, in postmodern Britain, in the well-appointed bathroom.

Of her father she said, "Daddy was gay, you know."

I said, "Yes, I figured that out."

She said, "Poor Daddy. And poor Mummy too, of course."

We reminisced at length, laughing, about the Do Drama Co., the films we had loved, the stars we fantasized ourselves to be. Darla brought out the album of the photographs taken with my very own first box Kodak: herself as Frog Prince and as Stella Dallas, and so forth. There was one of the two of us, as Joseph Cotton and Jennifer Jones in a tableau of discovery (*I can remember!*) over which we guffawed, and one of us as Cary Grant and Ginger Rogers. These she offered me, and I accepted with an effusion of thanks.

"We weren't really gay, were we?" she murmured, a little wistfully, I thought.

I said, "I think adolescent girls are naturally given to crushes. There's a whole literary subgenre on it."

"I did have to wonder, you know, because of Daddy . . ."

"I think we were practicing, but it was romance we were practicing for. I've had deep friendships with women, but I was never physically attracted to them. Except for you of course," and she laughed a throaty thanks.

"I was mad for guys; some of them *very* inappropriate."

"Oh, yes. Been there," I said.

"Yes. Wouldn't it be a wonder to have a friendship with a man! As well as sex, I mean."

By which I suppose she meant to tell me that her marriage was imperfect, though as I say she seemed relaxed and happy, handling a silver coffee pot and delicate bone china cups.

Now, waiting for the train to Brussels and Liege, I stow the photos, rearrange my gear. I will spend four days in Liege before returning to Brussels for Leo's conference of ageing eggheads. Jetlagged, nervous. I have brought along Alice Munro's *The Progress of Love*, but my mind will not settle to it.

I never remember its being hot in England. I never even remember its being bright.

Brussel Zuid

On the platform I am surprised to see a floor of polished granite; the worn stones of the platform across the way are more familiar. Aboard, the turquoise Formica of the little table between the seats seems an anachronism (it is I who am the anachronism), and the zipper pull on the women's handbags strikes me as extravagance. I never knew anyone in Belgium with a zipper to her handbag!

Familiar: houses built in the middle of fields with windowless, flat sides as if they expected immediate row-neighbors. The pillbox hat of the conductor, wound twice with gold braid. Strange: a mammoth sign, *KUMPS AGRO*, probably the name of some corporate food marvel. It has the braggadocio of spray-can graffiti.

We are approaching Liege, the track high above the houses, a gravel pit, cypress trees in the form of exclamation points.

8 JUNE
Hotel Ibis

*Place de la République Françai*s

Out of toothpaste, and the hotel offered me only shampoo. It was 6 p.m. The anxiety of this petty lack ballooned as if to prevent me from functioning. To find an open pharmacy seemed a triumph. I tried to buy a map but all I could find was an expensive book, as if I were going to settle here. Everything is smaller than I remembered, the warren of narrow streets, the shops full of plastic and polyester—and me a stranger in the place of my birth. At the hotel I was given a minimal map. My room leads past basin and bed to a window that looks out over steep-pitched roofs. I had diarrhea from the moment of arrival.

9 JUNE
Café Ibis

Today the streets are surface-strange but deep-familiar, as if covered over with layers of the intervening years. T-shirts and TV sets at every turn; a multiplex showing six American movies; McDonald's sells quarter-pounders and Belgian beer.

Yet I step onto cobblestones and the tilt and texture are known to my foot. I turn a corner and without thought predict: there will be a door with a gothic window, a Virgin in a niche, a passageway with an arch across the space. And they appear: window, Virgin, arch. Over and over I play this duet for memory and city: there will be a flatiron building, there will be a fountain, there will be a view of the river from an alley paved in stone. Sometimes this foreknowledge extends to things ephemeral, which might have been expected to alter in fifty years!—a striped awning, a newsagent, a pot of geraniums.

I circled the center cautiously toward my old street but turned left on Croisiers: there will be the wrought-iron gates, the playground, the redbrick walls. The fine old brick seemed neither more nor less shabby than it was then. The fingerpaintings taped on the windows could have been the same. Several score of five-to-eight-year-olds were in the yard; a game of soccer, jump rope, *boules*. A couple of girls gossiping in a corner on a bench. Uniforms of gray with yellow shirts. Back then it was navy with gray socks. I remember the weight of the strap that held my slate to my books. Patrice had a lacquer pencil box in which she smuggled candy. She shared it with Julienne and me as we sat gossiping on that bench.

At this corner the University will be to my left and the river to my right. The apartment building will be on the quai straight ahead. My heart was beating heard. I meant to write "hard" but let it stand. Listening to my heart I turned at the river balustrade. And was disoriented by the street sign: "Quai Roosevelt." Which could not, of course, have then been the name. I stood, head pounding with the effort to remember the name of the street I had lived on, but could not. So concentrated was I on this failure that it was a long while before I understood I was looking up at my balcony, its blue and amber leaded panes.

It is just the same. It is someone else's but utterly my own. Above the French doors an arch with a casting of two lions and a plaque like those on which a date is inscribed, but it is blank. As it was fifty years ago.

I moved away—*I am not ready!*—along the quai toward the market, which was a market. The butcher has refrigerated cases, but the awning opens out over the sidewalk as it did, "*Specialiste de l'Alimentation Italienne.*" I turned onto rue de l'Agneau knowing a split second before I did so that here would be an antique shop ahead. *Antiquités* in gilt, a gold hand pointing. And now I was in a time warp because not only was the shop there, but its windows held the same objects that, in my childhood, sat in living rooms and cafés. Chinoiserie, umbrella stand, fringed lamps. I pushed in and wandered among this paraphernalia of the past, and in the back, in a wooden trough, I found a treasure: a thick portfolio of photographs, glossy, mostly eight-by-tens—the discarded stock of some newspaper, I think—of the streets I had just come through, circa 1940 to '45. I bought the whole portfolio for two hundred and fifty dollars, a madness, no hesitation. I don't know how I'll get it home.

I'd left the camera in the hotel on purpose to see without intention. But tomorrow.

10 JUNE, STILL HOT

Anguiles aux verts in the Café St. Denis

Over coffee at the Vinâve d'Ile, in front of the fountain where my father used to hold me to dip my feet—flanked by four spewing lions and topped with Virgin and Child: I was up at dawn (the opposite of jet-lag, full of anxious energy) to retrace my steps with the camera: virgin, arch, the schoolyard empty now but for a pair of skateboarders who must have scaled the fence; the market, antique shop. At a photo shop I bought half a dozen more rolls of film. Bless my smart-focus new SLR. *Beignets* and chicory-laced coffee, then at nine to the library where a pretty, bemused assistant helped me find a pre-war map of the city. Which yields the inevitable-seeming news that the street we lived on was called Quai des Étas Unis.

"Look. I have lived all my life in the United States and didn't know it!" She was both pretty and amused.

LATE—I TURN ON A DIME.

I went back to the Quai Roosevelt fortified with my camera and took pictures in a 360-degree arc: a *péniche* with a cargo of sand passing under the Pont des Arches, its Stalinesque statues, the Institut Zoölogique across the river. My balcony. My leaded panes. My lions. I crossed, mounted and peered at the names on the doorbells. Bottom to top: Saveola, Safarian, Lacassel, Widart. A shiver, knowing what I would see next. On the top button, Hoffman. A Germanic—and familiar—and a Jewish—name.

I stood dithering whether to push the bell. I could not decide. I turned away and stepped aside for the woman laboriously mounting one foot on each step and then the other. An artificial leg, it seemed, a plastic bag of groceries in one hand while the other hoisted her by the railing. Dyed black hair twisted into a coronet, double chin. Bright-eyed. Short. *Saftig.*

"Hello, Lotte," I said. She stopped and heaved for breath. "I don't suppose you'll remember me."

Ill-chosen phrase! She did not *recognize* me, which is another matter. Remember! Such cries and grasping, clasping of arms and backs, such kisses, hugs, such hanging on, such tears on both sides. *Lotte, Lotte,* and *Simone, Simone, ma chère enfante, ma petite precieuse, ma petite coquine, mon chou.* I stood on the stone steps, a woman of sixty smartly dressed in silk and linen, an expensive camera around my neck, *her dear baby, her precious little one, her little minx, her cabbage.*

What is it like to solve the mysteries of fifty years in an attic over a cup of tea? I remember an image of the Big Crunch, when time will run backward and entropy will be reversed: the shattered pieces of the cup will snap together and jump intact back to the table. It is like that.

Our exchange was a little halting. Lotte's English never got beyond the grammar book, and she laughs at my French, which she says has the flavor of the forties. On the other hand, I'm sure I have a French vocabulary esoteric and arcane (*jouissance, silence imposé*) that is "postmodern" beyond Lotte's wildest imagining. What is missing is the youth and adulthood in between, the syntax of an ordinary life.

They never found, or at any rate, never identified, my father's body, but he was officially designated a hero of the *Résistance*. It is said he helped several dozen Jews escape, mostly by pretending a professorial absent-mindedness, churning out scholarly work so innocuous that he was not suspected. Lotte and her husband were among those he tried to help, but they were stopped at Antwerp, and for reasons never explained, her fake papers were accepted but his were not. She was dismissed; he was sent to his death at Auschwitz. That is why Lotte returned shortly before my mother died. "I couldn't see any point in going anywhere else."

And did she remember Vanderleven? Did she indeed! "*Un flamand tapageur*"—a flamboyant Flem. Whether he made pro-Jewish speeches or whether my father ever defended him, she couldn't say. "I know it was he who warned your papa that he was suspected. But I don't know how he knew. He could have let something slip himself!"

"He had a big mouth."

This made her rock with agreement. "*Une bouche pas assez bouché*," she said. A mouth not plugged-up enough.

All this in the slant-sided living room on the top floor, to which Lotte and her prophylactic heave themselves up again every time she must go out. A blood clot took her leg—nothing to do with war; the ordinary course of things is also dangerous to life and limb. She does not want to leave this upper floor. The window still gives onto that tessellation of shining roofs. The china rabbit wears its fur of flowers. The bowl in the form of a raddichio is still unbroken. I wept over these things, of course, and of course she offered them to me, and of course I said that that was not the point.

Did they try to find me? Who would have done so? How would they have done so? A father and daughter fled to the coast and disappeared. The records of the Resistance were partial, inaccurate and dispersed. To Lotte it never occurred to do anything but mourn. Why should it have been her responsibility? It was mine—fulfilled now half a century on.

Nor were there grandparents to find me. My father's parents had not survived the First World War, and my mother was long estranged from hers.

"She disbelieved, you see, which was, oh, shocking! to her parents." She came from a tiny village in the province of Cantal. Lotte could not remember the name of it, *Brisage? Brissein?* It was rye- and potato-growing country, caught in a punitive vision of the afterlife. My mother was the clever girl who went to the Lycée in Paris, where she lost God and found my father, a suitor unacceptable on two counts, as an unbeliever and as a Walloon. Her people disowned her, and the rift was never healed. "She was stubborn and came from stubborn stock."

Lotte said that my father wrote to these pious parents after my mother died, but received no reply except that one day a tract arrived in the mail, with a Cantal postmark but no return address, on the unrelenting torment of the damned. If they thought it would hurt him, they were both right and wrong, because it made him honor her atheism more fiercely.

"You see, that was her friendship with Dr. Saurraute. Well, these days—I suppose you can't be shocked to know that the doctor was a homosexual."

"No, I can't be shocked by that," I said. "Relieved, in fact. I was afraid there was a liaison with my mother."

"So? Oh, no. Dr. Saurraute was disowned by his parents too, and so her 'godlessness' and his 'perversion' made a special bond between them."

"Not one my father minded."

"*Ma petite!* Your father often said he did not know how he would have lived through your mother's illness without Dr. Saurraute."

"Or without you."

"Or without me," she shrugged. A little *moue* of self-deprecation, so Lotte-in-itself that I laughed for the memory of it. "Or without you," she said.

But I have no idea if this generous inclusion represents the truth. Was I necessary to my father's grief? Or a burden without which he might have lived?

I said, "I know my mother died of a liver ailment. Was it cirrhosis?"

"*Elle avait quelque chose aux foie,*" Lotte replied.

"I know." I asked, "Was it a result of alcohol?"

"How, of alcohol?"

"I mean was she a . . . did she . . . drink too much?"

"Ough." Lotte's sound was a throat-clearing of dismissal. "It was a war! All of us would have been happy to drink too much if we could get it. Oh, she liked her tipple." Here she began to laugh in a conspiratorial way. "We would add a thimbleful of schnapps to the tea if we had it, or sneak a bit of your father's cognac to the coffee. You may be sure that Dr. Saurraute brought a bottle when he came!"

She fairly shook with merriment, and I let it go.

When it grew late and I said I must let her rest, Lotte made me wait while she dug in a cupboard underneath the goose teapot, removed boxes of coupons and old envelopes, the *embarras* of an old magpie woman—to come triumphant up with an ancient shoebox that had inscribed on one end in blue cursive: *La Dame du Mode.* I could not breathe. It was as familiar to me as the hands into which she placed it. *La Dame du Mode.* Had my life depended on it I could not have told you what logo was printed on that box, but when I saw it, I knew my childhood had been saved inside. Four paper dolls in eighteenth-century gowns, a wood-block puzzle of two lollipop-eyed infants in undershirts and bulbous shoes. Three photographs: my mother and father on their wedding day; one of my mother in a park with me as a baby in her arms; one of my father fishing in the

Ardennes, younger than I ever knew him. The worn Tarot pack. A powder compact of which I have no recollection. A perfume bottle in cobalt blue, still smelling the smell of her, dead fifty years.

This I accepted. These things I will take home with me.

10 JUNE

Still bright, sudden drop in temperature, surprising and familiar.

Tourist of my origins, I have been by taxi to the *Maternité Publique* where I was born (now a *salle de musique*); on foot to the *école normale* I attended, the raised yard still with its view down to a Stella Artois café; by cab again past the *Palais des Congrès* to the little municipal cemetery and my mother's plain grave.

This must be like history itself. You go to a legendary place and all the salient features are still there, the rivers, the twist of streets. But the feel of it is different, the light falls in a different way; proportion was misrepresented. If we could travel back in time we would know that we had history right and wrong in just this way; the facts preserved, the past a foreign country.

Then back to Lotte's for coffee. She bustles; she finds me an eclair. She frets that she can't let me see inside the apartment where we lived. The Lacassels who live there are away. Lotte sniffs when she speaks of them, flings her hand in a dismissive manner. They have a mansion in the Ardennes; this is their city pad. A lawyer for Coca Cola. An expert on the European Union. I can see no reason for her disdain but a generalized loyalty to my parents who once held *soirées* in that sainted space.

Last, about four, saved as the *pièce de resistance,* we went together to the University—which is to say, just around the corner.

When I was a little girl, my father would take me by the hand and mount with me through the central of the three granite arches. He conveyed, or I assumed, a fullness in the chest, a feeling awed or holy. This was the palace of learning. This was where thought was born, enlarged. That feeling gripped me with the force, now, of both its presence and its loss. The vast foyer is upheld by half a dozen pillars. Beyond these, facing us as we entered, was a marble wall deeply engraved:

Universitaire Liègeios
Morts pour la patrie

My father's name was carved under the *Faculté de Philosophe et Lettres*, along with those of *Francine Mathieu, Didier Scuvre, Georges Dekan*. None of these names have the slightest resonance for me.

"*Voila l'épreuve*!" Lotte said. *There is the proof.* The proof: as in, the convincing evidence, the trial to which belief is put, the test run. Proof of the pudding. Proof of purchase. Page proof, meaning *that which may not yet be accurate.*

We climbed the stairs toward his old office, wandered through corridors nearly empty at this hour, stopping to look in a few open doors. I saw that Lotte hung back when I introduced myself to a professor—not a fear of antisemitism, surely, now, but the old deference of class.

No one remembered him. Until on the top floor back (they do expect the oldsters to mount the stairs!) a Professeur Lankrok, wizened to the look of pine bark, held my hand in both his hands. Like Lotte, wept, like Lotte called me *chère enfante* and *ma chère madame*. My father had put his life at naught for the honor of the country and his fellow man. My father was a saint, and my mother was another. I had no memory of this gently enthusiastic husk, not even of his name. My survival was a miracle, he said, meant by God to honor the memory of a pair of saints.

Such love, such friendship, and such heroism. May I believe it? In this century, for me, family and sacrifice are discredited. *Leave it to Beaver* syrup and John Wayne smarm—to *me* they are lies. So how may I know whether Lotte's memory, old Professor Lanrok's recollection, don't distort in the same set of ways?

Perhaps, now, I don't know about my parents the things that people with ordinary lives don't know about their parents.

Lotte offered to feed me, but I knew the leave-taking would be long, and I was right. *Mon chou, ma petit, ma petite precieuse.* At six o'clock I was at the station for a bowl of the peasant soup my mother called *hutsepot*. On the platform a Scout troop was singing boisterous songs.

Why do I remember one thing and not the other, this and not that, when this seems to have no significance and that might mean everything? I have heard that a pathway in the brain is dug deeper by each remembering, the way a path across grass is made by the passage of feet. Leo will know if this is a discredited notion. It would not explain why after fifty years I can recognize the shape of Lotte's moue, and not know the name of the village from which my mother's exile began.

12 JUNE
Hotel Vaderlaand

Down the stone platform of Bruxelle Zuid came a long-legged amble that put the word *mosey* in my mind. Leo Aczél scanned the cars, flung a wave at me, and spread his arms. Gray now, still out-at-elbows, still sartorially out of date, eyebrows grizzled and unruly, his head hung slightly forward on his shoulders, uncannily just as I remember. I stumbled into his hug and—swear!—recognized the muscles of his chest under a tweed coat and a slight thickening of flesh; the smell of his neck, sweet musk, the spread of his fingers across my spine. Remember, yes, but also recognized. This is he. No other. Foregrounded. Close-up of these eyes, this mouth, this face. The rest becomes mere context, out of focus or out of frame.

Transit: Vienna–Budapest

1989

The food in the dining car of the Vienna-Budapest Express is dry, meager and expensive. The Muzak veers from *csárdás* to Michael Jackson and back again. They aren't hungry anyway. Nevertheless Leo is carving chunks off a thin slab of *schnitzel;* Simone is shoving half a dozen shrimp around a boat of *pörkölt* broth. He sips a half-glass of Bitburger Pils, she nurses a glass of Perrier. Already they've established a habit of heading straight for the dining car. Leo is nervous on trains. Already Simone has understood that this has to do with his having starved on trains when he fled Hungary in '56. Four decades have not undone that fear. If he can eat, then he knows he will be allowed to alight unhindered. They order extravagantly and make garbage across Europe west to east.

She is saying, "I knew I had left him to die."

He says, "You did not *abandon* your father. You *obeyed* him. He ordered you to do exactly the same as those Jewish parents who sent their children with the *Kindertransport.* To *survive.*"

"I'll think of it that way."

"Too right."

They aren't hungry because they are slightly stupefied with desire. Her sleeve is rucked above her elbow and his hand strays to her arm, stroking between desultory attempts at the food. His fingers are dry, the bone at thumb-base prominent, the nails opalescent like the interior of a shell. The follicles of her forearm read his fingerprints and send liquid information through her thighs. He watches the delta of sinew on the backs of her hands, across which the veins run in a lightning bolt, sifted with age-freckles. Her skin has the lax malleability of worn leather. He kneads it gently, watches it creasing and stretching, lifts his hand briefly to his face to catch her smell.

Now he is talking about that journey on foot from Budapest to Tatabánya, train to Györ and across into Austria. "I had papers, but hardly any money, and of course the papers registered me as Communist. There were identity checks all along the line; nobody could know whether we'd get through. We were afraid if any of us got off the train for food, we'd be challenged and not allowed to get back on. In the bigger towns, vendors would come to the train with sandwiches or chocolate, and there'd be a murderous competition among the refugees."

"When I first met you in Binghamton, I thought you'd come as a child. A Chicago street kid."

"I worked at it, to put out that impression."

Anybody European can see they are one more "senior" American tourist couple. The hemisphere is thick with those. Up until the nineteen-sixties, aging American women aspired to the condition of Greek peasantry: black crepe dresses, thick-heeled shoes, a kerchief. But in the sixties they took to soft trousers and pullover tops—a geriatric revolution that, unlike flower power, maintained its sway. Men, too, used to become more formal as they aged, and sometimes dapper. Now these two are wearing nearly identical slacks and tops, she a burgundy scarf, he in navy. His hair is gray; hers is well on its way to being white.

Under the table his running shoe crosses hers and the calf muscles of both shiver at the contact. They have so little history together that they rehearse it endlessly.

"When I recognized you that day in the mail room, I thought: I'll kill him. And then I fell into your arms."

"You were wearing a knit dress with huge pockets. You kept burying your hands in them."

"I don't remember that."

"You sat against the window and your hair was a fuzzy halo."

"Are you sure? No, I cut my hair that winter."

"A flaxen Afro. Yes, I'm sure."

"Do you know—I still have your sketch of a flatworm. It was on a mimeo of the Jepson job announcement. I'll xerox it and send it to you."

"No, I'll come to Missouri for it."

The light is probably aslant outside, probably through deep forest that it's a scandal not to notice. The meat is made to disappear by a formally uniformed arm. Maybe they can do better with a few greens, a little radicchio. But not much. She wipes a drop of salad oil from her lip with the back of an index finger; he catches her eye; both pairs of eyes are suddenly in flash-flood, awe, the newness, the unexpectedness of it.

The sweets tray is flourished at them, and now they do laugh to find that they can deal with dessert. He forks into a *dobos torte*; she takes a *lepénye* with tart cherries and sweet buttercream. He is talking magnetic resonance imaging and PET scans, the capacity to watch in motion the color-coded dynamic of a brain. He is describing how the frontal lobe lights with pleasure, the r-complex burns with anxiety. She is opining that her neocortex is currently bathed in purple light.

He is talking ontogenetics, the organism in its passage from embryo to decline. He is asking, "When is death? It's a decision we have to make for social reasons. Brain-dead, sure. But what about the ganglion? If I separate the head of a moth from its thorax—I use moths, not butterflies; the students aren't as squeamish—and stimulate it, the nerve fires. So the nerve is still alive. For how long? Then is the moth alive that long?"

"They used to scare us as kids by saying that the hair keeps growing in the grave."

"And the fingernails."

"That's right. Do you think that's where the idea of the afterlife came from?"

"No, no. I think *that* came from unwillingness to believe in death at all. And all the same we think we have to know when the moment comes. Whereas it demonstrably happens over time. Of course, people equate the soul with the brain, because they can't separate the ego from the *ergo sum*."

They slacken more comfortably into their chairs—he because he has eaten, and she because he has scarcely taken his touch from her arm for the past five days, and so will not remove it soon; both, because the countryside they have wasted and ignored is dotted now with drab houses in the twilight, meaning that in half an hour they will arrive on the bank of the Danube known as Pest, where they have a too-expensive reservation at the Intercontinental, and where they can spend a long evening, a whole night, before setting off on the Hungarian lap of their stunned and inattentive tourism.

Coffee. She takes from her briefcase and spreads across the table a hodgepodge of photographs. A few are tintypes, some black and white portraits mounted on cardboard, others glossy street scenes, creased. The biggest pile are color snaps.

"Look," she says. She takes a shiny news photo, circa 1944, of a bombed-out Liege street with the windows gaping behind the charred facades, and sets on top of it a fresh color snapshot of a window in that same street. The contours of the building are jarringly similar without being a perfect match. The window is now full of bright detritus, a fringed lamp, a mounted boar's head, a grandfather clock with blue moons on its face. Gilt lettering on the window says, "Antiquités," with a gold hand pointing into the rubble of the doorway in the next façade.

"Fantastic," he admires.

She selects another, a print of a matron standing before a stall in the open market. Her mammoth hat festooned with puffs of tulle, she crosses her arms in a proprietary stance. Indifferent behind her, a Nazi soldier smokes at the river railing. Matching the openwork of the rail, Simone sets over this a color shot of a boy skateboarding in the same spot, head down, prone into the wind of his own making. The angle of his trajectory is unclear; in another couple of seconds he will plow into either the woman or the soldier.

Simone says, "I'll trim them, but roughly. It's to startle, not to fool."

"How did this idea come to you?"

“No notion. I’ll need to take classes in photography.”

“Maybe not. You have an eye.”

“Oh, but. The academic habit is too strong. You know that much about me.”

They fumble for each other’s hands on either side of the railway coffee. Neither remembers that the coffee was also awful in the faculty lounge of Harpur College in December of 1963. She remembers from more recently the hollow where his lifted clavicle meets the muscle of his neck. He remembers the surprising heft and handful of her breast. The conductor announces Budapest in German, Hungarian, English, French, and Italian.

Leo says, “Home.” Simone, mouth slightly parted, nods.

CHAPTER 13

Broken Home

1991

Almost two years, and his daughter had not yet met his—what?—lover, fiancée? "Partner" seemed to be the current term, but for Leo it implied the male grit of those Westerns he had devoured in post-war Budapest.

It wasn't that he didn't want them to meet, or that he kept Simone a secret from Lizbett. It was that Simone had lived alone for thirty years and developed a tendency to make quick decisions, whereas he had lived with Anika, for whom any plan might be rescinded in a flash of blame. So although he fully intended to take his *partner* down to Florida sometime soon, it had become second nature to hold off, delay, drag his heels.

That first year he spent a week in Jepson, and she came twice for long weekends in Hanover, while he went down to Florida alone to visit Lizbett, her husband Vince, and Eudora, who was four, and who called him "Dadag."

By the end of that first winter he and Simone had settled into a habit of reading by the woodstove in his Hanover bi-level, which sprawled across a stony acre outside of town, and where she hinted at retirement. He was simultaneously stricken with caution at these hints and dismally certain she would change her mind. He confessed what he knew were contradictory impulses, but Simone gently dismissed this. She observed that if it were not possible to feel two things at once there would be no poetry: *Do I contradict myself? Very well . . .*

It's not as if they were sedentary. That summer they traveled back to Europe and also to California, about which Simone harbored romantic fantasies, and was disappointed to find crowded with highways and restaurant chains. They developed a habit, so it became a joke between them, of studying the real estate windows wherever they went, pointing out the *For Sale* signs, translating the house prices into dollars. They picked a home for themselves in La Jolla, one in the German village of Eltville, another on a hill in Pest. They even—on a whim of Simone's—toured a multi-million-dollar mansion outside Tucson, on a hill where they were the only viewers, in shorts, and the real estate agent was wearing an upsweep and a suit. They liked Tucson. But also Antwerp, and a little village they found in Sussex called Rottingdean.

The next year Simone put in for retirement and began shipping her books to Hanover, though they agreed they would eventually settle somewhere else. What they did not directly say was that his house, in spite of its open aspect and big rooms, was crowded with memories of Anika.

Nor, still, did he quite trust Simone's moods. When she was playful, or moved, he half expected her to turn and point out some innate shortcoming of his, even pull out the scorching American vocabulary that had always sat a little awkwardly in Anika's accent: *bastard, dork, wimp.*

So, yes, he admitted to having been verbally abused. You couldn't spend a few decades in America, let alone in neuroscience, without being familiar with that term. So what? He considered that half the children in the world and a fair percentage of lovers male and female had been abused since the beginning of time. He had stayed in his marriage because of the damage done to his wife, which was partly the fault of the naïve Hungarian revolutionaries of which he was one, and partly the fault of the murderous Soviets, and partly the fault of an America that betrayed its friends. It could not be right to discard her for that damage, to strand her in this country—toward which she was also verbally abusive. He figured he and America could take it.

But he was left a little raw, a little apt to expect a cliff-edge, and when this feeling overtook him, he retreated inside himself.

And that, Simone did mind. She said, admonishing, "Leo, I'm *here*."

He said, "I'm afraid you'll wake up one morning and realize I don't measure up."

"Uh-huh," she said, "except that's not what's going to happen. What's going to happen is that one morning you'll wake up and realize I'm a permanent fixture."

She also said from time to time, "When do I get to see Lizbett?"

He'd shrug and roll his shoulders. "I want to give her time to get used to the idea."

"You said she doesn't object."

"No, no. She's fine with it. But I don't know . . . for example, whether Eudora remembers Anika. She was two when her grandmother died, but she's precocious. Seeing you might dredge up all that turmoil. And I don't know what Lizbett knows about the German measles episode." He didn't say that this was the sort of thing Anika might have thrown at her daughter in a fit of pique. "Or what you went through," he added, lame.

"I'll ask her. For heaven's sake, Leo. Lizbett's an adult."

"Yes, but she was a child, and those guilts, even resentments . . . those can last."

"She and I will talk about it."

"You're probably right. We'll plan a trip. Soon."

It was a fact that Lizbett did not object to his having a new woman. She remembered the lady at the zoo, and she encouraged him: "It's better than moping around the lab." Still, August in Florida would be sticky-hot. After that, Eudora was about to start kindergarten, not a good time for disruption. In October Lizbett would be overwhelmed with midterms, and Lizbett's jerk of a husband was always on edge through the holidays, more than likely to be drunk.

So when Simone sold her little house, when Leo himself announced his retirement and began the difficult process of handing off his lab, Simone and Lizbett still had not met. But in the winter of the second year, when Lizbett called to say she was pregnant—in fact, four months along—Simone finally called him out on it. "Why don't you want me to meet your daughter?"

"It isn't that. I just don't want to walk you into a situation."

"What situation do you think I can't handle? For chrissake, Leo . . ."

"Well, she has the pregnancy to deal with, and a full-time job . . ."

"We can help out. What *is* the problem?"

Her voice had an edge sharp as a shell. He had never heard that in her before, and it frightened him. "Anyway her husband is an asshole."

"God knows I've learned how to be cordial to an asshole!"

"I know, but . . ."

"No, all that's bullshit. You're afraid she'll like me or afraid she won't. You want her all to yourself, is that it? You don't want to make it real, because if you take me down there you'll have admitted we're a couple. *Something*! I don't know what's the matter with you."

Indignation stopped his throat. They were dressing for dinner. They had a reservation at their favorite restaurant just across the border in Manchester, Vermont; an hour by the shortest route, but they usually stretched the trip to an hour and a half, taking a right angle instead of a straight line because that would carry them down through the pretty villages and trees of Green Mountain. Now he decided to take the shorter highway. He'd have canceled dinner altogether, except what would they do stalking around this place?—she in her sleek black outfit and earrings, he already in the turtleneck that was his only concession to dressing up.

He said nothing more, didn't suggest that it would be cool on the way home and she should bring a wrap, didn't remind her to bring her keys. Pulling out of the driveway he gunned the motor like an adolescent, and took the driveway faster than he needed to.

"Seatbelt," she said, steely.

All right. He'd take anybody on in a silence competition. He briefly considered turning the radio on, decided not. If there was to be silence, let it be. They pulled on to the highway and she said nothing though she must have realized he was not taking the usual route. She kept a rigid stare, he passing every car he could, until he realized they'd be a half hour early and would have to hang around the bar.

They were—what, fifteen minutes?—on the US 6 tarmac before she said, to the windshield, "The truth is, you can't make a decision whether you want us to meet or not. You're incapable of making any decision. You won't even decide where you want to live. It might commit you to something, God forbid."

The car jumped forward the way she hated. *Emotional acceleration,* she called it. He spat out, "Really? Well, where do you want to live?"

"I don't know!"

"No? I thought that was your point."

"My point is, you can't even hold a real conversation about it. To you it's all a game."

"I thought it was a game we played together."

"All right, that's partly true. But at some point you have to get serious. Or would you rather drag around in Anika's wake for the next ten years?"

The bile of thirty years' contention rose in his throat again. "Okay, let's have the discussion. Where do you want to live?"

"Not like that. We'll talk about it when you're rational."

He, rational? He was nothing if not rational. He operated on pure rationality, which this suddenly unveiled harridan ought to know. He burned rubber on the turn into Manchester and again in the parking lot.

They were still twenty minutes early, an eternity to sit waiting, fuming, Simone making stilted chitchat with the bartender and a couple to their right. To their left a young woman—girl, really—in hot pants and a skimpy top sat on one stool with her foot on the next, baring an expanse of thigh and chattering into one of those flip phones. The inappropriate idiot young! He resented his turtleneck, which suddenly itched. He pulled at it.

Dinner carried on in the same vein. Simone was brightly false with the waiter and even the water-boy. To each other they spoke only of food, though they ordered their usual favorites: goat cheese soufflé, tuna carpaccio, salmon in *mille feuille*. It was all cardboard. His teeth strained to grind it, his throat didn't want to pass it, his stomach rose acid in protest. He told himself this was ridiculous, they were just having a stupid quarrel. For a moment he couldn't remember what the quarrel was about. But then Simone lifted her napkin to the corners of her mouth, one corner and then the other, with an irritable, prissy air, and his rage came back again: a hundred and twenty dollars for a reflux of goat cheese and marjoram. He over-tipped as a hedge against his desire to make the waiter suffer for it.

He drove home in the dark, just slightly loose, as if he had had too much to drink, which he had not, though he'd considered a *digestif* the Silver Fork called the "Order Me A Cab." He'd have drunk it, too, if he and Simone hadn't laughed over the name once before. He didn't want her laughing now.

He remembered how he had driven in the dark in the months after Anika's death, down to New York, west all the way to Chicago, opera blasting, feeling the freedom, the guilt overpowered by music. God, he had loved those nights. He turned on the radio but it was the wrong hour for opera, and his tapes were all at home. He found some classic rock and turned up the Eagles full blast, but it didn't have the right effect. *Take it to the limit, one more . . .* He cut it off mid-phrase.

At the house, Simone went straight to bed. He poured a drink and took it out to the patio where he sat and stewed on the chaise. The bedroom light, he saw, stayed on for a long time, then went out, and half an hour later went on again. Good. He didn't want her to be able to sleep. He took in that satisfaction for a while, and then the fear came back again, a shadow of the old certainty that she would walk out on him. His anger wanted another cognac but his stomach didn't. Rage and fear mixed in him. He twisted for how long he didn't know, and then he dozed. Woke disoriented, remembered the anger and the fear, and came to a realization that he struggled to keep at bay, and then struggled to face: that Simone was right. Not entirely right, but near enough. He had spent his youth and most of his middle age trying to be an exemplary father, to protect Lizbett from a woman who also deeply loved her but could not show it because what she had been through left no emotions available to her but fear and anger. That had been his mission: to bring Lizbett up as a strong woman, neither her mother's nor anybody else's victim. He had succeeded. Well, mostly succeeded; near enough. Now he didn't, in fact, want to share Lizbett with the other woman in his life. He sat with this insight for a while and then he dozed again, sinking into the welter of his feelings, dreaming he knew not what.

The sliding door woke him. Simone had a cup of coffee in each hand. She set one in front of him and sat, silent still but looking tousled, a little wan. Suddenly the anger was gone and the fear took his breath away. Now he didn't speak for fear he would say the wrong, the annihilating thing.

It would be a red sunrise. Sailor's warning. They watched until it was time to turn away from the ascending sun.

Simone said, "It would be crazy to spoil this."

Fear and anger dissipated like a summer squall. "I know."

"I don't want to intrude on your relationship with your daughter."

"I'll get tickets today."

"There's no rush. I was wrong. It's up to you to know when you're ready."

"No, you were right. I guess my impulse is to protect her even from you. It's stupid. She'll love you in no time. And she's not somebody who needs protecting."

"We can wait."

"No. I just want one promise. Any time we quarrel, we resolve it. If it separates us we get back together, however long it takes."

"Done."

Lizbett taught social studies at little Flagler College down in St. Augustine, Florida. The college was housed in the former Ponce de León Hotel, a spectacular bauble of a place, bequeathed to higher education by an old Standard Oil tycoon ("Sort of like Jebadiah Jepson,"

Simone said, and predicted that she and Lizbett would have a lot to talk about). Lizbett herself had grown into a calm, no-nonsense sort of professional, as if in compensation for her childhood, though she continued to invite chaos by picking an erratic husband with a black brush moustache. Why did that handsome-bad-boy look attract so many otherwise sensible women? Leo did not buy a lot of psychiatric claptrap. Still, it sat there, blatant: Lizbett was in love with, and apologist for, a man much like her mother: volatile, unpredictable, and often out of work. She had always looked to her father for steadiness, for reliable affection. Might she not, out of the aforementioned guilt and resentment, find Simone a usurper of her father's love?

They flew to Jacksonville, rented a car and drove down to St. Augustine. When they arrived it turned out that Vince was away on some unspecified business trip. Lizbett was distracted, apologetic, which was not her style. She and Simone were cordial enough to each other, but not as if they welcomed each other like old souls. They talked administration or semiotics, they denigrated meetings and praised affirmative action—academic chitchat, not friendship. It was May, already hot in the daytime. The most intimate thing that happened was that Lizbett took Simone off to find a "tankini," which turned out to be a smart beach outfit that lit up her platinum hair. After that Leo thought, hoped, the women grew a little easier with each other.

With Eudora there was no such holding back. Eudora was a child determined to be taken seriously, and Simone was serious with her. She had endless patience for reading, and Eudora an endless appetite for being read to. "Again," was her refrain, and Simone would read again—the three classic S's: Seuss, Sendak, Silverstein—and on to *The Adventures of Pippi Longstocking* and *The Little Prince*. After a few days Eudora was "reading" back to Simone stories she had in fact memorized.

Then there was the camera. Simone had a fancy new Hasselblad with a screen to show Eudora the pictures she'd taken of her. Eudora began to develop the repertoire of funny faces that afflict children as soon as they discover self-consciousness. And Simone was, surprisingly, willing to let her handle the costly device. Eudora learned to balance it on her knees so her hand would reach to the shutter-button. She took pictures of the carpet or Dadag's ear or the left half of a stuffed koala bear.

Now Lizbett began to recall the Binghamton Zoo. "I met Simone when I was younger than you are now," she told Eudora. "She used to take pictures of all the animals. Or pieces of them."

"You remember that?" Simone asked.

"Oh, yeah."

Later, to Leo, Lizbett said, "Were you and Simone lovers back then?"

"Absolutely not."

"Why not? Isn't that supposed to be the birthright of your gender?"

It took him only a beat to see that this was a reference to Vince and his "business travel." "Because I was faithful to your mother," he said sternly. And then, relenting, "Not that I didn't want to."

"Uh-huh," said Lizbett.

They had been in Florida less than a week when Vince arrived, and the atmosphere of the household shifted. Lizbett became unnaturally cheerful, full of plans for places Leo and Simone might take Eudora. Now and then Eudora could be seen in a watchful mode, studying her father, but whether out of wariness or hoping for his attention Leo couldn't tell. Vince of the dashing moustache teased Lizbett in a way that made clear he wasn't really kidding: her cutoffs, her haircut, her marinara sauce. To Leo and Simone he spoke, with the appearance of great friendliness and enthusiasm, of the money to be made from renting food-court furniture to malls. It was wonderful how many sentences could be formed on this subject. The only conversational deviation was to the possibility of acquiring tracts of cheap land in South Dakota. Leo did not ask where the money for these ventures was to come from.

But the second night after he came home, sitting over the linguini and *vino rossi*, Vince chided Simone for her mere sparkling water and then said in a jovial way, "I understand Liz screwed up your plans when she was a little girl."

Simone said, "I'm sorry?"

"When she gave you the German measles and you lost that baby, right? You must've hated her."

Lizbett caught at and resettled her glass. "Eudora, sweetie, go get Snuffles ready for bed, ok?"

"It's nothing she can't hear. You're pregnant, for God's sake. Dora knows that."

"Go on, sweetie." Lizbett smoothed at the tablecloth. "Simone, I'm so sorry. It was a husband-and-wife confidence, you know?"

But when Eudora had obediently slipped from her chair and disappeared to her room, Simone faced Vince. "Lizbett was not responsible for that. It was a virus."

"Of course," Lizbett laughed, ran her fingers through her forelock. "I never thought it was my *fault*."

"But then you didn't have any kids," Vince pressed Simone. "Ever. That must have been rough on you."

"Look here," Leo said, but he didn't know who he wanted to protect, or from what, or how.

"It was very hard for a while," Simone agreed. "But I've thought about it a lot over the years, and it's clear to me . . . that, if anything . . . that illness rescued me. If I'd had a child—maybe disabled, maybe blind—I'd never have been able to leave that awful marriage. I'd have been trapped. Not by the child, you understand. But by the stupid mistake I'd made marrying a cruel man."

There was a moment's silence. Then Leo thought to say, "And she wouldn't have been here to rescue *me*." Which gave Lizbett a chance to stand, saying, "Coffee in the living room, everyone. Vince, you can clear while I make it." The rest of the evening passed back to food-court furniture.

All the same, the trip was spoiled. The queen bed in the guest room became suddenly too small, and though the nights were still cool Simone complained that the damp made a Brillo pad of her hair. With three days to go, they took Eudora out to Chuck E. Cheese, to old Fort St. Augustine, to one of the dispirited "museums" on the coastal highway (*The very Cadillac in which Jane Mansfield was beheaded!*). Leo said "What can you do? It's Florida."

They left with relief, except for a moment of guilt-edged charm at the airport when Eudora asked Simone with great solemnity, "Are you my grandma now?"

Simone said, "I expect that partly depends on you. Do you think that would work out okay?"

"Uh-huh," said Eudora.

That was May. In July they learned that Lizbett had been offered the chair of her department, and that she had accepted, to begin a month before the baby was due. Was that a good idea? Leo ventured. "Sure. It's always good for me to be busy," she insisted. Vince would help out while she adjusted. "I'll bounce back in a week," she said.

By August Simone was busy sorting and combining their books and Leo wrapping up a project in the neurophysiology of the *Lolliguncula brevis,* the only cephalopod that lived in brackish water (because, yes, it had been a condition of his taking the job at Dartmouth that he could switch to octopuses) when Lizbett called again, her voice that deadly calm that presages hysteria—so Leo's mind went immediately to hospitals, Eudora dead in the road, miscarriage—to say that Vince had left her. He had taken the Volvo that she had chosen and paid off over five years because it was considered safe for kids. She seemed particularly pissed about the Volvo.

"What happened?"

"Nothing."

"There must have been some . . ."

"No fight, nothing. It was like he went out for cigarettes and never came back. Except he stuck around long enough to say, '*I don't think I'm cut out for fatherhood.*'"

"Figured that out, did he?"

"I told him nobody's cut out to be a parent! It happens and then you deal with it."

"He never dealt with Eudora."

"Right. And of course he took the balance of the joint account."

"Don't worry about money, kitten . . ."

"I'm not worried. I get a raise; I'm insured to the max. It's just, you know . . ."

"Take some time off!"

"No, Dad. That is *exactly* what I *don't* need."

"Do you think he meant it though? Maybe he'll spend a few nights in a Best Western and have second thoughts."

"What, like a five-year-old runaway? You know what? Somebody walks out on his eight-and-a-half-month pregnant wife, I'm not so sure she ought to put out the welcome mat!"

At which point Leo was encouraged that she'd had enough of Vince. But the next thing she said was, "Could I talk to Simone?" and when he handed over the phone, he could tell from Simone's responses that Lizbett was in tears on the other end. "I know," Simone kept saying. "You're feeling exactly what you must right now." And, "It'll take time." And, "Shall we come down? Well, say when you want us, we'll be on the next plane." And finally, "I'm so sorry. He's a shit."

What Leo could not have foreseen was that Simone would fall in love with the baby.

She was there, in the room, when the little girl was born: Lizbett's choice, with Leo's blessing. Was he a tiny bit jealous? Probably. But he was not cut out for the visceral fluids of birth; he knew that. He busied himself with putting up new gutters, buying tar for the roof, trimming back the azalea bushes where they'd gone blowsy. Simone came back from the hospital glowing, in spite of a night's lost sleep.

"She's just gorgeous. She has Lizbett's eyes and Vince's hair. She's perfect, everything, ten fingers, little rosebud mouth. Although Lizbett's going to call her Zelda! Do you think that's bad luck?"

"I don't believe in luck."

"I know. But you've got to see her, Leo. Her little toenails!"

"Did she mention Vince?"

"She said he'd be pissed off it was another girl. Then she laughed. Honestly, Leo, they're both *fine*."

The guest room had been turned into a nursery, all yellow and abstract birds, so Leo and Simone were in a motel, expecting to stay a week. Now Simone suggested they rent a beachfront condo for a month. They'd be able to take Eudora swimming and look after the baby while Lizbett worked.

It was a good idea. Lizbett had spent the summer setting up her new department duties and the deputies for her two weeks of leave. Predictably, she had overestimated her stamina. When she started afternoons back at the college she came home haggard. She was determined to keep up a front with her colleagues, and she was avoiding altogether the friends that she and Vince had shared, so she was often cloistered in the bedroom with baby Zelda and Simone while it was Leo, now, who read to Eudora and played the same winsome/boring games he had played with Lizbett: hide and seek, Snakes and Ladders, teacher and student. Eudora did not mention her father. Together he and Eudora went out and picked, and Leo paid for, a silver three-year-old Audi to replace the pilfered Volvo.

After a few days back at the University, Lizbett's milk dried up. She was inconsolable for a day and then as suddenly consoled, and at that point Simone began napping on the couch until the 2 a.m. feeding, leaving Leo alone in the condo until she came back just before the sky began to pale.

Did he feel abandoned? Probably. Mainly he worried. He worried that his paper (his last! paper) would get to the proofing stage and he needed to oversee it. He worried that the state of limbo he felt these mornings were what retirement would always feel like. He worried that Simone had left in Hanover a promising—no, brilliant—series of photo montages that she needed to take seriously, and get to galleries. He worried that Lizbett had lined up a phalanx of undergraduate sitters who were too young to entrust with an infant, that Simone's love for the baby was an unhealthy displacement, that that shithead Vince had been right about her: she'd never got over the loss. He worried that Lizbett would become too dependent on Simone, or that she would come to resent Simone's help as an intrusion, or that the baby would become too attached to Simone and ultimately bring about a maternal tug-of-war in which he would be enlisted as King Solomon. That the whole situation, back to '56, back to '42, was trip-wired with danger: he and Simone and Anika had all been victims of war, and Lizbett had inherited, and Eudora and Zelda would absorb, the secondhand harm coming to be known as *intergenerational trauma*.

Mainly he worried that if he voiced all this to Simone, her temper would flare again, and if he didn't, he would contract resentfully into himself. He feared this last the most, so he started gently one evening on the balcony of their condo, before Simone was due to head to Lizbett's for the night. The Atlantic lapped thirty yards in front of them, not so gently.

"I worry you're exhausting yourself, and you'll get so attached to the baby it'll be a *wrench* when we have to leave."

Simone replied, not without edge, "It's possible. Why don't you alternate nights with me?"

He had imagined several responses, but not this one, so sensible, so assertive. It seemed to block him from any response but acquiescence. *He*, as if he hadn't been the caring parent all his life!

They added a month to their rental contract for the condo. He chose the Monday, Wednesday, Friday feedings; Simone took Sunday, Tuesday, Thursday. They figured Lizbett could manage Saturday on her own. After a few days on his watch, Leo surprised himself by anticipating little Zelda's cry, picking her up from the bassinet most nights before Lizbett had stirred. Then he would warm a bottle, pour a cognac, and sit sating them both on the back porch in moonlit calm. He watched the miniature hands pulsing at the bottle, the wispy cirrus clouds traveling out to sea. People always said that grandparents like to see the grandchildren come, and like to see them go. But these nights were of a peacefulness that reminded him of nothing except possibly Andromeda, his last, favorite, *brevis* squid. He was at peace. He rocked, the baby suckled; when it was over he went back to the beach house and slipped under covers warm with Simone's breath.

Now Simone and Leo would sleep in, have a leisurely brunch, then pick up the baby from home and Eudora from school. They would bring them back to the rental, swaddle the baby on a beach chair under a vast umbrella and let Eudora dabble in the surf for an hour or two. Leo was not too old for sandcastle construction, and Simone could dribble towers to an impressive height. Lizbett was sometimes excessively grateful, sometimes she would shoo them off, declaring it to be bonding time. Then they would wander the coast in their rental car, sampling oysters and crab legs on the weathered porches of seafront restaurants.

One afternoon, threading the streets of St. Augustine with both girls in tow, they turned onto a narrow peninsula between two equally narrow spits of water, one a brackish river and the other salt. A row of rather grand old clapboard houses stood with their backs to the river, facing toward the sea. It was a glorious day, just on the hinge between summer and fall, the sky the luminous azure of old heraldry. The azaleas were long finished blooming, but there were bright red hibiscus along the walks. You could just hear the surf from here; sea gulls dotted the sky. And in the middle of this block, facing the street but with its back yard giving onto the lapping water of the inlet, was a particularly yellow, many-windowed house with a For Sale sign in the lantana bed.

Leo would later claim that the car stopped of its own accord.

The style was hodge-podge, a little too plain to be Victorian, a little too gracious to be Colonial, with half the ground floor taken up by a bank of windows into what must be a "Florida Room." Each of the doors and windows carried a pane of stained glass: amber verticals interrupted by ice blue triangles and yellow disks. The ground floor was raised some five feet above the grass. Lantana burst orange and lavender and hosted bumble bees. There were wide steps up to a generous covered porch, and in the middle of the hip roof was a single sleepy-eye-shaped dormer.

Simone fetched Zelda out of her car seat and Leo freed Eudora, and they mounted the porch, where a wood-slatted swing had been abandoned to accommodate, perfectly, a five-year-old and a woman with a baby on her lap.

Leo tested the floorboards. "That's a crawl space. They don't dig full basements down here. Too easy to flood."

"Mmm," said Simone. "It's in bad need of a paint job. A *professional* paint job, not a job for a sixty-five-year-old."

"Sixty-four."

Simone rocked the porch swing. "Hold on tight, Eudora." Then to Leo, "It'll be worse inside. Gunked-on paint, probably. It'd need a deep clean."

"A *professional* deep-clean."

"*Touché.*"

Together they peered into the larger windows, which were partially obscured, but they could see a sweep of wide-plank oak with darker wood framing the baseboards. Teak, maybe. What Leo could see of the wall was papered in *trompe l'oeil* hibiscus (*Definitely have to get rid of that.*).

Simone handed him the baby while she took pictures of the glass. Through the bevels of the heavy door he could see a fantastically carved newel post. Low, not to wake Zelda, Leo whistled.

"What?"

"Look at this. There must have been big money here at one time."

"Jesus. What . . . what do you think it would go for now?"

Teasing: "What, are you in the market?"

"Of course not! Just curious." Eudora peered in the view finder while Simone kneeled for a low-angle shot.

"Two hundred and fifty thousand."

"Oh, Leo, you always underestimate. Twice that."

"Oh, Leo," Eudora said. She had grown lean and brown, but still in her flashing curiosity reminded Leo of Lizbett in the pushchair years. She scooted on the porch floor with her bare legs, and suddenly let out a yell. Leo held the baby while Eudora screamed and Simone removed the splinter with the tweezer she conveniently carried in her purse.

"No harm done," Simone said.

Eudora accused, "Mama puts peroxide."

"When we get home."

And it was time to go home, but they did not. Simone ran her finger over one of the stained-glass transoms. "Anyway, you need double-glazing, place this old, and it gets down into the forties." She took back the stirring baby.

"How do you know that?"

"Lizbett told me. Oh, I forgot; we need to get Eudora a winter coat."

"Are we going to buy it?" Eudora asked.

"A coat for you? Yes."

"No, this house."

"Oh, no, Sweetie. Dadag and I are just fooling around. We look at houses all the time."

"Let's check out the back," Leo said. "Maybe I can see into the crawl space."

Simone shielded Zelda's face from the sun as they descended. Eudora hopped down the steps, sliding her hand along the rail. "Splinters," Simone reminded her.

"Bees," Eudora said.

Camelia bushes continued along the side wall, their wilted petals on the grass. "Probably needs sodding," Leo observed. The window into the crawl space was too dirty to see in. But up the back steps he found a windowed door that allowed a view onto a covered porch where the planks were in better shape. He tried the handle. "Hey, it's open!"

The interior door was locked, but he could see in, to a generous kitchen with a farm-style sink. Simone was beside him, camera dangling and Zelda still tucked in the crook of her arm. "The space is good," he said, "but you'd need to gut it and put in a new kitchen."

"Maybe you could save the sink. Open up to the dining room."

He peered at the ceiling, the just-visible newel post of a stairway up. "Damn. Carving on the *back* stairs."

"It's a lot of stairs for old people," Simone pointed out.

"Way too many." But now he'd spotted a ladder in the grass. He went down and picked it up.

"Leo, you're not!"

"It's good and steady." He lifted it, grunting, against the back of the house.

"Dadag, you're not!" said Eudora.

In fact the ladder was in better shape than the sill that supported it (or, truth to tell, the meniscus of his left knee). He climbed to an upper window where the shade had not been drawn.

"Wood floors all the way," he said. "Wide plank. Good bones!" And Simone laughed.

Simone descended and spread the blanket to set the baby in the shaded grass. She aimed the camera at the inlet, at movement in it that might be sea grass or might be a minnow kindergarten. Eudora was mimicking one of her mother's exercises; one step up, one step down. She carried rhythmically on while she turned her head in their direction.

"Is this a broken home?"

Leo wondered angrily who had talked to her about broken homes, but Simone said, "I expect so."

"Can we fix it?"

"Oh, I don't know about that, punkin."

Leo lay the ladder back in the grass and picked Eudora up onto his shoulders. The baby had begun to fuss by now.

"Florida!" Leo said.

Simone lifted a lock of hair to show how the damp had made it frizz. "All the same. It can't do any harm make a call."

"Just have a quick glance around inside," Leo explained.

Transit: Shore to Shore

1995

It's her sixty-fifth birthday, and Leo has rented a jet-boat for the afternoon, complete with shade over the cockpit and a deck for sun. He has even taken a lesson in advance, so he knows how to steer it out from the dock, over the sand bars and out to sea.

It happens—one of those coincidences Leo loves; he calls them "random symmetry"—that there's a hot-air convention south at Ponte Vedra, which means that by the time they're past the sandbars, the sky is awash with balloons, great buoyancies of purple, blue, vermillion. They arch over the water from horizon to horizon in a twitchy skydance. The seagulls inspect them, territorial.

Laughing with pleasure, Simone strips to her suit and slathers them both with sunscreen. She won't take up water-skiing at this age, but she can hang from a bar-on-a-rope that descends from the stern and let Leo pull her slowly through the salt cool water, out where the underwater mountains are too far down to see, and the water is now emerald and now midnight blue.

When she climbs back in and dries herself, he cuts the motor and produces a basket of pears and cheese. No more food, he admonishes, because they will dock in Flagler Beach for shrimp and oyster dinner with the girls. They toast her birthday, each other, their nearly finished rehab of the yellow house, peering back to identify their peninsula, at which they may or may not succeed. They dawdle on the deck while he slowly, slowly replenishes the sunscreen on her back, face, legs. But they are not alone on the water, and this boat has no lower deck. So Simone sits and gathers the leftover rinds and peels, tosses bread scraps to the gulls.

She remembers that bleak night from Ostend to Dover when she was a little girl in a coat that was too small. She remembers the way Winona Farnsworth wrapped her in a rough blanket, and the way she, Winona, described the trawler's black wake as "a clot being washed from a wound." But here is full sun, the vivid flashes off of overhead balloons, the sea blue to its depth. The boat's wake is more furrow than wound, and into this furrow she sows her handful of leftover bread. Immediately it is snatched by a ray, as fluid as silk in the wind. Order *Batiformes,* family *Rajidae,* says Leo, showing off.

Overhead a pelican floats, holding his heavy head forward on his body, as Leo does. He folds himself into a pod and plummets to the deep. As if in answer, two flying fish leap forth. The boat swings a wide arc and heads back toward shore and home.

CHAPTER 14

I Arrive Alone

2000

Her first journey is to the john and the second to the pill box and the third to the porch, where the fresh disasters of the world have been tossed by a black seventh-grader with the droll nickname of Laptop. She carries the news to the kitchen (*USS Cole attacked by Al-Qaeda; bodies of WWII airmen discovered on Greenland glacier*) and flips on the coffee pot that Lizbett readied for her last night. She goes back to the Florida room.

He is probably not awake. It was bad from midnight to two and four to five. For the moment pain sits in his face as an undertow. When the spasm comes again it will surge over his head and under his eyebrows that are still a full tangle of bleached seagrass; it will sink into the sockets of his eyes. She strokes the foot of the bed (fancy hydraulic hospital rental) and pulls up the covers on her couch.

In an alcove on the far wall hang a portrait of Darla in movie star regalia and the photo of Duck, the Vicar, and Winona Farnsworth in front of the trawler that brought Simone to England. On the near wall are two panels, each the size of her armspan, from her most recent installation, "Piece Work." One is of women of sewing, so contrived that they seem to be themselves stitching the photo segments together. The other shows a trio of women cooking slabs of meat over a blazing forest. Soon these panels will go to the gallery in Atlanta that represents her work.

She and Leo sold up and settled finally, as so many do, in Florida. They retired finally, as so many do, to where the grandchildren are. The house is too much house for a pair of septuagenarians, too many dust-catching crannies, too many stairs. But it has shade in the breakfast room and sunset over the river. To the east, the distant pulse of surf.

The bedrooms are all upstairs, so he is dying in the Florida room, which is a generous rectangle of windows and overweening plants, its furniture now reconfigured for the high-tech bed. Little yellow squares yap out instructions from the doors and mirrors. How people died before Post-it notes she can't imagine.

The pitcher is still full because he drank nothing yesterday. Nevertheless she takes it to the kitchen and changes old water for new. Pours herself a cup of coffee, glances at "The Living Arts" (*Christie's withdraws Gauguin forgery; a docudrama on the murder of JonBenet Ramsey*). Now, knuckles on the pine table, she stops briefly for a pain of her own, which is either colon cancer or diverticulitis or flatulence. The old are not hypochondriacal, they are *prescient*. This slicing at the ribs is heart attack, though perhaps not now. This swelling in the lymph nodes is cancer, just perhaps not here. She takes the coffee and the paper and heads back.

He's awake. His eyes follow her, and when she says, "Good morning, love," he rises to "G'morn," a gift. But it has cost enough effort to make him gasp for breath. If he becomes restless he may try to get out of bed though he is too frail to stand and she won't be able to stop him or hold him up. Therefore she will give him the Ativan, but not until she must, because she wants him with her. She reaches under the cover to massage his calves. Ten years ago—yea, six months—she knelt naked in the shower and soaped these calves in which the muscles plumped like chicken breasts. Now the flesh is flimsy as a stocking from which the leg has been removed. He is disappearing bit by bit. Where is he disappearing to?

"There was rain last night, everything smells of fresh-washed dust." Does that make sense? "Not a cloud left except those little wispy ones high up. Cirrus. Did you know the word 'cloud' comes from the same root as 'clod'? I looked it up." Does he smile? "I can see they look like boulders or lumps of dirt."

Dust unto dust.

She pulls up a chair and dandles his hand. The flesh over his face, for all that it is shrink-wrapped to the bone, cannot diminish the square substantiality of his head. "Marina will be here any minute, and then Lizbett said she'd stop by with the girls on their way to school." She resettles his pillow, which may or may not make him more comfortable, but comforts him. She asks, "Do you want anything?"

He says clearly, "Life for you."

She holds the limp hand to her forehead. Something, either the hand or the forehead, registers a heartbeat. His torso contracts, the scapulae closing in on the clavicle. She says, "Shall I get the morphine?"

He says, "First Marina."

"All right."

He says, "We spoke of this."

Then the pain comes, rolling from the hip, shuddering up his spine and snapping at his nape. He grinds his teeth. He has no grip, so she grips his hands and the shudder passes into her. She thinks of how the kids stand on the sidewalk fingertip to fingertip passing a wave one to the other. He subsides, falls back, his forehead slick.

From the front door Marina calls, "Halloo," and comes in plump and open-faced, as she comes every morning and afternoon from the hospice where she does the same things as she does here, day after day, year after year. Marina never runs out of energy or customers. She plants herself on her snow-white Nikes. Her azure eyes suggest an Irish ancestry. In fact she is a Ukrainian refugee. Simone can't remember which pogrom is responsible for her being here. In any case it is contingent. It is nowhere written that a girl who fled a certain batch of Soviets should become nurse to a man who fled a different batch of Soviets.

"Everything smells so fresh. Did you hear the thunder?" Marina speaks a perfect idiomatic English and gets everything right except the sound of *th,* which she pronounces arbitrarily as *d* or *sh* or *z.* Simone's throat thickens at the echo of Eastern Europe.

"Oh, yes. Half the night."

"Now it's your turn," Marina says to Leo. Up until two weeks ago she would hoist him, legs dangling over her forearm, set him in the rented chair and wheel him along the waterway. Now she just lifts his top half, cradling his head while with the other arm she tucks the sheet. Then she lifts his legs and does the bottom half.

"He needs the morphine," Simone says.

"I see that." Marina apologizes, "The dose is pretty high. I'm not sure we can up it yet again." The problem is that too much makes him incoherent but not enough lets in the pain. It's always the problem, Marina says. Marina says that morphine is not addictive, but the body does adjust to it. Then you need to adjust the dose. But you must proceed with care; an overdose can kill the patient you are trying to help. Marina says. Now she takes a little bottle, expertly inserts a needle and snaps her finger against the glass. The thimbleful of elixir is drawn up. Marina rolls Leo gently onto his side and flicks the needle into his buttock neat as a dart.

"Go take your walk," she says. I'll give him a sponge and a shave." Marina shoos Simone as she does every day, saying as always, "It's important you keep up your strength."

Simone takes Riberia south, then west to Marine (retracing Laptop's paper route), north along the water, and discards her sandals on the boardwalk to dig her toes in the amber sand. *The sea is there, and who shall drain its yield?* Sand fleas and coquinas at her feet scurry into the wet. The shore presents itself as an undulating line but, really, she thinks, there is no such boundary. All things flow into each other. Under the water the sand continues, under the sand the water seeps.

The beach, pocked with last night's rain, smells both organic and immaculate, luminous grit made of the crushed carapaces of several trillion dead things. Sometimes Lizbett and the girls stomp on the shells; they say they are "helping God make sand."

As for helping God, Simone thinks, our prospect is not good. The oysters have begun to disappear in Apalachicola. Red tide is choking the Gulfside bays, and we will probably continue to produce and devour while the planet burns and drowns—and so disappear ourselves, the victims of our own success.

Yet, she thinks, nothing dies; it's simply snipped or melted into its elements. When we have enlightened ourselves into extinction, we will dissolve and evolve through millions of years into some other form of consciousness. When the "immortal" Shakespeare has proved ephemeral, and her own collages disintegrate into their molecules—there will still be water, there will still be light.

It's too cold for swimmers and too early for the uproar of the Jet-skis. To her left a great blue heron stalks, companion to the fisherman casting his rod. Skittish but arrogant, the bird makes a semicircle of hieroglyphs in the sand. From time to time the fisherman tosses it either a waterlogged bait shrimp or a fish too small to keep. Like the man and the bird, she and the man companionably ignore each other. In five years she has seen him catch, at a generous count, two dozen grunt fish and three flounder large enough to put in his pail.

When she gets back she plucks the mail from the box and carries it into the vestibule, where her life-sized collage of Leo is framed at floor level so you meet him eye to eye. At some point Leo was doing something helpful—unloading the dishwasher or cleaning the cat box—and she said: *You really are a reconstructed male.* Then it occurred to her to make a life-sized "reconstruction" from the portraits and snapshots of him she had taken—hundreds by then. In fact it had needed some twenty thousand photographic snippets of the right tint or texture to complete. When it was shown at the Corcoran Gallery, the *Washington Post* called her "the Chuck Close of photomontage."

She turns to the mail, lets the ads and pleas for money slide unopened into the wastebasket. But one is a delicate blue air letter that she slits open. Jade Singh in Jaipur never fails, once a year, to insist that she come to visit. Today she also writes of her sister Jewel, now teaching at the university in New Delhi and of her husband who has expanded his transport business (involving camels). Simone thinks of the bright-eyed twins she met a quarter of a century ago, who remind her how the stone strength of women comes from an accretion of the ordinary: friendship, children, meals, invitations—stitched together in whatever thread or fiber is at hand.

Of course, people hand out invitations all the time. You risk terrible embarrassment if you take them at their word. Thinking of India, she remembers the molting camel in Binghamton, and thinks what a monster it would be, a full-sized loose-limbed collage of that slobbery beast. The labor of a year. She has become so used to the rhythms of the sickroom that the sudden leap of ambition stops her heart. She sets Jade's letter on the hall tree and goes on to the Florida room.

Leo is dozing, clean-shaven, and Marina is seated in the Papasan chair behind *The Times.* "Imagine. They've found four bodies from the Second World War, up in Greenland, and their plane. Someplace called Comanche Flats."

"Frozen all that time?"

"It doesn't say. Not, is my guess. Summer comes even in the Arctic." Then, "They're saying this Cuban boat boy Elian is a miracle, his mother, all the others drowned like that."

"Yes." Some get to the boat or the shore in time and live to a ripe old age, perhaps in Florida. Some don't.

"God help us if he grows up to be the Pope," Marina says.

Marina folds the paper and smooths the spine so that you couldn't tell it has ever been opened. Leo, in the scant decade they have been allowed together, has never shut a section of newspaper without crumpling and skewing the fold. Simone is visited with the understanding that such irritations are the stuff of loss. She hugs Marina, who says, as always, "I'll stop by this afternoon." She says, "Zhis afternoon."

Simone sees her off and steps into the study. She tilts the blinds to soften the light. She is working with digitized images now, which she posts on her website, Anachron.com. When you pull up the site it says:

Brief history of the Twentieth Century:

WWI

WWII

www

That was Leo's joke.

Simone turns to face the wall of shelves. Sooner or later she should go into one of those retirement "homes"—rendered so Martha Stewart now, so like a genteel mansion in the suburbs. But what would she do with the books? Here are a full ten feet of shelf packed with her erratically kept journals, which no one will ever now read. Here is a massive volume from which the gilt lettering has flaked off. Her first English dictionary. The book she's carried farthest, across the Pond and the country to Florida, which Auntie Toffat back in Hove bought for her . . .

She is suddenly astonished at the breadth of such a gesture! Who'd have thought that Auntie Toffat, that practical, dull-witted woman, would see the intensity of such a need? She opens it to the page marked by a crumbling card with keyhole-punches along one side. This is stuck in a page of *O*'s, and on the card is written: *Opsimath: one who begins learning late in life.* She has no recollection of the word. Yet it might have been set there for an oracle, of a life in which everything—authentic love, and family, and her life's work—were granted late. She lifts it out, and there slips from behind it a snapshot of a woman's torso, arms thrusting forward a baby that is squinting in the sun. A forties shot, from the crinkle-edges of the print. On the back it says, "Daddy's girl—4 ½ months" in faded pencil. Simone has no idea who this baby is or where she'd have come by the photo. It's not good enough to use. But—she sticks it back and replaces the dictionary—imagine Auntie Toffat being so kind!

Late February is spring in St. Augustine. It's not yet eight but the sun is sixty degrees into its arc. Outside again she clips a handful of azaleas and one lush magnolia blossom and sets these in the Florida room in front of one wall of windows. Next to them Leo's glasses are splayed on the book he laid there three weeks ago. From the bed begins the grunting moan that can last an hour or more, the metronome of hurt.

When Lizbett comes she is bearing another pot of soup, which Simone doesn't need and Lizbett did not have time to make, but which she accepts with gratitude because what it signifies between them is the nothing they can do. Lizbett, divorced, is the Dean of Students at Flagler College up the road in its sumptuous shell of a twenties hotel. She is substantial, swarthy, sexy—the adult version of the stolid toddler Simone knew in Binghamton forty years ago—showing no sign of the schizophrenia that emptied her mother's mind. Nor is the universe under any obligation, if a toddler gives German measles to a pregnant woman, to turn that child, grown, into a friend and daughter. There is no mandate that a childless woman should be offered a pair of grandchildren. The gifts are arbitrary, like the losses. Simone sends Lizbett for coffee for herself, juice for the girls.

Eudora, twelve and dragging her way through middle school, hangs at the door—it isn't cool to show any emotion re hospital beds. But seven-year-old Zelda wraps her boniness around her grandmother, smashes her face stomach-high. Simone collapses back into the chair to take her weight. Zelda is an octopus; she seems to have more than the requisite number of limbs. Five years ago Eudora behaved like this, and five years from now Zelda will be sullen and withdrawn while Eudora will have discovered compassion like a new continent.

"What's on for today?" she asks. Eudora from the door says "Nothing," while Zelda begins a chatter of field trip plans. The second grade is collecting shells; their teacher calls it Marine Biology. Zelda has a starfish and a blowfish and two dozen sand dollars that she bleached in a margarine tub. Silent Eudora has long sun-bleached hair pulled high on the crown, lips in a pout to avoid the wire of her braces. Her clothing is all branded; her budding breasts belong to Calvin Klein, her thin wrist to Guess, her long feet to Puma. Eudora roots herself at the doorframe while Zelda's chatter opens Leo's eyes.

"Grandad knows you're here," Simone says. "He likes to listen to us talk."

Lizbett, returning, asks, "Shall I give him the morphine this morning?"

Simone hesitates.

Leo says something: "Spoke."

"Thanks. He did have one bad spasm already." She pulls open the drawer beside her bed and takes out a cardboard palette of blue pills.

"Oh, good, you got the buccal sort." Lizbett pushes one from its foil trap. Lizbett does not believe in shielding children. Besides, the buccal delivery system is so low-key. You take the pill on the tip of your forefinger as Lizbett now does, slide it inside the gum and under the tongue, lodge it there and remove your finger. The pill will dissolve at some technologically predetermined rate and deliver the morphine into the system over the next four hours. It's so much less dramatic than the hypodermic—although, of course, your tension raises because it would be so easy to do every time he hurts.

Leo's girls can't stay, they are off to their separate school days, they will be back later. But no, Eudora says she will not be here this afternoon.

"Me'n Laptop're going down to the Fish Bar."

"Laptop and I," says Lizbett.

"They're putting on a leap year fry."

Zelda singsongs, "Dora's got a boyfriend."

Eudora scowls and chips at the doorframe. "Laptop's *gay*." The scorn is for her sister's density, not for Laptop.

Lizbett instructs them to kiss their grandfather, which they both do with a touching caution, as with a breakable antique. Eudora allows Simone a hug of her board-stiff torso; Zelda tangles her in limbs again. Lizbett holds her for a long minute while they share, though they do not say, that it's a blessing to have become such friends. Zelda's ponytail and Eudora's blonde fall and Lizbett's dark crop glister retreating in the sun.

This, then, is the comfort coven: Marina, Lizbett, Simone, Eudora, Zelda.

Simone takes their cup and glasses back to the kitchen, rinses them. She goes to Leo, smooths his pillow, smooths his pate. His eyes are closed and his breathing shallow. The cardboard palette of pills is still on the nightstand. She takes it and pushes out another pill. She puts the palette in the drawer. Closes the drawer.

The notion of a "happy ending" is a lexical paradox. *Happy ending* means "happily ever after," which means "happy without end," whereas she and Leo have always known that there is only one end for a sand flea, husband, father, lover, species.

The inside of his mouth is damp and slippery, smooth as a newborn. Lizbett's pill was on the left so she slides to the right. Rides it down an indentation in the still-firm gum between the roots of two molars, presses it under the tongue. Slips her finger out and leans to kiss him. His breath is slightly metallic. She holds his flaccid hand to her beating brow. She gazes at the expanse of window beyond his bed.

Saint Augustine said that Christ was conceived of Mary as "sunlight falls through glass." Simone wonders if they still make glass by melting sand. The beach, cremated into windows, is made of the transparent bodies of sea-creatures? And is that cremation then the worldly equivalent of purity?

Many times she has sat looking through this window expecting Leo's white Nissan to appear, willing it in sight when it was not there. Now she expects it to appear although he is dying while she holds his hand. There is no reason to suppose that she will stop waiting for it at this late date.

His glasses—outsized hornrims, because he was always a few decades out of vogue—sit in front of the window on a splayed copy of *Anachron: The Photomontages of Simone Lerrante*. Leo's glasses will have to go to whatever organization collects them to recycle, because his sight was skewed in some different way than hers. Yet his eyes have looked through them at the images that she concocted out of the misfit of the war and the consumer world. All things flow into each other, altering with the current's crookedness.

She is holding his hand. She is telling him, over and over, parts of their story, in and out of sequence. About the time she stumbled into him and let loose with the waterworks. The fractured memory of snowlight on his crumpled sleeve. The camel in Ross Park Zoo, whose slobber she caught in close-up on her Polaroid. How Lizbett strained against the confines of her pushchair. The hotel in Budapest with the river view. His choice of that ludicrous too-small shower cubicle for his declaration of undying love. How the Romany kid at St. Peter's Square tricked her into hoisting him for a look at the Pope while the father went for her hip-pack. How she longed to tell him, all those years ago, that she was leaving Martin Puig. How the furious little bureaucrat in Vienna lectured the homeless man who had asked for a cigarette. How they journeyed back to see Lotte in Liege, and how she has now thought of the camel for one of her "reconstructions." How Zelda was born weeks after her father took off, the jerk. How the day they found this house, trash flower petals in the yard and varnish crumbling, they sat together on the seafront to decide whether they were too old to take on one more broken home. She wonders aloud whether they were fooled, their generation; whether those schmaltzy Jewish exiles in Hollywood had got it right: that the important thing is to find one person till death do you part.

She touches the thick fringe of his eyebrows, the thinning on his crown, the stubble still growing on his sharpened chin. He deeply sighs, and with that exhalation seems imperceptibly to shrink. There is all at once in his face an undertow of something not speaking pain so much as affirming absence. She has for a moment the sense that she too is sucked upward in the force of it—she feels the whirring of the fan at her back—looking down on the two of them, he in bed and she at his bedside, holding hands. Then he disappears from her—upward?—into the cirrus clouds (clods, dust unto dust), and she settles stiffly back down into her body once again. She places her free hand over their two clasped hands and presses this packet of hands. Happily. Ever after.

That is as good as ending gets.

Acknowledgments

Simone in Pieces began in the late 1990s as an academic satire, which I read at the University of Alabama (hosted by the intrepid Michael Martone) and which was published in the Black Warrior Review shortly thereafter. The story was meant to be a postmodern in-joke, but as sometimes happens, the plot surprised me by taking a hard turn into grief. I found that in order to understand it I had to work out the whole life story of the narrator. When I laid out that story for my husband Peter Ruppert, he said, "Oh, that's your next novel." He was right in everything but the "next." Other books intruded: a different novel, a memoir, the editing of several essays, two updatings of textbooks. In between, I worked at Simone's life piecemeal, in the same way she seeks to find and build her self. One of my ideas was that we are created by our encounters with others, some of which touch us only slightly, some profoundly, as we also affect others lightly or crucially, building ourselves by will and happenstance. If we are lucky and awake, such encounters help us to full lives. Working out this idea in short and long passages from many points of view, I wrote much more than made the cut, and some of Simone's outtakes are scattered here and there in magazines.

Of course, such a literary trek means that, like my heroine, I was helped along the way. So I have more people to thank than I will remember, but I am grateful first of all to my son Alex Eysselinck for fact-checking my British life and voices. Also to my husband Peter, always my first and kindest reader; to my brother Stan, who honed his editing skills over decades at the *Los Angeles Times*; and to my BFF Julia Kling, who has read everything I've written over the course of sixty-five years, and who keeps me on track with her mantra: "Please just tell the story." I am dependent for valuable guidance on my writing group PerSisters: Rosellen Brown, Garnett Kilberg-Cohen, Tsivia Cohen, Maggie Kast, Peggy Shinner, Sharon Solwitz, and Sandi Wisenberg.

Thanks to my infinitely patient agent, Margaret Sutherland Brown; to Dennis Lloyd at the University of Wisconsin Press, and to my team there: Sheila McMahon, Jessica Hasan, Alison Shay, and Jacqueline Krass; to Josh McCall, who built a handsome new website for me; and to my publicity director, Julia Bocherts at Kaye Publicity.

Some further acknowledgments:

"The Love Song of Johnny A. Purdy" is based on "The Love Song of J. Alfred Prufrock" by T. S. Eliot.

The calendar of events in "Lady Lazarus" for the Cambridge winter of 1956 is taken in part from the published journals and letters of Sylvia Plath; some of the characters there and in "Transit: Suttling–Cambridge" are named after those in her short story "Stone Boy with Dolphin."

Larry Achzel's neurology experiments in "Memoirs of a Survivor" are loosely borrowed from Steve Rose's *The Making of Memory*.

For an understanding of suppression, disassociation, and memory recovery I am indebted to Lenore Terr's *Unchained Memories*.

John Grant generously helped me to understand Kai Maginnis's time in Vietnam.

"Deconstruction" incorporates as homage several phrases and paraphrases from the article "Like the Sound of the Sea Deep Within a Shell: Paul de Man's War" by Jacques Derrida, which appeared in *Critical Inquiry*, no. 14 (Spring 1988).

The following sections of *Simone in Pieces* appeared in slightly different form in the following publications:

"Deconstruction," *Prairie Schooner,* Winter 1999 (winner of the Lawrence Foundation Award).

"Regular," *New Letters,* Spring 2001.

"Oracles," *Prairie Schooner,* Summer 2004 (winner of the Reader's Choice Award).

"Chronotope," *Prairier Schooner,* Summer 2006 (winner of the Reader's Choice Award).

"Blackout" ("The Love Song of Johnny A. Purdy"), *Narrative Magazine,* Fall 2008.

"White Space" (first prize, short story contest), *Narrative Magazine,* Spring 2009.

"Home Help" (first prize, short story contest), *Narrative Magazine,* Winter 2017.

"Lady Lazarus" and "Transit: District of Columbia–Columbia, MO," *New Letters,* Spring 2020.

"Newcomer," honorable mention, story contest, *Narrative Magazine,* Winter 2022.

"Straight Home," winner of the *Narrative Magazine* prose contest, Winter 2022.

I am grateful to these magazines for permission to reprint.

Simone in Pieces, in an earlier version called *Simone in Transit,* was runner-up in the 2023 Red Hen Prose Prize.

JANET BURROWAY was born in Tucson, Arizona, raised in Phoenix, and began college at the University of Arizona, where she weighed the careers of writing, acting, and fashion design, and from which she was chosen one of the earliest "Guest Editors" at *Mademoiselle Magazine*. She transferred to Barnard College, then went on to Cambridge University (England) on a Marshall scholarship, and to the Yale School of Drama (RCA-NBC Fellow 1960–61).

She taught 1965–71 at the University of Sussex, England, where she also designed costumes for the university's Gardner Arts Centre and for the National Theatre of Belgium. She returned to the United States in 1971 and taught at the University of Illinois; the Writer's Workshop at the University of Iowa; the Florida State University at Tallahassee (1972–2002); and most recently in the MA/MFA Writing Program at Northwestern University. She is a Robert O. Lawton Distinguished Professor Emerita from FSU, and in 2014 she received a Lifetime Achievement Award in Writing from the Humanities Council of Florida.

She is the author of some twenty books, including nine novels, three children's books, essays, poetry, and a memoir. Her three earliest novels have been reissued from Michael Walmer Publisher in the United Kingdom, and others are forthcoming. Her poems, essays, and stories have appeared widely in literary magazines and newspapers in both the United States and the United Kingdom, including

MS., *Narrative Magazine*, *New Letters*, *Prairie Schooner*, *Pushcart Prizes XXVII*, *The Guardian*, the *Chicago Tribune*, and the *New York Times*.

Burroway's *Writing Fiction: A Guide to Narrative Craft* (tenth edition, University of Chicago Press) is the most widely used fiction writing text in America and has been translated into Simple and Complex Chinese and into Vietnamese. *Imaginative Writing: The Elements of Craft* (Pearson 2023) is in its fifth edition.

Her plays have been seen in Los Angeles, Chicago, and London, as well as regional theaters, and her novel *Opening Nights* was made into a serial drama for PBS in 1998. In the early 2000s, her three children's books were set to symphonic music by composer Philip Wharton, which has been performed throughout the Midwest, as well as *The Perfect Pig*, also by On Site Opera at Little Island in New York City. She has since collaborated with Philip on a variety of art songs and a song cycle. Burroway has given readings and lectures in some ninety venues in the United States, England, Sweden, China, and UAE, mostly at universities but also at bookstores, festivals, and on Zoom.

The author's son Alex Eysselinck lives in London and, with his wife, Tricia Howard, has raised two grown daughters, Eleanor and Holly. Her elder son, Captain Timothy Eysselinck, died in Africa in 2004. Tim's daughter Thyra is now doing graduate studies at the City University of New York.

Burroway has lived in Phoenix and Tucson; New York City and Binghamton, New York; Cambridge, Sussex, and London, England; New Haven, Connecticut; Ghent, Belgium; and with her husband of thirty-plus years, Utopian scholar and film critic Peter Ruppert, in Tallahassee, Florida, and Lake Geneva, Wisconsin. They now live in Chicago.